Robert Edric was born in 1956. His novels include *Winter Garden*

KT-408-280

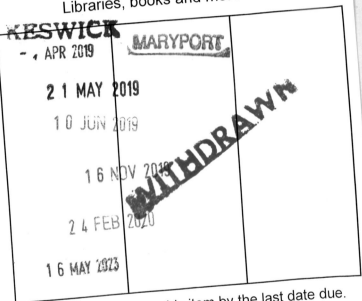

Cumbria

County Council

Libraries, books and more.........

KESWICK	MARYPORT	
- APR 2019		
2 1 MAY 2019		
1 0 JUN 2019		
1 6 NOV 2019		
2 4 FEB 2020		
1 6 MAY 2023		

WITHDRAWN

Please return/renew this item by the last date due.
Library items may also be renewed by phone on
030 33 33 1234 (24 hours) or via our website

www.cumbria.gov.uk/libraries

Cumbria Libraries
CLIC
Interactive Catalogue

Ask for a CLIC password

For Tony and Teresa Armitage

The Fens, 1954

Part I
Summer

1

JIMMY DEVLIN WOKE TO THE SOUND OF AN ENGINE IN THE yard below, followed by a man shouting. Devlin rubbed his eyes, yawned, stretched, waited. The engine was switched off and then stuttered for a few seconds, the noise like stones rattling in a tin. The same voice shouted again, louder, angrier. What was it his mother used to say? Only bad news ever arrived before noon.

Devlin went naked to the window and looked down. The stale smell of the bed clung to him, as though he'd draped one of the unwashed sheets over his shoulders.

Beneath him, the man climbed from the cab and walked to the door. A Bedford, probably ex-Army. Definitely ex-Army, which would account for the engine noise and the over-run. The flat wooden back was empty except for a tarpaulin and a pile of rope. Blue smoke hung in the still air.

The man knocked on the door with the side of his fist and shouted again.

Devlin opened the window and leaned out. 'What you after?' he shouted down.

'You Jimmy Devlin?'

'What if I am?'

The man shook his head and turned back to the lorry.

The passenger door opened and a fat, blonde woman swung her legs to hang awkwardly above the running board.

'What's he saying?' she called to the man.

'Another smart alec who wants me to guess if it's him or not.' The man shook his head again, spat heavily and turned back to Devlin. 'You coming down or what? I'm getting a crick standing like this.'

'Who's she?' Devlin shouted.

The woman was fitted close into the tight space, her heavy thighs pressed against the stripped dash.

'None of your business who she is,' the man shouted. 'She's my wife.'

'And who are you, while we're at it?'

The man grinned at this. 'I, sonny-Jim, am the man whose letters you don't answer.'

'What letters?' Devlin knew exactly what letters.

'Landlord's letters, bailiff's letters. Notice of Eviction letters. That's what letters. Starting to ring any distant bells in that tiny little skull of yours?'

'No idea what you're talking about,' Devlin said, his mouth dry, knowing he'd said too much.

The man went to the small window beside the door, shielded his eyes and looked inside. 'Probably them same letters you've got stacked all neat and tidy on the mantel wishing they'd go away. Which they won't. A bit like me in that respect, because I'm going nowhere, either. You coming down or what? I spend half my life shouting through walls and doors at idiots like you and it's starting to wear a bit thin. I'm Skelton, by the way, seeing as how you're asking. Bailiff.'

Devlin ran a hand down his pale chest and stomach. He took a step back from the window and left it swinging open.

It was already warm. Not yet six on a summer's morning. Sunlight fell in a beam across the dust-filled room, over the threadbare carpet and on to the faded, peeling wallpaper. A pattern of roses. It seemed to him as though nothing had ever changed in that room for fifty years past, longer.

He dressed and went downstairs.

He opened the door and pointed the slender rifle he now held at Skelton.

The man had gone back to where his wife sat and the pair of them were sharing a cigarette. The woman's hair was piled high beneath a transparent headscarf.

'What's he got that thing for?' she said loudly, indicating the rifle.

Skelton turned and looked Devlin up and down. 'You think I never been threatened before, boy? And by bigger men than you. Besides, look at it. What is it?'

'A gun,' Devlin said.

Skelton laughed. 'Steal it from the funfair, did you? It's a rat gun, that's all. And even they wouldn't run too fast at the sight of it. You wouldn't even touch a rabbit at twenty yards with that thing.'

'Don't you be too sure of that,' Devlin said. 'Plenty of rabbits already made that mistake.' One rabbit. Wounded, and already diseased when he finally caught up with it at the Moulton drain. Killed with the rifle stock and then thrown into the water.

'Apart from which,' Skelton went on, nudging his wife, 'it'd probably have to be stuck halfway up the rat's arse for the poor little bugger to even feel it.' The pair of them laughed.

Then the man came to Devlin, put his hand on the end of the thin barrel and pushed it to one side. 'Right,' he said. 'You've made your point, son. Time to get down to business. Fact is, Jesse

James, I've taken a bit of a shine to you, and so because of that I'm going to do you a big favour here and pretend none of this gun business ever happened. I've seen it all, me, and I know where trouble lies deepest and where it blows away on the first wind. And bear in mind I'm talking about *your* trouble here, boy, not mine.'

Devlin lowered the rifle. 'It's not even six o'clock,' he said.

'Ten past. What's that got to do with anything? Besides, best time of day for this kind of work. You have worked out, I suppose, that I'm here on behalf of Harrap to evict you.'

'Evict?'

'Don't push your luck, son. Even *you* know what that means. And if you don't, then you've seen it written out often enough over these past few months to know what was coming. You're out.' He gestured at the rundown farmhouse. 'By order of the Court. Old man Harrap wrote to you about your arrears. *I* wrote to you about your arrears, and then the County Court wrote to you about your arrears.'

'Harrap said when he rented me the place that I'd get good pasture on the bottom half,' Devlin said. 'I was going to let it on.' It was a pointless, futile argument, and he knew this before he'd finished speaking.

'Not my problem,' Skelton said. 'Besides, look at you. Since when were *you* a farmer? None of you Devlins were *ever* farmers. You might have played at it, once, but that's all. What, you think good pasture just grows and the money pours in on the back of a bit of cutting now and then?'

'Harrap said—'

'Don't matter one jot what Harrap did or didn't say. You were the one who signed the lease on the place and he's the one still shy five months' rent.'

'I was going to pay him—'

'When the cows came home. You already said.'

Beyond the man, in the lorry, the woman slid heavily from her seat on to the running board and then to the ground. 'Just tell him to go, and have done with it,' she shouted to her husband.

'She's right,' Skelton said. 'I'm not here to argue the toss. I'm here because I've got a legal duty to throw you out and then to retrieve goods to cover all costs and—'

'Costs? What costs?'

'"What costs?" he says. What costs? Well, for a start there's the unpaid rent, then there's the costs of the Court, the costs of old man Harrap's solicitor's clerk, and then my costs in coming all this way out here to waste my fucking breath in telling you all this and to carry out my legal, Court-sanctioned duties. All of which, incidentally, you would already have known if you'd opened even one of them fucking letters.'

Devlin considered all this. He had known it was coming, but had not expected it to come at six o'clock on a summer's morning. He usually woke around eleven and got up an hour or two later.

Skelton's wife came to him. She wore heels and walked unsteadily over the cobbled yard.

'Why don't he put that thing right down?' she said, nodding to the rifle Devlin still held.

'He won't fire it,' Skelton said. 'Peacetime hero, that's all he is.'

The rifle felt like a toy in Devlin's hands.

'He's let the place go something rotten,' the woman said. She looked around her and pulled a face at everything she saw.

Lines of tall grass and overgrown nettles and dock grew along every building. Windows were broken. The door hung off the barn, and its tile roof sagged along its entire length.

'Too busy shooting rabbits, probably,' Skelton said.

'Since when was he a farmer?' the woman said. 'None of them Devlins ever amounted to *anything*.'

'We already done that bit,' Skelton said.

Devlin thought he detected a note of lukewarm sympathy in the man's voice.

'Why don't you go back to the cab?' Skelton said to his wife. 'Me and Al Capone here just need a few words in private.'

The remark angered the woman. She started walking away, but then stopped and turned back to face them. She looked directly at Devlin and grinned.

'I only came to see what this one looked like,' she said, her smile growing. 'You do realize that this was the mouthy little bastard that knocked up Mary Collet's youngest, Barbara. Kid was born two months back, a girl.'

'You sure about that?' Skelton said. 'Don't look as though he's got it in him. You sure? She's ripe enough, I'll give you that. Word is, she gets about a bit. Flighty. It could be anybody's.'

'She's lying,' Devlin said.

'You watch your mouth,' Skelton said.

'Not her,' Devlin said. 'The Collet girl. And that bitch of a mother. Besides, it wasn't me. Last I heard, it was a man from Wisbech way. You seen the colour of my hair, my eyes? Well? You want to take a closer look at the kid. Pound to a penny neither of you got the first idea about its eyes.'

A baby girl. Two months. The first Devlin had heard.

Skelton and his wife exchanged a glance.

'He's got a point,' Skelton said.

'It's science,' Devlin said. 'The eye-colour thing. Medical. You want to get your facts straight before you start accusing people of things.'

Skelton took out a cloth and wiped his face. Then he held open the jacket he wore to reveal a brown envelope.

What else was it Devlin's mother used to say? And if it *is* bad news arriving before noon, then it'll come in brown.

'This is for me to give to you.' Skelton pushed the envelope into Devlin's free hand.

'Telling me what?'

'Telling you what you've long since known and expected. Besides, I know all about you – I make it my business. You're a man who won't be told.' He flicked the envelope. 'It's to inform you that I've been here and that I've carried out my designated duty and kicked you out on your arse.'

'And all the other stuff?'

'What other stuff?'

'"Goods to the value" stuff.'

'I'll take whatever I can find and then let those bastards at the Lynn auction house sell it off cheap to everybody who knows what you've been up to here these past months.'

It had never been Devlin's intention to become a farmer. All he'd wanted was somewhere to live and to settle himself for a few months. He'd known the day he'd arrived at the place – a walk of two miles from the nearest bus stop; one service a day except Sundays in either direction – that nothing would ever come of it. And he'd been proved right.

'There's nothing in there,' he said, motioning to the building behind him.

'Oh, there's always something,' Skelton said. 'I took all the clothes from a defaulter in Whaplode last week. Rag value. Just about covered the diesel, but it was something.' He looked around him at the dilapidated buildings. 'You've probably got some bits and pieces of equipment worth a few quid to somebody.'

11

'All here when I came,' Devlin said. 'Harrap's.'

Skelton spat again, waving a hand at the corn flies gathering close to his face. 'I thought the old bastard was just that little bit too keen to get you out.'

'What?' his wife said.

'Told me we could sort out all the reimbursements later.'

'You could have this,' Devlin said, raising the rifle.

'That? Scrap metal. Besides, I got a box full of real guns and rifles already.'

'Go in and have a look round if you don't believe me,' Devlin said. 'I brought nothing with me. Nothing *to* bring.'

It was a victory, of sorts, and for the first time during their encounter, Devlin felt pleased with himself.

'He thinks he's got one over on you,' Skelton's wife said. 'And I'm telling you here and now – Mary Collet will swear in a Court of Law that he's the father.'

But that was the mother, not the daughter, and Devlin sensed his second small victory.

'And once she knows you're out on your ear,' the woman went on, 'she'll send one of her boys – or perhaps all three of them – to keep you moving on. By all accounts, you're a nasty little piece of work and nobody will shed any tears when you pack up and disappear.'

Devlin raised the barrel of the rifle until it was pointing at her face.

'You should have left her at home,' he said to Skelton. 'Where she belongs.'

'You going to let him talk to me like that?' the woman said.

'I was talking to him,' Devlin said.

Skelton rubbed his unshaved chin and sighed. 'You know where all this is going, boy?'

'No, you tell me. Where *is* all this going?'

'Well, the way things stand, straight back to the Court and the magistrate who signed Harrap's eviction order in the first place. One thing you should have learned by now – you don't *ever* get to turn your back on debt. I suppose that comes of you being a Devlin. And before anything even gets anywhere near the magistrate, it goes first to the police over in Boston, Spalding and Lynn. You don't know it, but you just made everything that much worse for yourself. There's always *something* to seize against a debt.'

'The police?' Devlin said.

'*Now* he's listening,' the woman said. '*Now* you've got his attention.'

'What have they got to do with anything?' Devlin said. 'You said it was between me and Harrap.'

'Never said any such thing. You owe money. And if there's something else that should have penetrated that thick skull of yours by now, then it's the simple fact that the law is always on the side of money and them what has it and them what's owed it. Always has been, always will be. Harrap's got it and he's owed it. And he's got some big friends, that man.'

'The law won't waste its time on me,' Devlin said.

Skelton laughed. 'Oh, you'd be surprised what *they* waste their time on.' His face was slick with sweat again. 'Look, we're the only ones wasting time here. You just pay me something on account – one month's rent, say – and all this can be pushed back into the paperwork. I'll stick my claim in to Harrap and then he can take it back to the Court. Pay nothing and we're all on a different path completely. Pay nothing and even if—'

'Assault with a deadly weapon,' the woman shouted suddenly, surprising them both.

'What?' Devlin said.

'You heard me. You're still waving the thing around. Always gets them moving a bit faster – the police *and* the Courts – if there are one or two other charges to tack on, especially charges concerning weapons.'

'I haven't even fired it,' Devlin said.

'Not the point. You still threatened us both with it.'

'Hardly,' Skelton said, seeming to surprise himself with the word in Devlin's defence.

Angry at the woman's interventions, especially after all she'd said before, and now that the encounter was surely coming to its end, Devlin raised the rifle and jabbed it towards her.

Uncertain what was happening, Skelton said, 'Don't be stupid, son. You got all the letters. Truth be told, you probably even read them and started to work things out. You brought all this on yourself. The last thing you want to be doing now is waving that thing in people's faces. Ask me, you're your own worst enemy.'

'He don't need you to tell him that,' his wife said.

Devlin almost laughed, and he slowly swung the rifle from the woman to her husband.

Seeing this, Skelton shook his head and said, 'Go on then, son, do us all a big favour and pull the trigger.' He spread his arms, opening the front of his jacket.

'For God's sake, don't encourage him,' his wife shouted.

'He won't fire,' Skelton said. 'He's not got *that* in him, either. In fact, I doubt if he ever—'

And before the man could say any more, Devlin raised the rifle a few inches and pulled the trigger and Skelton shouted and clutched the top of his arm.

'The little bastard's only gone and shot me,' he said. He

14

inspected the cloth of his jacket and shirt and then the palm of his hand for any sign of blood.

'He drawn any blood?' his wife said.

'Not that I can see.'

It seemed yet another insult to Devlin.

'He still fired it. He still threatened you and then aimed it and fired it.'

'Shut up,' Skelton shouted at her.

There was a moment of silence.

'What?' the woman said eventually.

Skelton pulled a finger from beneath his armpit. The faintest smear of red. 'He did, he shot me. That's a first.'

'And there'll be a hole. Two holes,' the woman said.

'What?'

'In your jacket, your shirt.'

Skelton took off his jacket and rolled up his shirt sleeve. The small-calibre bullet had grazed him. Nothing had entered his flesh.

'I can feel it,' he said. 'The bullet. In my shirt. You stupid, vicious little bastard. You think the law are going to ignore something like this? I was giving you a chance up until this, but now you've got everything you deserve coming to you.' He spat on his finger and wiped his small wound. Then he rolled down his sleeve and put on his jacket.

The man and the woman went back to the lorry and climbed inside. Skelton shouted for his struggling wife to get a fucking move on.

Beside the doorway, Devlin propped the rifle by his leg and raised his arm to wave at them. And he stood like that, still waving, until the lorry left the yard and turned back along the top of the embankment in the direction of the Spalding road.

15

2

HE CAME BACK TO THE ABANDONED TIN CHAPEL AT THE end of the Bystall Bank road. It was another hot day and he carried a sack. Sweat ran in circles beneath his eyes and in lines across his cheeks to his chin. He stopped at the first sight of the sea beyond the road. All around him boundaries were lost and the sea, land and sky were confused in a shimmer of heat haze.

A distant figure stood at the chapel wall and Devlin dropped his sack and crouched behind a low bank of levelled thorn. It was unlikely that the man would have seen him from that distance. A few sheep grazed the open marsh on either side of the isolated building.

Devlin lit a cigarette and lay back, careful not to let the smoke form above him.

When he looked ten minutes later, the figure was gone. Devlin searched all around him, but saw nothing. The dry clay where he lay stained his clothing and he brushed at this, but to little effect.

He waited a few minutes longer, then picked up the sack and continued towards the chapel. The disused path ended as he walked and the marsh grass felt soft beneath his boots. The sheep raised their heads to watch him, but none of them was alarmed by his sudden presence among them.

He waited again at the toppled fencing which had once marked out a small graveyard and searched the open land beyond for whoever might have been there. The high sun was reflected in the remains of the chapel's only window, most of which was broken and gone.

The grass between where he stood and the chapel door had been recently cut. When he'd left the building six hours earlier, the stems had risen to his knees; now everything was flat and drying.

He went to the seaward side of the building and pushed at a piece of loose sheeting to let himself inside. At the height of the day, the place was like an oven, and even now, late in the afternoon, it remained uncomfortably warm. Throughout the night, the tin walls and roof cracked and ticked as the flimsy structure cooled.

He went to one of the few remaining benches and stretched out on this. A lidless drum full of water stood beside the simple pulpit. Devlin dipped a jar into the drum and poured the water over his face, repeating this several times before examining the jar and drinking from it.

'I knew it would be somebody.' The voice came from the door end of the chapel.

Devlin froze, and then continued drinking. 'It's always somebody or other,' he said. He turned slowly to see an old man holding a scythe, its blade on the floor between his feet.

'I saw you coming along the sea road. You saw me at the grass and so you stopped. You waited and smoked. Then you thought I'd gone, so you come on.' The man came to another of the benches and lowered himself on to it. 'Old bones,' he said. He propped the scythe against the wall.

'Who are you, then?' Devlin said. 'Old Father Time?'

'I've heard that said often enough. That or the Grim Reaper. Take your pick. I keep an eye on the place, that's all.'

'What for? Been deserted for as long as anybody can remember.'

'Fourteen years, not that long. Nineteen forty. Wartime regulations. Cleared the congregation out to Friskney or Wrangle. Happy to go, most of them.'

'So why bother now?'

'My father used to preach here. My mother was treasurer for the Chapel Guild. She was baptized in the sea here. Name's Samuel. I was supposed to inherit wisdom.'

'I see,' Devlin said. He didn't, not really.

The old man half raised his hand and then lowered it. Then he indicated the jar Devlin still held. 'I wouldn't mind a taste of that.'

Devlin refilled the jar and went to him.

'It's warm,' Samuel said.

'What were you expecting?'

Samuel shrugged and went on drinking, handing the jar back to Devlin to fill again. Water ran down his chin on to the vest he wore.

'You got one of them fags going begging?'

Devlin gave him one and lit another for himself.

'Where you get your tobacco?' Samuel said.

'Scrounged, mostly.'

'Tastes it.'

Devlin shook his head at the remark.

'What's your name?'

'Smith,' Devlin said. He tapped his nose. 'Keep *that* out.'

'I had three brothers,' Samuel said. 'Solomon, Amos and Isaiah.'

'And?'

'Nothing. I was just saying. How long you been sleeping here?'

'Who says I'm sleeping here? Hardly a hotel, is it?'

'That's your blanket pushed up the back. The place is full of empty tins, bottles and ash. *Somebody's* sleeping here, and I'm guessing by the state of you that it's you.'

'What's that supposed to mean?' Devlin said. He brushed again at the clay on his legs and arms. 'It's only a bit of mud.'

'And the rest,' Samuel said. 'Don't worry, son, I know when to keep it buttoned. You're on hard times, that's all, and we've all known *them*.'

Devlin wanted to tell him that he'd got it all wrong. 'Hard times all round,' he said.

Three weeks had passed since he'd left the Harrap place. And in all that time, no one had come looking for him. All of Skelton's threats had evaporated into thin air.

On the day he'd gone, he'd walked seven miles; the next, four. He'd considered following the Witham to Tattershall and landing at his sister's place. But he hadn't seen the woman for three years, and he doubted her husband hated him any less for all that passed time. Absence and the heart and all that. And so instead he'd turned at Boston and followed the signs for Wainfleet. At the end of the second day he'd fallen asleep in a sluice shed, and when he'd woken he'd seen the chapel in the distance, remembered it from his solitary Sunday-school visit as a child, and had come to it as though it were a sign, a beckoning, comfortable home.

The smoke from the cigarettes filled the warm air above the two men and was marbled in the dim light. In Devlin's mind, he had left Harrap's of his own free will. No one had followed him

19

and no one was looking. The tie was severed and that was all that mattered. And every day that passed convinced him further of this. That bastard of a bailiff had said nothing to nobody. And certainly not about his scratched arm. And why hadn't he said anything? Because he'd be a laughing-stock, that's why; stood to reason. You could get injured worse than that any night of the week in any bar between Grantham and Lynn. And besides, he probably wasn't even supposed to have had that fat tart of a wife in tow. Probably breaking half a dozen regulations just by having her stick her nose into the official proceedings.

'Soldiers,' the old man said unexpectedly, drawing Devlin back to him.

'What about them?'

'They've had it harder than most. Do your bit, did you?'

Devlin nodded.

'You hardly look of an age.'

'I'm twenty-nine,' Devlin said, making his own quick calculation.

'Where were you?'

'Germany. Crossing of the Rhine. You heard about that, I suppose?'

'Heard about it all, one way or another. You settle to anything since?'

Devlin leaned forward, his head low, his eyes on the floor. 'You ask a lot of questions,' he said.

'I suppose I do. It's not even as though I don't already know the answers to most of them. I'm sixty-nine. If I don't know it all by now, when will I? You're here, aren't you? As far as I can see, all you've got to show for the past nine years is a blanket, the clothes you're stood up in and whatever else you're humping around in that sack.' He nodded at the sack still standing beside the loose panel.

'Potatoes, mostly,' Devlin said.

'Be the size of peas this time of year.'

'They are.'

Neither man spoke for a moment.

'I look after the sheep,' Samuel said eventually. 'Out on the marsh. Lambing time. Used to be a full-time job before the war came along. Now they only want me at lambing, and sometimes to help at the markets. There's still every shortage you'd care to mention and yet the price of mutton is half what it was ten years ago. It makes no sense. Or if it does, then it makes no sense to me.' He paused and looked away from Devlin. 'You get any idea about touching one of them and I'd be obliged to bring the law to you.'

'Everybody threatens the same.'

'Perhaps, but I'm serious. There's still a Police House in Wainfleet. They'd be here in the hour.'

'But only once you'd spent three hours walking to get them,' Devlin said.

'There is that. What, and you'd be long gone by then?'

'What do you think? Stop worrying. Killing a sheep – more trouble than it's worth. Not at today's prices.'

It was a joke and Samuel smiled. 'My daughter's eldest was out there. Italy. Killed. You can't begin to imagine the grief that landed on us all. Buried over there. She hasn't so much as laid a bunch of flowers on his grave. Imagine that. Nineteen, he was. Same as you, probably, when you did your bit. Grief like you was living in a constant storm of wind and rain. A year to the day, she tried to kill herself. Cut her wrist. Boston hospital for two months. They wanted to move her to a place towards Gains-borough, but I told them I wasn't having any of that. Been looking after her more or less ever since. Her husband – call him that – went off with a woman from Grantham way. Biggest waste of space I ever knew.'

'You hear it a lot,' Devlin said, as though he too had a tale as dark and as all-consuming waiting to be told.

'I suppose you do,' Samuel said. 'I cut the grass over at Saint Margaret's, and once a fortnight at Saint Mary's. Summer work, mostly. The winters are long.'

The names meant nothing to Devlin.

'Keep yourself busy, that's the main thing.'

'If you say so,' Devlin said.

'Not exactly the life and soul, are you?'

'And you are?'

Samuel laughed again. 'No, I don't suppose I am, come to think of it. Overrated, happiness.' He handed the empty jar back to Devlin. 'I wouldn't mind another.'

Devlin fetched him more water.

'What will you do?'

'Do?' Devlin said.

'When you leave here. I don't suppose you're planning to live here for ever.'

'I'm waiting to see what turns up,' Devlin said.

'Oh, that always happens. Good or ill, something always turns up. Good or ill, there's always something coming along the road towards you. I suppose all your plans are gone. My daughter's boy, he wanted to be an engineer. Studying for the work when he got his call-up. He said we had to build for the future. Every word he said, you could believe in. When he was killed, all that went with him. Her, me, everybody. Each time I go out, I tell her when I'll be back, and then I have to make sure I get back to the house on the dot. Sometimes, when I'm early, I go and sit somewhere and wait. Speaking of which . . .' He rose stiffly to his feet. 'I ache in every joint,' he said. 'You can hear me creaking.' He stood and flexed his shoulders, swinging his thin arms. 'I suppose I should wish you luck, but the stuff's in short supply these days, especially for the likes of you and me. And even when it does show its face, it rarely comes up to muster.'

'You got that right,' Devlin said.

The old man walked to the chapel door. 'You want to draw your water from beyond the Bystall pump. Cleaner. That stuff you're drinking will sicken you in a week.'

'I'll be long gone by then,' Devlin said.

Samuel pushed open the chapel door and stood framed in the afternoon light. 'I can't even ask you back for a proper night's sleep and some decent rations,' he said. 'The girl. Strangers, see?'

Devlin said he understood.

'We all have our cross to bear,' Samuel said. He looked hard at Devlin for a moment, and then at the building around him. 'You wouldn't believe how full this place used to get on Chapel anniversaries, celebration days.'

After that, he let himself out.

When Devlin went to the doorway a few minutes later, the old man was a distant figure on the bank road, already half lost in the heat, and looking to Devlin as though he were legless, somehow floating above the lost course of his own path home.

3

DEVLIN WENT TO RETRIEVE HIS RABBIT GUN. HE HADN'T been thinking straight on the day he'd gone from Harrap's, but straight enough to know that if either Harrap or Skelton *had* set the police on him, they would be easier to dodge without the actual weapon in his hand. He was a smarter man than most, and certainly smarter than either Skelton or Harrap would ever give him credit for.

But approaching the Outmarsh Bank, he knew even from a mile away, from beyond the old brickworks, that everything was wrong, that everything had changed since he'd hidden the gun.

A dozen pieces of earth-moving machinery – bulldozers, mostly, and a pair of bucket dredgers – were lined up across the top of the bank above the drain, and at least a hundred men either sat on these or worked across the nearby slope.

He drew closer, until the noise of the machinery and shouting voices filled the air. He climbed the bank and watched the slow progress of the dredgers, their belts of buckets scooping the heavy grey clay from the water and laying it behind them in a saturated trail.

He had hidden the rifle inside a pile of pipes beside a deserted brick-built store a hundred yards from the old pump. Now there were no pipes and no store and no pump. Everything had been flattened, churned to mud and then flattened again. The land for another hundred yards on all sides was criss-crossed with the pattern of the giant tyres.

He went closer to where the store had been. Not even its foundations remained. A convoy of lorries carried lengths of cast-concrete piping to the drain alongside him. The men sitting on these looked down at him where he stood, and Devlin watched them go by.

A solitary man wearing a shirt and tie beneath his overalls and carrying a rolled chart walked a short distance behind the final lorry. He came to Devlin and stopped beside him.

'Lost something?'

'There used to be a shed here.'

'Used to be.' The man swung his chart from side to side.

Devlin considered the distant men for a moment. 'You're widening the drain,' he said.

'Among other things. Should have been done decades ago. The flooding, see?'

The flood had come last winter, covering a wide area, drowning livestock, ruining livelihoods, killing people.

'What happened to the shed?'

The man shrugged. 'You looking for work?'

'What kind of work?'

The man nodded at the men now gathering by the lorries. 'Labouring, mostly. The machinery does most of it these days and you won't be let anywhere near any of that.' He stamped his feet on the ground as though testing something. 'Well?'

'I wouldn't mind,' Devlin said. 'For a few weeks. I could use the money.'

'Everybody gets paid a week in arrears. You got your cards?'

Devlin shook his head. 'Lost everything in the flooding. I'm still waiting for them to come through.' He surprised himself at the ease with which the lie came.

'We've been told to take on casuals. Locals.'

'That's me,' Devlin said. 'Both counts.' He held out his hand to the man.

'You ever done this kind of work before?'

'Worked all my life on the land. Apart from a bit of soldiering.'

The last remark made the man look up at him. 'We've all done a bit of that,' he said. 'One way or another.' He leaned to one side and looked up and down the drain, sighting something along his outstretched arm. 'See that man standing on the bonnet of that lorry? Foreman. Go and see him. Tell him Mister Tindall can vouch for you.'

'You hardly know me,' Devlin said.

'Perhaps, but I see enough men like you to know you better than you might think. Besides, we have rotas to fill. What was it you were looking for?'

Devlin turned to look at the man on the distant lorry, waving his arms and shouting at the labourers around him.

'Nothing much. I was just looking, that's all.'

'Go and see him. He'll tell you when and where to get started. Tell him the bit about being flooded out. He's ex-military himself, so . . .'

'Right,' Devlin said, and set off towards the lorries.

Upon his approach, the man on the bonnet shouted down for him to stay where he was. A succession of smaller tipper lorries came slowly up the low bank and then along its rim. They carried sludge from the dredgers and laid it in mounds over the adjoining fields. When they had passed, the man climbed down and approached Devlin.

'Tindall sent me,' Devlin said, as though he already knew the man well. 'I'm looking for work.'

'That's *Mister* Tindall to you.' The man considered Devlin and shook his head at what he saw. 'We only take on *bona fide* grafters.'

'I can graft.'

'Go on.'

'I worked on the Steeping Bank and then the Wainfleet Staunch at the Havenhouse Station. Dug the channel *and* laid the rail bed.'

'I can check up on all of that easy enough.'

No he couldn't.

'Feel free,' Devlin said. 'Went straight into the work when I was demobbed. Forty-six. After two years' Active.'

The man nodded at everything he said. 'And since then?'

'Bits and pieces. The flood put an end to most of it.'

The man screwed up his face. 'I can start you as a casual,' he said. 'Paid weekly. You just do what you're told and no complaining.'

'It's what I'm good at,' Devlin said.

'We'll see. You got any work clothes?'

'Not on me. I wasn't expecting to be here.'

'Follow me,' the man said, and led Devlin to a caravan parked below the embankment.

He pushed open the door and then pulled a face at the smell inside. 'There's overalls, boots and hats. New regulations say we've got to wear hats. No one does. If we're due a Ministry inspector, word will get round. If there *is* an inspection and you're not wearing a hat, then that's you gone, capiche?'

'Capiche,' Devlin said. He wondered if he ought to salute.

Beyond the caravans a line of men had been digging into a

ditch and throwing the wet clay into one of the waiting tippers. At the foreman's approach they'd all been sitting on the slope, smoking and talking.

'Find something your size and then come and get me. I'll fill in your forms.'

Devlin explained about his cards.

'I hear that same old story ten times a week. All I really need is a name and an address.'

'"No Fixed Abode" do?' Devlin said.

The man clicked his lips. 'Smart lad like you – you'll find somewhere.'

Devlin went into the caravan and searched among the scattered, mud-stained clothing for a pair of overalls that fitted him. He found boots and a helmet, and a belt which he pulled tight at his waist. He put on a pair of stiff gauntlets and considered his reflection in a dirty mirror. He looked like a different man completely and smiled at what he saw.

Going back outside, he sought out the foreman.

'At least now you look the part. I'm Thompson, by the way. I'm the one who tells you what to do, and I'm the one you say "Yes, sir" and "No, sir" to. Are we clear on all that?'

'As water,' Devlin said.

Thompson looked into the water below them and shook his head. He told Devlin to join the men digging nearby.

Devlin went to the men and those closest to him introduced themselves. It was clear to Devlin that they were all just waiting for Thompson to leave before stopping work and settling themselves back on the bank again.

When Thompson finally went, the man beside Devlin asked him where he lived. When Devlin said he was looking for somewhere, the man took him along the slope and pointed to the high frame of the distant Crescent Sluice.

'See that? Track on the left, running in from the coast. Half a mile on the right. Ray Duggan's farm. Flooded out and never properly brought back. He lets out rooms to make ends meet. If you're interested.'

Devlin thanked the man and memorized the directions.

He worked at the shovelling for the rest of the day. At noon the others ate the food they'd brought with them. Seeing Devlin had nothing, the man who'd told him about the farm shared his own dry sandwiches.

They worked until four, when a whistle blew and everyone immediately stopped what they were doing. Devlin followed the others back to the caravan, where they all took off their work clothes and then washed themselves at several nearby stand-pipes. Devlin did the same, rinsing the worst of the mud from his overalls and boots.

Setting off towards the sluice, he carried the overalls on his back, drying them in the sun as he walked.

He followed the bank to the sluice and then turned along the track. Every muscle and joint in his body ached. He was expected back at the drain at six in the morning, another half-hour's walk. Men did this day after day after day of every month of every year of their long working lives.

As he walked, the caked mud peeled and fell from his clothing and boots and skin. The rotting-vegetable smell of the drain stayed with him every step of the way.

4

ARRIVING AT THE FARMHOUSE, DEVLIN WAITED AT THE gate and studied the place. The fields around it were unploughed and weed-filled. Furniture and waste were piled and scattered in the yard surrounding the building. Another flooded farm not yet recovered. Devlin's first thought was that the place was empty, but as he watched, the door opened and a woman came out. She carried a wicker basket and started pegging washing to a line.

Devlin watched her, careful not to attract her attention. But something caught the woman's eye and she stopped pegging. She raised the sheet she had just hung and looked directly at Devlin.

She watched him for a moment before taking a few paces towards him. 'What you looking at?'

Devlin unfastened the tied sleeves of his overalls and shook more dirt from them. 'I'm looking for Duggan,' he said.

'Which one? There's my husband and there's his father.'

'I was told there was a room to rent. I'm working on the drainage.'

The woman said nothing in reply to this.

Devlin guessed her to be in her mid forties. Her hair fell

loose over her face. There was dirt on her cheeks. Her legs were bare. She wore canvas shoes, a pinafore and an apron.

'You want my husband,' she said.

Picking up his helmet and gloves, Devlin went closer to her.

'What's your name?' she said to him, and Devlin told her.

'I'm Alison Duggan. I can't say anything one way or another until Duggan gets home.'

'You got a room or not?' Devlin suddenly felt weak on his legs. 'I've been either walking or shovelling all day.'

'So? I still can't say. Look around you. We're not in a good way here.' She motioned to the discarded furniture. 'Can't even get it to burn with petrol.'

Devlin saw where several of the mounds had been scorched and then left.

'Duggan poured it on, but the stuff was saturated. Under water for a week, most of it. We lost everything.'

'It'll dry in time,' Devlin said, turning his closed eyes to the sun.

'I daresay. Last man we had staying here went off owing a week's rent.'

'I can't give you a penny until I get paid, but after that I can give you something in advance.'

'It's not open to negotiation. My husband will tell you exactly what and when you pay.'

'Where'd you learn long words like that?' Devlin said.

'"Negotiation"? Oh, I know words much longer than that. And soon I'll be living somewhere where I get to use most of them.'

'Boston?' Devlin said, causing the woman to smile.

'Yeah, that's right. Boston.'

She was still considering the remark when a much older man

31

appeared round the side of the house behind her. He called out to her and she immediately fell silent.

'Who's he?' the man shouted, coming to stand beside her, almost as though to protect her from Devlin.

'He's looking for a room.'

The man embraced her and kissed her cheek. The woman stiffened at the gesture, her eyes fixed on Devlin.

When the old man released her, she returned to where the basket of clothes still stood beneath the line. Water had already pooled on the ground around it, drying at its edges.

The old man came to Devlin.

Devlin saw that he carried a heavy book which he had so far held behind his back.

'I'm Duggan,' he said. 'Any business here, I'm the one you're seeking.'

'The drainage sent me,' Devlin said. *Seeking?*

'The drainage. I see.' Then the old man raised the book he held and waved it in Devlin's face. 'Know what this is?'

Behind her father-in-law, the woman covered her mouth and shook her head in amusement.

'I'm going to guess at a Bible,' Devlin said.

'Then you're guessing right. You're a shiftless, know-it-all smartarse – I can see that much just by looking at you in your hand-me-downs – but if you can't put your hand on this book and swear to act honest and decent and pay everything you owe, then you can turn right round and walk all the way back to wherever it was you started from. And after that you can walk ten miles further and forget you were ever here.'

'I'm as honest as the next man,' Devlin said, more to prolong the woman's amusement than to appease the old man.

'That's not saying much in this part of the great wide world.'

Devlin shrugged. Another pointless argument. 'You sound like a preacher,' he said.

'That's because I am one.'

Devlin doubted this. 'Ordained?'

'What's that ever been worth? I'm a man of God.'

'I'll bet,' Devlin said, but in a low voice that only the woman heard, causing her to turn away from the pair of them.

'The world hereabouts is changing faster than men can walk,' the old man said. 'Especially since the flood. The simple fact is, even honest men need to be led back to firm ground every now and again.'

'And that's what you do, is it – show them the way, all those lost and wandering honest men?'

The old man looked at the piles of waste all around him. 'This, all this – this was God's lesson to us all. You don't agree with that – I can see that, too – but that's what it was. What else would it have been?'

'If you say so,' Devlin said. He turned to the woman, who moved along the sagging line, hanging out smaller pieces. 'That what she believes, too, is it?'

The old man seemed suddenly uncertain of himself. 'I know she laughs at me,' he said. 'Both of them do, her and Duggan. It's an easy thing to do – mock a man of conviction. You and all your engineers and diggers, you think you've got all the answers, all the power and reckoning in the world. Well, that's exactly what you thought and believed until the water came overtopping everything you'd put in place last time to keep it out.' He ran out of breath and wiped a sleeve across his face.

'I've only been at the work a day,' Devlin said. 'Nothing to do with me.'

'Makes no odds.'

Devlin wondered what the old man's rant had achieved. 'I only came looking for a room,' he said.

'Then come in and look at it,' the old man said. He called for the woman to accompany them and she picked up the empty basket and followed them into the house.

'You smell that?' he said when they were inside. 'Floodwater. Take a house this old five more summers to get rid of that smell. And then it'll be back at the first bit of dampness. You'll never keep the wet out of the bones of a place like this.'

The sharp odour caught in Devlin's throat.

'You get used to it. Keep a few doors and windows open. It's worst in the early spring when the first heat comes. The winter will kill it off again.'

Devlin wafted the air with his hand. He'd smelled the same in a dozen other houses. He looked at the waist-high tide mark around the room. In places, the plaster had already been scraped away to reveal the lathwork beneath.

'Duggan started to strip the place out,' the woman said. 'Not much point, to my mind.'

The boards beneath Devlin's feet sagged where he walked and he tested the spring in the wood.

'Joists are still good,' the old man said. 'You might go through the boards in a few places, but that's all.'

'And here's me thinking you'd have people queuing back to the road to rent that room.'

'Needs must, I suppose,' the old man said. He sat at the table and placed the Bible at its centre. 'Swear on it,' he said to Devlin, tapping a finger on the gilt lettering.

'Swear what?'

'That you're an honest man.'

34

Devlin sat opposite the man. 'And suppose I say it and then burst into flames where I sit?'

'Then we'll know two things for certain,' the old man said. 'One, that you're an out-and-out liar – though not many set any store by the truth these days.'

'And the second? If I burn.'

'That the place is drying out faster than we thought.' He laughed at the remark and both Devlin and the woman joined in. The old man's laughter became uncontrollable and turned into a bout of coughing and then breathlessness from which he struggled to recover. He motioned for the woman to pat his back, and she came to the table and did this.

Watching her, it occurred to Devlin that she struck the old man with her cupped hand considerably harder than was necessary.

Eventually, the old man grew calm and sat breathing deeply for a moment.

The woman went to the sink, leaving the men together at the table.

'How long do you reckon you'll stick at the work?' the old man asked Devlin when he was finally able to speak. 'It's hard work, the drainage. Look at your hands, you're not going to last the month. And then where will the rent come from?'

'I'll stick at it until something better comes along,' Devlin said.

'And what would that be? These are hard times all round. The politicians try to tell us different, but they're the biggest liars of all. Hard times, and likely to get even harder.'

'If you say so,' Devlin said.

'I was right about you and that mouth of yours. I knew it the minute I saw you in the yard. What you running away from? The law?'

'Who says I'm running away from anything?'

'You just did. You aren't anywhere near as clever as you like to think you are. I'm not saying that you're stupid, but then again I never believed that being stupid was the opposite of being smart.'

'You've lost me,' Devlin said.

'I lost you the minute you tried to get one over on me,' the old man said. 'But do it anyway.'

'Do what?'

'Put your hand on this book here and tell me you'll pay up on time while you're living under my roof.'

'Whatever you want,' Devlin said and slapped his hand down on the Bible.

'Say it,' the old man said. 'We're all waiting.'

5

DUGGAN CAME BACK TO THE FARM TWO HOURS LATER. HE
drove a flat-back lorry whose uneven load was loosely sheeted.

From where he lay, Devlin heard murmured and then raised
voices in the room below. This was followed by Duggan coming
to the bottom of the steep stairs and shouting for him to go
down to them.

Devlin went down.

'You need to go,' Duggan said to him before Devlin could
say anything.

Devlin looked at Duggan's father, still at the table, who
avoided looking at him, pretending instead to study the crumpled
newspaper he held across his knees.

'I'd have told you straight off,' Duggan said. 'Except I was
out.'

'I swore on the Bible to pay my rent as soon as I'm paid,'
Devlin said.

Duggan smiled. 'The old fool makes everybody do that. It
doesn't mean a thing. Probably even told you he was a preacher.'

'I am,' Duggan's father insisted.

'I've unpacked all my stuff now,' Devlin said.

'What does that amount to? You've only got the clothes

you're standing up in and the ones the drainers hand out. Besides, you won't stick at it a week, man like you.'

'He already told me that,' Devlin said. 'Besides, you're both wrong. I'm a trained mechanic. They'll have me working on the machines, the engines, before long. I've only been there a day. You wait.' It seemed a fair argument to him.

Duggan laughed at this, and then he grabbed Devlin's hand and turned it palm up on the table. 'Now tell me you're a mechanic. You're casual, that's all, and a week of that kind of work will see you long gone. And my rent with you.'

'Not me,' Devlin said. 'Besides, I need the money.'

Duggan let go of his hand and Devlin resisted the urge to rub where the man's strong fingers had dug into him. He considered another way. 'I was flooded out just like you,' he said.

'Where?'

'Over beyond the Three Towns drain close to Sutterton.' The place had been in all the papers.

'Never heard of it,' Duggan said.

'So?'

Duggan dropped heavily into the room's only armchair. The aroma of cooking meat and vegetables filled the house.

No one spoke. Duggan studied Devlin closely.

Devlin decided to act, seizing whatever small advantage he might have gained from the lie. 'You say everything as though it's the gospel truth,' he said. 'So what if you don't believe me? So what if you never heard of the place? We were flooded out, like hundreds of others. We lost the house and the family split up to stay wherever we could. At least you three got back to your own home.'

'This dump?' Duggan said, looking around him.

'At least it's something. It's more than some ever did.'

'Any kids?' Duggan said.

Devlin shook his head.

'So how come you ended up here?'

'The drainage pointed him at us,' Duggan's father said. 'Perhaps they wanted to make up for the last one they sent.'

'No one's seen hide nor hair of *him*,' Duggan said. 'And, believe me, I've looked. And what's worse, the thieving little bastard owed money everywhere I asked.' He turned to Devlin. 'I *will* find him, incidentally – just in case you were thinking of following in his tracks.'

'And when you do . . . ?' Devlin said, more to encourage Duggan than to hear his answer.

Duggan made a strangling motion with his hands. 'Guess,' he said.

Alison Duggan started laying the table. Before Duggan's return, it had been agreed that Devlin would pay for a single evening meal each day, nothing more.

'Tell me where your mother's staying now,' Duggan said unexpectedly as the three of them sat and waited for their food.

'Why her?'

'Because if you do scarper, then I'll know where to start looking. And if you run past her, I'll see what *she's* got to cover the cost.'

Devlin hadn't seen his mother for two years. He had no idea where she was now. The last he'd heard she was living somewhere in Terrington Parish, close to his sister. 'She lost most of everything she'd ever owned in the flood,' Devlin said. He was beginning to wonder if the flood might not be an answer to everything: geography *and* history wiped clean and ready to be made anew. As far as Devlin was concerned, he'd been abandoned by his father when he was five, and by his mother ten years later.

'So *you* say,' Duggan said. He picked the dirt from the hairs on his forearms.

'You think a son would lie about a thing like that, about his own mother?'

'It's what you are – a liar,' Duggan said. 'We already established that much.'

'And what's this place?' Devlin said. 'You make it sound like a four-star hotel, room service, all that.'

The room he had been given was bare except for a sheetless bed, a dressing table, a chair and a small wardrobe. There was a mirror on the wall in the shape of a flower, and on the wall by the solitary window, a small black cross. He had taken this down and put it in a drawer. And then a minute later he had retrieved it and hung it back on the wall. Besides, it had left a mark on the wallpaper, and a cross of any sort was still a cross.

For a second time, Duggan looked hard at Devlin. 'I recognize you,' he said. 'Our paths have crossed.'

'It's a small world,' Devlin said.

'Oh, it's that all right. It'll come to me.' He closed his eyes for a moment.

Devlin watched the slow smile form on Duggan's lips.

'Were you Army?' Duggan said.

'Lincolnshires. Like I said, Engineers. You?' It was what men did.

'Royal Norfolks. I was overseas for two years. Then back here, and then down in Colchester.' He continued looking directly at Devlin as he said all this.

Devlin guessed the man to be eight or nine years older than himself, ten at a push. He had a tattoo on each forearm, military insignia, the blue ink blurring beneath the hairs.

'Perhaps our paths crossed then,' Devlin said. He pretended

to read the newspaper in the old man's lap, as though he might divert Duggan's calculations.

'Perhaps they did,' Duggan said. 'It'll come to me. It always does. You need a good eye and a memory for faces in my line of work.'

Devlin resisted asking him what that was.

Alison Duggan put a bowl of steaming potatoes on the table, followed by a plate of sliced meat, and the four of them ate. Devlin waited until the other three had helped themselves before scraping what little remained on to his own plate.

The old man looked at this and said, 'That all you want?'

'Perhaps he lost his appetite,' Duggan said.

Devlin told Alison Duggan that the food was delicious and she shook her head at the remark.

When the meal was finished, Duggan's father said, 'We applied to all the Boards for compensation. They told us straight off that we had nothing coming. Lost everything and no one was to blame. Act of God, see? We had no insurance. Who does?'

'We were in the exact same boat,' Devlin said, glad to be back in these calmer waters. Feeling suddenly brave, and guessing that he would be allowed to stay, he said to Duggan, 'So, what kind of work *are* you in?'

Duggan sat picking at his teeth for a moment before answering. 'This and that,' he said.

It was what Devlin had guessed, what he had wanted to hear. Three small and seemingly insignificant words, and yet he now knew precisely where he stood with the man.

'What is it – scrap, salvage? I saw your load. I daresay it's a good time to be in that particular line.'

'It's been worse,' Duggan said. He looked closely at the speck of food on the tip of his finger.

Salvage merchants. Scavengers and thieves making a small fortune in the receding waters of other people's lives.

Devlin weighed up his chances. 'I could give you a hand,' he said. 'If ever you needed it, I mean.'

Duggan shook his head. 'You'll be worn out from all the digging and fetching and carrying you'll be doing at the drainage. Besides, you've got to know what you're doing, otherwise it's a mug's game.'

Right, Devlin thought, but said nothing.

After a short silence, Duggan's father said, 'What you get, then?' to his son.

Duggan was reluctant to talk in front of Devlin. 'A few bits and pieces, scrap mostly,' he said. 'I'll offload it in the morning. Might make a few quid, might not. Depends.'

'It's something, I suppose,' the old man said.

Duggan lit a cigarette and blew the first mouthful of smoke into Devlin's chest, where it struck him like a cloudy fist.

Point taken, Devlin thought. He looked down at the smoke, which first caressed his arms and face and then sank down over his stomach and into the space between his legs.

6

A WEEK PASSED. DEVLIN LABOURED AT THE DRAINAGE. He slept at the Duggans' run-down home and he ate with them each evening. He was unaccustomed to the heavy work and it exhausted him; most nights he was asleep by nine. He listened to old man Duggan's convoluted Bible talk and withstood his son's constant jibes and complaints. The food hardly varied from day to day. When Alison Duggan served up fish one night, both Duggan and his father refused to eat it, adding bread to their potatoes instead.

No one at the flood repair work recognized his potential and he remained a labourer. When he tried to tell the foreman of his military experience with engines, the man laughed at him and said, 'You and a million others, chum, you and a million others.' The water was always cold and the mud always filthy, clinging and heavy. He was never free of the stuff. He washed himself each day with a hose in the Duggans' yard, but it stuck to him and dried on him wherever he missed it.

After that first week, as Devlin and Duggan sat together one night listening to a football match on the radiogram, and as Duggan's father slept and snored in the chair beside them,

Duggan leaned towards Devlin and said, 'I might have a little job in the offing could use some extra muscle. You interested?'

'When?' Devlin, as usual, was tired. The football finished in ten minutes.

'Tonight.'

'What sort of job?' Devlin could see Alison Duggan in the yard outside.

'What does that matter? Yes or no?'

'I suppose so,' Devlin said.

'No need to sound too keen.'

'I mean yes,' Devlin said, rubbing his face.

Two hours later, as darkness finally fell, Devlin sat beside Duggan in the uncomfortable cab of his lorry as they drove beyond Kirton before turning off the road towards the Welland, where the old and new sea banks met.

A mile from the river, Duggan pulled over and switched off his headlights.

They waited without speaking. After ten minutes, a solitary light shone on the horizon. Duggan started up the engine and they continued slowly towards the water. The path was uneven and ill-defined. A steep bank fell away on one side.

'You look worried,' Duggan said as he briefly lost control of the wheel on the soft ground.

'We'd be down that bank and under the water in five seconds flat,' Devlin said.

'Three, probably. Cheer up, misery, nearly there.'

They stopped closer to the solitary light.

Duggan turned off the engine again and climbed out, careful not to slam his door. Devlin did the same.

Duggan pointed at the light. 'Dogs,' he said.

Devlin looked around them. Beyond a low hedge, machinery

stood covered in tarpaulins. The same machinery he saw every day along the drain. He followed Duggan beyond this, to where bundles of piping and sheets of metal lay stacked.

'Start loading that,' Duggan told him, pointing to a mound of cisterns.

'That's not scrap,' Devlin said.

'What, you thought we'd come all this way in the middle of the night to do an honest day's work? Besides, that's common land. As far as I know, all this gear's been dumped here.'

'They'll trace this back to you in hours,' Devlin said, guessing.

'Us,' Duggan corrected him. 'More like days. Besides, what do you take me for? By the time we get back to our beds, this lorry will be as clean as it is now. You going to start loading or what?'

They carried the cisterns, followed by as much of the piping as they could manage to load. Devlin did most of the work while Duggan went off to search the remainder of the site, coming back with several jerry cans of petrol and coils of fabric-coated wiring.

'Good money for that,' he said as he threw the coils into the cab. 'You've got to box clever these days.' He stood for a while looking at the distant light. 'Night-watchman gets himself over there for a bit of the other most nights. I know the tart. We got at least two hours. Most nights he sleeps off his hangover until he drags himself back here an hour before the foreman arrives.' He smiled and rubbed his hands together. 'Not that he'll be here for much longer after this little caper.'

There was a night-watchman at the drainage works depot. Devlin had spoken to the man. He wondered how long it would be before Duggan started asking him questions about that particular little set-up.

Eventually, the bed of the lorry sagged on its axles and Duggan told him to stop loading.

The journey back along the narrow track took twice as long with the weight they were now carrying. Reaching the road, they turned towards Holbeach.

After a further long silence, Duggan said, 'It's finally come to me.'

'What has?'

'Where I've seen you before.' Duggan smiled at the realization.

Devlin tensed at the remark. 'Where was that, then?' The words dried in his mouth.

'You was in the Colchester barracks nick. Military.'

'Not me,' Devlin said.

'You got a twin, then. What was it you were in for?'

'I already told you—'

'And I heard you. What was it? Pilfering Army goods?'

Devlin turned to look out into the passing darkness. Isolated lights shone in the distance. The lorry's headlights barely illuminated the road ahead of them.

'I knew it,' Duggan said. 'How long was you in for?'

'End of hostilities,' Devlin said. He'd served five months for stealing fuel and selling it to a garage owner in the town. Red petrol, easy to spot, not much harder to trace. Everybody Devlin knew was at it. Perhaps not *everybody*, but a good few. He'd been caught making his third delivery to the man. Caught, charged, tried, found guilty, imprisoned, all in the space of a week. The two others he'd been with had both avoided capture and had gone on stealing and selling the fuel until their discharge a year later. Devlin had hoped they might have compensated him for keeping his mouth shut, but nothing came, and both men went back into the world without him even knowing where or when.

'What about you?' he said eventually to Duggan.

'What about me what? Did *I* serve time, you mean? Hardly. No, I used to deliver in and out of the barracks and the prison. A bit of black-market stuff now and then. But I always knew exactly how far to push it, see? Most of the redcaps in that place were as bent as Essex. *You* just didn't know the ones to get on your side. Besides, how old were you?'

'Eighteen, nineteen.'

'Christ. Conscript? And I bet that's as far as you ever got – Colchester nick. Am I right?'

'So what?' Devlin said.

'You take offence too easy, son. Most of the blokes I know have been inside at one time or another. Some of them for long spells. Stealing petrol? They wouldn't take two steps out of their way to get involved in that little lark. And especially not in the last few months of hostilities. I knew a quartermaster-sergeant once, stationed in Italy – Naples – and he said that nine-tenths of everything that was ever delivered to him went AWOL the first night it was there. Said it was like trying to stop a river. Said he was happy if he held on to what was left. You got caught, that's all.'

They arrived at the outskirts of Holbeach and Duggan turned on to the fen road towards the South Holland drain. 'Not far now,' he said.

And even as he spoke, Devlin saw a line of trailers and lorries parked on the roadside ahead of them.

'That's us,' Duggan said. He pulled up alongside the line.

Devlin saw then that it was the trailers, lorries and dismantled machinery of a travelling fair.

'You stay put,' Duggan told him. 'I mean it.'

He climbed down and walked away, vanishing in the darkness.

He reappeared ten minutes later accompanied by two men and a woman, all of them Devlin's age. Despite the night air, the men were naked from the waist up and the woman walked with a sheet held over her shoulders. All of them, Devlin guessed, had been asleep.

Duggan motioned to him to go out to them.

The two men, Devlin now saw, were nearly identical in their appearance, both dark-skinned and black-haired.

'Meet the McGuire brothers,' Duggan said. 'And sister. They might be gyppos, but they try not to be too dishonest where I'm concerned, and, better than that, they take everything I need to move on in a hurry and pay cash-in-hand. No hanging about with this crew.' He put an arm around the shoulders of each brother.

The men, taking no obvious offence at what Duggan had just said, looked suspiciously at Devlin, then one of them shook himself free of Duggan and pushed a finger hard into Devlin's chest, causing him to stumble back against the lorry's hot radiator.

Duggan laughed at this. 'He's stronger than he looks,' he said, meaning Devlin.

Both brothers laughed.

Then the three of them went to the back of the lorry and Duggan unfastened the tarpaulin.

The woman came closer to Devlin and he saw that she was younger than he had first thought, eighteen or nineteen perhaps. Her hair and skin were as dark as her brothers'.

Devlin introduced himself.

'So?' she said to him.

The McGuire brothers pulled themselves up on to the bed of the lorry and started throwing down the cisterns and lengths of piping.

Having climbed up to look inside the cab, the girl came back to Devlin and said, 'I'm Maria. I'm their sister. They're Patrick and Colm. Patrick is the elder by a year.'

'How old are you?' Devlin wondered why he'd asked.

'How old do you think?'

'Twenty?'

'Then twenty it is.' She watched Duggan and her brothers for a moment. 'What work do you do?' she asked him.

'Drainer,' Devlin said, pleased at how easily the word now came. 'Are you with the fair?' He nodded to the parked trailers.

'On our way to Cambridge. We do the circuit. It's why Duggan likes to sell to them. This time tomorrow we'll be forty miles away. They'll only give him half of what he'd get from any of the local dealers.'

Devlin saw the simple efficiency of it all.

'You his new skivvy, or what?' Maria said.

'I lodge with him, that's all.'

She watched her brothers again. 'People are scared of him,' she said, her voice low.

'Duggan?'

'He has a reputation. He turns nasty. One minute he's all smiles and drinks-all-round and the next . . .' She clicked her lips.

'Thanks for the warning,' Devlin said.

'What warning? You knew that much already. And if you didn't, then more fool you.'

'I suppose so,' Devlin said. He took out his cigarettes and offered her one, which she accepted, leaning close to him as he lit it. He caught her sharp scent. She brushed the long hair from her face as she smoked.

They were interrupted by Patrick coming back to them and pulling her away. Devlin was about to protest at this rough treatment, but he saw by the way the girl looked at him that he should say nothing. Patrick cupped a hand to her head and whispered something to her. Maria then reached beneath the sheet she still held over her shoulders and took out a roll of banknotes. She opened this and counted through it, giving the notes she peeled away to her brother, who took them and went back to Duggan and the unloaded cisterns.

Maria came back to Devlin. 'Neither of them can read or write,' she said. 'I doubt Patrick can even count to ten.'

'Unless it was pound notes.'

She laughed at the remark. She pushed what remained of the money back beneath the sheet, and as she did this, the material swung loose to reveal one of her breasts to him. It took her a few seconds to pull the sheet back into place and hold it at her shoulder.

'I was asleep,' she said.

'I see.'

She picked a shred of tobacco from her lips.

Duggan came back to Devlin and waved the money in his face. 'She's the bookkeeper,' he said. 'You want to watch her – one word from her and the pair of them would cut you into little pieces. You know what I'm saying?'

Maria smiled at Devlin. 'It's true,' she said.

'Tell him what happened to that car dealer over in Bicker,' Duggan said.

'He looks like he's got a brain in his head,' Maria said. 'Let him imagine it.'

Duggan laughed as though it were the funniest thing he'd ever heard. Devlin imagined the money in his hand had something to do with it. Then he went back to the lorry and threw the tarpaulin and ropes back on to it.

'How much did you give him?' Devlin asked Maria while they waited.

She shook her head. 'That's between you and him.'

Devlin nodded to the cisterns and wire and piping all now scattered along the verge. 'It can all be traced,' he said.

'So what?' she said. 'This is where we found it – all dumped by the roadside.'

'Where will you sell it on?'

She shook her head again. 'You ask a lot of questions,' she said. 'Perhaps you're not as smart as you look.'

Devlin wondered if this was a compliment or an insult. 'Duggan says the same,' he said. 'About the questions.'

She turned her back on the others. 'Seriously, you want to watch him.' She drew hard on the last half-inch of her cigarette. 'First sign of any serious trouble and he'll push you in front of him.'

It was something else Devlin had already worked out, but he appreciated hearing it from her. He could say nothing in reply to this warning as Duggan and the brothers came back to them.

'He's been trying to take a squint underneath the sheet,' Patrick said loudly. 'Dirty little bastard.' The man pinched Devlin's chin and then held a finger into his cheek. 'I'm only kidding,' he said. 'You look like you're going to piss yourself.' He looked around at the others. 'He's trembling,' he said.

Devlin slapped Patrick's hand away and then swiftly wrapped his fist around the pointing finger, bending it backwards until the man cried out. It was an instinctive reaction to the

51

provocation and only as the two of them stood there like that did he start to consider the consequences of what he'd just done. At the very least, he imagined, the other brother would grab him and pull him away.

But Colm remained where he stood, and, to Devlin's surprise, he laughed and said, 'Go on, break it. He needs teaching a lesson.'

'You don't even want to be thinking of doing that,' Duggan said.

Devlin heard the fear in Duggan's voice.

He squeezed Patrick's finger tighter for a moment and then released it.

Patrick clasped his hand beneath his arm for a moment and then tested bending the finger. 'You going to let him get away with that?' he said to Colm.

Colm said nothing for a moment. 'He got the better of you for a few seconds, that's all.' He nodded to Devlin and then held out his own hand to him.

Devlin did the same and the two men shook.

'I'll have a word,' Duggan said to Patrick, but then Patrick also laughed and held out his other hand to Devlin, releasing the last of the night's small tensions.

Then Maria surprised them all by pulling out a single note from beneath her sheet and giving it to Devlin.

'What you doing that for?' Patrick said to her, as amused as he was angry at the gesture. 'We already paid Duggan.'

'You were a pound short,' Maria said, making no attempt to hide the lie.

'Wouldn't be the first time you'd come up light,' Duggan said. Then he pushed Devlin towards the lorry. 'We're off,' he said. 'He's got a hard day's work in the morning.'

The summer dawn was already brightening the sky in the direction of the sea.

As he went, Devlin half turned and held up the note to the girl.

In the cab, Duggan said. 'Christ, boy, you just escaped a fate worse than whatsit. I reckon she's took a shine to you. Did you see the look on that bastard Patrick's face when you had his finger? Believe me, there's a few pints in that little story for the foreseeable.'

They manoeuvred on to the road and drove back towards Holbeach.

After a long silence, during which Devlin felt himself falling asleep, Duggan said, 'Seriously, you want to watch yourself with that pair. She keeps a bit of a rein on them – the money and everything – but you go poking too hard and you'll find out exactly where you stand. And next time, I might not be there to help you out.'

'Is that what you did, then?' Devlin said.

'We go back a long way. It counts for something.'

If you say so.

Then Duggan laughed and started to sing, keeping Devlin awake for the rest of the journey home.

7

FOR A FURTHER MONTH THROUGH THAT LATE SUMMER
Devlin and Duggan went out every second or third night to
conduct more of Duggan's business. It seemed to Devlin that
Duggan knew every thief and dealer and opportunist within a
fifty-mile radius of the flooded-out farm.

It was a rule of Duggan's never to return home with anything iffy on the lorry. He was by nature a careful man, and he
repeatedly told Devlin what a risk he was taking simply by
allowing Devlin to accompany him on all these excursions. It
was all veiled threat and warning with Duggan, and Devlin
understood this.

On occasion, when a deal fell through or when Duggan was
beaten below his lowest price, he would stop the lorry in some
isolated spot and offload whatever he was carrying on to overgrown verges or into the dilapidated outbuildings of other
abandoned farms, to be collected later.

'Watch and learn,' he also frequently told Devlin. And so
Devlin watched and he learned, and if his time with Duggan,
the man's father and his wife had lasted beyond that final warm
month of the year, there was little doubt in Devlin's mind that
he would eventually have made himself into the sort of man

Duggan had long since become. It was an uncertain kind of reasoning – Devlin understood that, too – but it was exactly the kind of reasoning that served and motivated him best. They all lived in an unsettled world, and a world which, despite what the newspapers and radio announcers kept telling everyone, was still uncertain of the way ahead. The real trick, Devlin reasoned during his month with Duggan, was to find the best path through that maze of uncertainty and opportunity and to make sure that you maintained at least some kind of forward momentum, however weak or faltering. Looking after Number One – that was all that counted in Duggan's world.

'Dawn of a New Age?' Duggan once said to him, pronouncing the capitals and spreading his hands in a mocking theatrical flutter. 'Don't make me fucking laugh.' The war might be long gone and the country might finally be getting up off its fucking knees ten years later, but they were still hard times for most. Hard times for most and yet at the same time a world of golden opportunity for those men – those *self-made* men – who understood how to take advantage of those times. That was what Duggan called himself – a self-made man.

He told Devlin that their elders and betters had had their chance and that they'd squandered it. Now it was up to men like Duggan and Devlin to seize whatever opportunity presented itself. Was he right or was he right? Devlin knew better than to disagree with any of it. It still rankled that Duggan shared as little of the profit of all this boundless opportunity as possible, but what choice did he have?

Uncertainty, doubt and anxiety were strange notions to Duggan; all that really mattered to him was making money, getting one over on others and looking after that Number One.

'All you really need is to know the man you're dealing with

better than he thinks he knows himself,' he told Devlin. Weaknesses and strengths, that's what counted. Know *them* and you're halfway there. Know the man and you know the deal. People have secrets and weaknesses. People are greedy. Do unto others before they do unto you. That was a particular favourite and Duggan always laughed when he said it.

Duggan's kingdom stretched from Wainfleet to Anwick, and from Walcott all the way down to Peterborough and Wisbech. Weigh up the pros and cons, make a decision and stick to it. Simple as. And from Spalding they went as far east as King's Lynn and Downham Market. Men knew men who knew men, and once all those interconnections – stealing and selling and buying and selling – were made, then those men were all dependent on each other. You scratch my back, I'll scratch yours.

To begin with, most of those others were suspicious of Devlin. But Duggan vouched for him, and Duggan's word was a powerful thing in that world. As the weeks progressed, Duggan gave the orders and Devlin did more and more of the donkey work.

There was nothing Duggan wouldn't steal or buy if the opportunity arose. There was no profit, however small, he wasn't prepared to grab and then increase. He kept his ear to the ground. The bush telegraph never stopped humming. A few pints here, a few pints there, that ear to the ground, a few quid slipped into somebody's pocket, a few favours called in, a nod and a wink and those opportunities just kept on coming.

One of Duggan's biggest earners was all the flood defence and new drainage work being carried out in every direction. Empty fields turned into storage depots overnight. Machinery and building materials were delivered and re-routed and used up and gone and no one ever seemed to keep a proper tally.

Ministries of Building, Housing and Agriculture and the MOD – all of them competing with each other, and all of them too busy with the work at hand to chase up and make good any discrepancies on their dockets and rosters. It was a world in which Duggan and all the others like him walked like shabby princes.

On one occasion, Devlin accompanied Duggan to a field five miles beyond Friskney where forty donkeys stood grazing in the darkness. Actual donkeys.

The man who appeared out of the night to talk to Duggan looked like another gypsy, and after a brief conversation Duggan handed over the folded notes from his breast pocket. It was a trick of his always to have the money to hand and to take it out and hold it close to the face of the man who was arguing for more. Most deals were completed with spat-upon palms and Duggan was always careful to wait until the other man had either gone or turned his back before pulling a face and wiping his hand clean. Protocol, he explained to Devlin – another of his favourite words. Watch and learn, watch and learn.

Following the exchange, the gypsy disappeared back into the night as quickly as he had come out of it.

'Now what?' Devlin asked Duggan, standing at the gate and looking over the inquisitive donkeys, most of which congregated close to where the two men stood. Duggan called them 'Jerusalem racehorses'. 'We're waiting,' he told Devlin. Devlin wondered if the animals had come from the beach at Skegness. He had ridden on them as a small boy during the only family holiday he remembered. There was probably still a photograph of him on one of the creatures in a drawer or a tin somewhere. He wondered if their appearance in the field beyond Friskney had anything to do with the end of the summer season at the resort. It was still a year of four quarters in places like Skegness, three of them much harder and more precarious than the other one. The holidaymakers might be back for the three months of high summer, but the rest of the year was hard and empty for the place.

An hour after the departure of the gypsy, another lorry arrived and a second man came to Duggan. There was further negotiation and this time the new buyer took money from his own pocket and held it in Duggan's face. Spit and shake and walk away. Business completed.

Back in the cab, Duggan gave Devlin five pounds and told him to consider himself lucky. 'I do,' Devlin said. He didn't. He asked Duggan to tell him about the deal.

'Forty sold and ten bob profit on each one. Six of the poor bloody creatures I gave him for nothing. At least, that's what I told him. All in the delivery, the dressing-up, see? I'd expected eight bob on each, eight and a half at best, and so the two bob extra over forty ups the ante and lowers the odds, see? Seller wins, I win, buyer wins. What could be better than that?'

When Devlin asked him who the man was and why he would want to buy forty donkeys in the middle of the night in the middle of nowhere, Duggan resorted to the usual 'Ask no questions' line. 'Ours is not to question why, ours is but to do or die. That's a poem, by the way. I bet you never had me down as a poet.'

They passed the next afternoon and evening in one of the Sutton Bridge pubs spending Duggan's profit. As usual, Duggan drank until he could neither speak coherently nor stand, let alone drive the pair of them home.

Several days after the sale of the donkeys, Duggan came home and dropped a bloody sack on to the table. Duggan's father, woken by his son's noisy arrival, tipped out the contents to reveal a dozen large joints of dark meat. Blood and dust coated the pieces, attracting the room's ever-present flies.

'Best beef, that,' Duggan said. Alison Duggan took the joints to the sink and washed them.

She cooked the pieces over the following days and Devlin ate what he was given.

'He thinks it's them donkeys,' Duggan said, causing his wife and father to laugh at Devlin. 'What does he take us for, savages?'

In addition to all his dealing and thieving, Duggan also let out pieces of land scattered around the farm, and once a week he and Devlin went to meet the men who owed him rent. Few of the men appeared to undertake any kind of farming on the land, but Devlin knew enough by then not to ask. The men were always prompt with their payments, and several invariably whispered in Duggan's ear, after which money was handed back.

One night, approaching the farm following a visit to the tractor yard outside Pinchbeck, Duggan said unexpectedly, 'You set your eyes on anybody yet?' He kept his gaze straight ahead as he spoke.

It seemed to Devlin to be an uncharacteristic thing for the man to say. 'No one in particular,' he said. He thought immediately of Barbara Collet and her two-month-old daughter. He had visited prostitutes in Colchester before his imprisonment – the barracks and Army bars had been surrounded by the women – but nothing other than his two or three months with Barbara Collet since.

'Looks to me like you're having a drought,' Duggan went on, clearing his throat. 'Young shaver like yourself, it's hardly natural. I'll let you into a bit of a secret, shall I? I see a tasty old girl over Grantham way when I'm in that direction. Distant, see? You don't want to go messing in your own back yard. Been seeing her on and off these past ten years, nearer twelve.'

It was only twenty miles away, but distance enough in that neck of the woods.

Devlin wondered why Duggan had told him this.

'No, I suppose not,' he said. If nothing else, it was a new understanding between them, these two men of the world. He resisted telling Duggan about the baby girl.

'You got to take things where you find them, that's my motto,' Duggan said, again sounding uncharacteristically uncertain of himself.

Devlin wondered if the backhanded remark wasn't intended as a warning of sorts, but could think of nothing to say in answer that might make things clearer to him.

'I suppose so,' he said.

The lights of the farm appeared in the darkness ahead of them and it was the last either man said on the subject.

8

HE STOOD WITH A GROUP OF LABOURERS WAITING FOR the grading shovels to warm up. The drivers pulled the tarpaulins from the machines and then poured paraffin over the engine blocks, setting these alight and then waiting a few seconds for the vaporous blue flames to burn off. Some of the engines started first time; others were kicked and sworn at while the waiting men watched.

Thompson came to them, a sheaf of papers in his hand. He shouted for the men to listen to him. Work would be listed and men allocated. He was only going to say it all once, he called above the noise of the engines.

'Right, gather round. Some nice little bits and pieces today. Listen for your name, do what you're told, and no complaints. You're mostly casuals – you know the score by now.' He took a pencil from his pocket and licked its tip.

The men around Devlin spoke in low voices. Few of them had any time for the foreman.

Thompson allocated half of them to the grading work. Meaning they would work alongside the machines, keeping them clear of the mud and vegetation that built up around them and pulling free anything more solid which threatened to get caught in the machinery and cause delays. The previous week, a man working with the graders had got both his arms caught in a roll of barbed wire that the machine pulled up out of the water. He'd been in Boston hospital for two days and then lost a further five days' work.

The foreman looked more closely at the men. Most of the labourers avoided catching his eye. He had his favourites and was vindictive towards others.

'You.' He was pointing directly at Devlin.

'Me?'

'That's what I said. Name?'

Devlin told him, surprised Thompson had already forgotten him.

'Well, you're new to me, Devlin, but you look as though you might have leadership qualities, am I right?'

The men around Devlin shuffled a few paces away from him.

'I said am I right? And before you answer that, it's only fair to tell you that I'm not a man who likes to be proved wrong. Am I making myself clear to you?'

'I suppose so,' Devlin said. Hedging his bets.

'Good. You see that lot' – the man pointed with his pencil to a distant group of workers waiting beside a single-decker bus a hundred yards from the drain where the marsh bank ran towards it.

Devlin shielded his eyes and looked at the vehicle.

'Good. I want you to go and keep an eye on that merry bunch. They're expecting you. They know what they're here to do, so it's up to you to make sure they do it.'

Devlin had spent the past ten days labouring up to his waist in water behind one of the dredgers. Anything would be better than that.

'You heard me,' the foreman said, smiling now. 'Quick sharp.'

The others parted around him as Devlin picked up his shovel and started walking.

Approaching the bus, he saw that it was from the Sea Camp borstal at Frieston Low. Day-release inmates sent out to help with the more menial work. Before that, they'd worked at clearing up after the flooding. Devlin had seen the boys over the previous weeks, but had never approached or spoken to them. They were invariably kept apart from the other labourers and given the work even the casuals like Devlin considered beneath them.

At his arrival, a warder climbed down from the bus and came to him. The man was overweight and panted heavily at every step he took. He said something to the gathered boys, but they paid little attention to him. Most were sitting or squatting on the ground and a pall of smoke hung above them. Some played cards on the flattened grass.

'I've been sent to supervise,' Devlin said to the warder. He wondered if he should hold out his hand.

'You've been sent to do exactly what I tell you to do,' the man said. 'Supervise? Who told you that? You? I'll give you this – you've got a sense of humour.' The man held out his own hand and Devlin took it. 'I'm Sullivan, by the way. And your presence among us here today is, as they say, obligatory. *I* supervise and you just keep what they call in the trade a watching brief. We clear on that much, at least?'

Devlin nodded.

'Don't look so worried, sunshine; you drew the short straw, that's all. Whoever sent you might have had it in for you, but play your cards right and this can be a cushy little number as far as you're concerned. You and me can keep our hands clean while these idle little bastards get theirs dirty. See that drain?' He pointed to the shallow drain running the length of the field alongside the bank. 'We're clearing it out. Another party started the work a month back and we're here to finish the job. We can easily stretch this one out for two or three days by my reckoning. It's water, that's all, and whatever *we* think we might be achieving, it'll come and go as it pleases, so we do what we're told to do, pretend it's work, and then move on to something else probably just as pointless. Where's the point in breaking into a sweat in that particular little scenario? Didn't we learn *anything* after this last lot?'

'The flood?'

'What else? I spent every day of last week – not me person-ally, you understand – filling sandbags. Sandbags, I ask you.' He looked around him at the scattered boys.

Devlin guessed there were thirty of them.

'Besides, you won't get much out of this lot. Blood out of a stone most days. What's your name?'

Devlin told him.

'Well, Devlin, this is how it works. I tell the lazy little bas-tards what to do, and then you sign off on my dockets for the work done. When it's time for a break or to leave, you can help me to count them all back on board and then sign off again. I can't make it any simpler for you.'

'No, I don't suppose you can,' Devlin said, mostly under his breath.

Sullivan turned back to the boys and started calling their names. Each one rose in a desultory manner and picked up a shovel or a bucket or a rake. They walked along the course of the shallow drain and then slid down into it until they were up to their shins in its stagnant water.

'You won't drown,' Sullivan shouted to them. 'And if you do, we'll clean you up nice and proper before boxing you up and sending you back to your mother.'

Devlin waited beside the man, wondering what was expected of him.

The last of the boys were sent to that part of the drain beyond the bank and started work there.

Watching them, Devlin saw that they did little. Six shovelfuls to fill a bucket where one or two was normal. Rakes and shovels splashed around in the water to no effect. Boys chopped at the surrounding low bank and then scooped up the dislodged soil from the water and threw it back on to the slope.

'I know what you're thinking,' Sullivan said. 'Why bother? Government, see? Home Office. This is what they call "rehabilitation".' He stretched the word out to each of its unbelievable syllables. 'Supposed to be teaching them something useful. Happening all over the country, apparently. Teach them something useful and they stay out of prison proper. Ask me, most of this lot ought to be taken straight there when their time's up at the borstal. They're laughing at us, every single one of them, because they know that all this ends when they're eighteen. After that, they get a clean slate and start all over again. Useful? I ask you. Digging out a blocked drain that some bone-idle farmer hasn't even *thought* about clearing in the past twenty years. How on God's good earth is that useful?'

Devlin nodded his agreement to everything the man said.

Mid morning, Sullivan rose to his feet and blew a whistle. The boys climbed out of the drain and sat in the sun.

'Half an hour,' Sullivan said to Devlin. 'It seems a lot. Used to be what they called "discretionary". You know what that means?'

Devlin did, but shook his head.

'It means *I* used to be the one who decided how long the break lasted. Me. New rules and regulations, see? Everything's written down these days. No good arguing with any of it. Besides, one of yours could do the work of ten of these idle little bleeders. They know it, I know it, and our lords and masters know it. Everybody knows it – the Drainage Board, your bosses, my governor, everybody.' He became more exasperated and breathless with each unhappy addition to the list. His argument was with everyone and everything. 'They even considered sending the farmers and landowners a bill for the work. Imagine that.'

'They could afford to pay it,' Devlin said.

'Oh, you been in that game, then, farming?'

'Not really. But once the salt's gone off the land, it's still worth money.'

'I daresay. What, and we're only adding to their coffers with all this?'

'None of my concern,' Devlin said.

Sullivan took a solitary cigarette from his pocket, lit it and smoked in long breaths. Devlin lit one of his own.

'Is this all we do?' Devlin asked him. 'Watch over them?'

'What more do you want? Believe me, we'll have our work cut out if one of them tries to leg it.'

'Here?'

'You think they don't try? We get two or three every month in the summer. Some of them are just kids. Shoplifting, petty theft. We even get them sent to us for truanting. Some of them take to the life, some don't. We even get a few who try—' Sullivan stopped talking.

'Try what?' Devlin said.

'You know . . .' Sullivan held a fist to his neck and tilted his head.

Devlin understood him. He looked along the line of resting boys.

'And you can guess who gets the blame for that, can't you?'

You, Devlin thought.

'That's right. Muggins here. Me and all the others. Apparently, we should have been keeping a closer eye, spotted the so-called signs. *What* so-called signs? It's the same when the little bastards start fighting among themselves. We should have seen that coming, too.' He pushed the last of his cigarette into the ground and looked at his watch. 'Twenty-two minutes.' He took out his whistle and blew on it. The boys rose slowly to their feet and resumed their work.

'Getting warm,' Sullivan said. 'Let's go back to the bus. We can see better from up there. I got a flask.'

Devlin followed him to the bus and the two men sat looking out at the expanse of the surrounding fields. Further along the main drain, the dredgers and graders were moving noisily along the embankments.

Sullivan took out his flask and poured them both a drink.

Devlin sipped at the sugarless liquid and pulled a face.

'I'm supposed to be losing weight,' Sullivan said, patting the tight globe of his stomach. 'Medicals. You wed?'

'Not yet.'

Then Sullivan clicked his fingers and said, 'You're Jimmy Devlin's boy. Thought I saw the likeness. You used to live over Moulton way.'

'I *am* Jimmy Devlin,' Devlin said.

'No offence intended. You know what I mean.'

'He buggered off when I was a kid. We haven't seen him in years. The odd story, but that's all.'

'He's still your father,' Sullivan said.

'Might as well be dead for all it matters. Neither use nor ornament to any of us. Never was, never will be.'

'I see,' Sullivan said. 'I still see him on the rare occasion, this bar or that. He used to take bets for the Corrigan brothers over in Wisbech.'

'That'd be him.'

'He's a popular man. You ought not to be too hard on him.'

Devlin tried to remember the last time he'd seen his father but the memory was beyond him.

'I wept buckets when we lost my own father,' Sullivan said. 'Worshipped the ground that man walked on. We all did.'

'Good for you,' Devlin said, again the words more mouthed than spoken.

'It's everything, family is,' Sullivan said.

'Not to everybody.'

Sullivan fell silent after that and Devlin did nothing to prolong the conversation.

After a few minutes during which neither man spoke, Sullivan said, 'I suppose you got your reasons, I'll give you that. And I daresay if you could get ten sensible words out of any of this lot, they'd tell much the same story. "Broken homes", they're calling it.'

Then Sullivan fell asleep where he sat in the warm bus.

Devlin went outside and walked to the closest of the boys, most of whom, knowing Sullivan's routine, had already stopped working.

'You come to crack the whip, then?' a boy of fifteen or sixteen asked Devlin.

Devlin made a whipping motion. 'I might have.'

The boy laughed. 'And how many of us do you think it would take to pull you down here and hold your face under a foot of water?'

Devlin smiled at the empty threat, turned and walked back to the bus.

9

THEY WERE BREAKING UP THE AIRFIELD BEYOND TATTERS-
hall. The Americans had recently gone home. Good riddance.
Shame. Either gone home or down to one of the new bases in
Suffolk. Jet planes, a different thing entirely.

Duggan suggested to Devlin that they drive over to the airfield on Sunday. Suggested – as though Devlin had any say in
the matter. Duggan's father insisted on keeping the Sabbath –
'That's what he calls it – the bloody Sabbath' – but Duggan told
Devlin it would be the only time to go. The unguarded pickings
would be rich, easy to load and even easier to sell on. Always
lots of hands held out for that kind of stuff.

But on the day, nothing came right. Even from half a mile
away Devlin could see that too many others had had the same
idea, and over thirty lorries and vans already stood parked along
the broken runway. Duggan shook his head and swore at everything he saw. Scavengers roamed the recently abandoned site
singly and in small groups.

'Waste of time us coming,' Duggan said as he drove along
what remained of the runway. Mounds of reinforced concrete rose
all around them. What little remained of the aircraft themselves
after all those years had been cut into pieces far too heavy to lift.

'This will all go to the contract boys in Peterborough and Lincoln,' Duggan said. 'I should have guessed. The broken concrete – worthless, that stuff, even with the steel in it – will go to shore up the Welland at the Coronation Channel, and the chopped-up metal will already be sold to the Sheffield mills. Good stuff, that. Aluminium. Light. They can smelt that back down. Shame, a ton of that stuff would have seen us sitting pretty. I should never have let you talk me into leaving it this late.'

Devlin laughed at the remark, but mostly at Duggan's disappointment.

'Besides, there's too many others here.'

'Do you know them?' Devlin said.

Duggan looked around them. 'I'll know some. I usually do. They'll be amateurs, most of them, spoiling it for the rest of us. I might get a bit of business done one way or another, but apart from that we might as well call it a day.' He pointed to the few remaining buildings in the distance. 'Might be something in there worth having a butcher's at. I've got a man in Corby who buys metal window frames sight unseen. Don't ask me why. We'll have a recce, shall we?' He climbed down from the cab and Devlin followed him.

After a few paces, Duggan turned and indicated the far side of the runway, where most of the others were now gathering. 'You go and have a shufti over there,' he told Devlin. 'And keep shtum. We're here for a look round, that's all. I wouldn't put it past the Lynn coppers to send someone in civvies.'

Devlin considered this unlikely, but said nothing. Not his place. Or was this Duggan doing what he always did and letting Devlin wander out into the open while he kept himself nicely tucked away in the background?

'I'll go and give the buildings a once-over,' Duggan said.

'Back here, half an hour. Anybody asks for me, tell them where we're parked up. Anyone tells you I owe them money, tell them I'm dead and buried.' He laughed at this and then turned and walked away from Devlin.

Uncertain what was expected of him, Devlin wandered towards the other men. Some he recognized from previous encounters with Duggan, but most were strangers to him – men who watched him come towards them and who then stopped talking as he passed them by. Mounds of cable and rotted sleepers stood higher than the scavengers. A column of giant tyres rocked where men climbed on it. The fact that the tyres had been stacked like this suggested that they'd already been sold and were awaiting collection. Men rolled smaller tyres along the concrete apron.

'Forget it,' a man said unexpectedly to Devlin as he watched this. 'We were here first.'

'They're aircraft tyres,' Devlin said. He remembered watching the sleek green-and-silver bombers coming and going from the place.

'You don't know what you're talking about, son,' the man said.

'If you say so.' Devlin walked to where others were peering into oil drums and then kicking them and rolling them around to determine if they might still contain something. Duggan liked oil drums.

Someone had lit a fire and a column of black smoke rose in a straight line into the still air. Devlin wondered why anyone would attract attention to the place like that.

A man with a dog on a lead came to him and asked him where Duggan was. The dog strained on the lead and growled and bared its teeth at Devlin.

'Who's Duggan?'

'*Duggan* Duggan. Don't play the smartarse. Me and him have got a bit of business. He said he might be here. I seen you with him a few times. You're his current skivvy.' He spat heavily at his feet.

'Get the dog away,' Devlin said.

'What, him? Wouldn't hurt a fly.'

Devlin motioned to the distant buildings.

'Got his eyes on the window frames, has he?' the man said. 'He's got a good nose for that kind of thing.' He looked disdainfully at the others around them. 'Half of this lot don't know their arse from their elbow. I even heard one of them say he was going to start loading up some of the broken concrete. Idiot. Where's Duggan parked?'

Devlin indicated the distant lorry on the runway.

'Tell him Billy from Holbeach Clough was asking after him,' the man said. 'I'll catch up with him. He knows where I am.' He kicked the snarling dog and the animal finally fell silent.

Devlin watched him go. He felt confident that he'd kept up Duggan's end of things. He was starting to talk the same language. It was a world in which he would soon belong in his own right. It had already occurred to him to suggest to Duggan that he buy a smaller van so that the two of them might work separately on occasion and increase their profits. Duggan would laugh at the idea, ridicule it, and only then perhaps consider it.

A man at the drums kicked one over and then slipped in the old viscous oil which poured slowly from it across the warm concrete. Others gathered around to laugh at him as he struggled to stand upright.

Leaving the small crowd, Devlin went back to the lorry.

Half an hour had passed. In Duggan's world, that might

mean an hour, or even two, or even a whole day if something else cropped up while he was away. From Devlin's vantage point, he searched for Duggan, but saw nothing. Distant figures moved among the buildings, but everything was distorted in the haze. He'd tell Duggan about the drums, the tyres perhaps, but little else. The man with the dog. Let Duggan decide.

He wound down the window to let air into the overheated cab, and as he did this a man came to the running board, climbed up and looked in at him. Devlin recognized him as the older of the two brothers – Patrick – who had bought the cisterns from Duggan.

'Duggan said you was here,' Patrick said. He pushed his head into the cab and looked around. 'What you seen?'

'Nothing worth the effort,' Devlin said.

The man laughed. 'Like that, is it? He's teaching you good.'

'He's over there.'

'I know. Colm's with him. You spent that quid yet?'

'What quid?'

'"What quid?" he says. You not too hot sitting in there?'

'A bit,' Devlin said.

'Listen, you ever fancy doing a bit of business with us on your own account, we're easy enough to find,' Patrick said. 'Autumn soon, we'll be laying up for the winter. Over at the wintering ground close by Swineshead. You can't miss us.'

'I work with Duggan,' Devlin said.

'"Course you do. I'm just saying, that's all. Things change. We all need to push a few bits and pieces to one side now and again.'

'I'll bear it in mind,' Devlin said.

'You do that. Got a fag?' Patrick reached into the cab and took the packet from the dash.

'They're Duggan's.'

'So? Hardly going to miss one, is he? Unless you told him.' He took several from the packet and slid them into his pocket. 'Anyway, best be off. Idle hands and all that. I'll tell Maria we met, shall I?'

'If you like.' Devlin looked again at the distant buildings.

Patrick dropped down from the door. 'Until next time, then.'

Devlin watched him as he ran along the edge of the runway to the other waiting lorries.

It was midday. He and Duggan had been out until almost one the previous night and then up again at five. He closed his eyes and felt the warmth on his face.

He was almost asleep when he was startled by a sudden banging on the cab door and someone shouting for him to open it. Expecting this to be Duggan, he opened the door and leaned out, but before he could say anything, and before he really knew what was happening, he was grabbed by his arm and half pulled from his seat.

An older man was trying to drag him down from the cab, but was already losing his grip. Then Devlin's shirt tore and the man fell backwards to the ground. Devlin banged the door shut, locked it and wound up the window.

'Open the door, you thieving little bastard. You and me got a score to settle. Where's my money? I'm owed. Where is it? I paid good money to the courts and to Skelton. Get out here.' He banged on the door with both fists.

'You've got me wrong,' Devlin shouted. He had never previously met Harrap. He had signed the tenancy agreement at Harrap's solicitor's office in Lynn. 'I don't know who you are. I don't owe you anything. You've got me mixed up with somebody else.'

'You lying little bastard. You bare-faced lying little bastard. You signed one of my contracts. Just because I never saw you before . . . Seven months you were there. Seven months. Two months' rent you paid. Where's the rest? You aren't getting away with this.' He went on banging on the door. By then, others nearby were turning to look.

Devlin could think of nothing more to say. He leaned away from the door.

'What you even doing here?' Harrap shouted at him. 'This your lorry? You got a lorry now, have you? Is that what you've spent the money that's rightfully mine on?' He ran out of breath after that and stood for a moment with his hands on his knees. Then he walked a short distance away and sat on a concrete block. 'Well, at least I've seen you now,' he shouted. 'I know you're still in this neck of the woods. At least now I can go back to the police and the courts and tell them where I've seen you. Don't worry, they'll catch up with you soon enough. I daresay even Skelton might want a few words with you. You think all this is just going to go away, then think again.' He took out a handkerchief and wiped his face.

Devlin looked beyond him and saw Duggan coming back along the runway towards the lorry. Harrap being there would only spell trouble and he felt suddenly anxious.

But then Harrap rose to his feet and walked a few paces away. He paused and turned to point an accusing finger back at Devlin, but then continued walking until he was lost among the others.

Devlin silently urged Duggan to reach the lorry so they could leave.

Duggan arrived at the driver's side several minutes later, having stopped to talk to the man with the dog. Devlin tried to guess what he might or might not have seen and heard of Harrap.

'Find anything?' Devlin asked him as he finally climbed into the cab, one eye on the group of men Harrap had joined.

'Nothing worth the effort. You?'

'Nothing.'

Duggan leaned forward over the wheel and then brushed dirt from his palms.

'I saw one of the gyppos,' Devlin said.

'So I gather. Where that pair are concerned, you say as little as possible. They put an arm around your shoulders, that pair, and then pick your pocket while you're laughing with them. I saw Colm. He said Patrick was prowling around somewhere. He's the one you've got to watch the closest. What did he want?'

'Just to know if you'd found anything.'

'Might as well get off home,' Duggan said. He took out the key and turned on the engine, sitting for a moment and looking at the smoke still rising into the air. Then he turned the engine off and said, 'You going to tell me, then, or what?'

'Tell you what?' At first, Devlin thought the remark was connected to what Patrick had said.

Duggan sighed. 'I'm going to give you the benefit just this once. The man trying to pull your fucking head off, that's what. I'll count to three.'

'Same old story,' Devlin said. 'I owe him a bit of rent, that's all.'

'Harrap,' Duggan said. 'I know him. Does things by the book. Stickler. You get the chance, you pay him. Not everything, just something. Is he likely to make trouble for you?' He looked directly ahead of them as he said all this.

'I can take care—'

'That's the point, see,' Duggan shouted at him. 'You *can't* take care of things like that. And the last thing I need is any of your old trouble following you back to me. We clear on that?'

Devlin understood perfectly all the calculations Duggan was already starting to make.

'He saw me, that's all. He doesn't know the first thing about you. It's not as though your name and address are on the lorry.'

'Don't get smart.'

'He saw me, lost his temper and started shouting the odds. That's all it was. It'll blow over. He's hardly likely to start throwing more good money after bad. It's not even that much money. I told him I'd pay him when I got the chance.'

'You said "more" good money.'

'He had me evicted.'

Duggan laughed at this. 'I can imagine. I never liked the man.' He looked at Devlin. 'That shirt's torn.'

'I've got another.'

'Perhaps, but you just lost the better of the two.' He turned on the ignition and drove off the runway and over the rough ground to the road.

10

'FACT IS, WE GO WHERE THE WORK IS. THE BOARD SAYS HERE, I allocate for here. The Board says there . . .' Thompson held up his palms and shrugged.

'Here, there, everywhere,' a man behind Devlin said, as though he were singing a song. Most of the others shook their heads at what they had already guessed was coming.

'Exactly. Here, there, everywhere. That's how it works.' Thompson looked hard at the man who'd said it. He took an envelope from his pocket, and from it drew a folded sheet and slowly opened this out, every small part of the drama another argument against protest. 'I have here—'

'Peace in our time,' the comedian said.

'Smeaton. I might have known,' Thompson said. 'The thing is, this is a serious matter. Apart from which, nobody else thinks you're funny.' He looked at the others gathered around him. 'This is men's livelihoods I'm talking about here. Do you want to hear what I've got to say, or don't you?' He shook the unfolded sheet in their faces. 'Right. Thought so.'

'Just get on with it,' someone else shouted.

The foreman waited. 'We've had an order for the work on the Nene Channel towards Sutton. Also work on and around the bridge and up towards the old sea bank towards the so-called nature reserve.'

A murmur of complaint rippled through the gathered men.

Devlin tried to place the work, the distances involved.

It would mean longer journeys, earlier starts, later finishes, and none of it on the clock. And just as the nights were starting to draw in.

'Got to be done. Order of . . .' Thompson looked at the sheet. 'Got to be done.'

'And I suppose you're the one deciding who gets to stay here and who goes to the new jobs,' Smeaton said.

'You all know how it works. If anybody *wants* to go, then let me know. Otherwise, it's those not on the permanent list. Or, failing that, those last in.'

Devlin on both counts.

'And what if we refuse to go?'

'Entirely up to you. I've got men queuing up at the office in Boston just waiting for the nod to get started.'

'You know already who you're sending off,' Smeaton said.

'Nothing's been decided yet. That's why I called you all together. I could just as easily have waited until the day beforehand and given it to you as a done deal. But I'm a fair man. Not my style.'

'You're a tin-pot little Hitler, that's what you are,' Smeaton shouted.

'That's his goose cooked,' the man beside Devlin whispered to him.

'If that's how you feel, then you know what you can do,' Thompson said.

'He's already done it,' the same man whispered. 'That's you and me off to Sutton, then.'

The work on the bridge was being carried out under the supervision of the Ministry of Transport and was renowned for being hard and without any opportunity for skiving.

It occurred to Devlin that there was a Ministry for everything under the sun these days.

'Anyhow, that's all I've got to say,' the foreman said. He folded up the sheet of paper – the fate of thirty men – and slid it back into its envelope and then put this back in his pocket. 'Ten days. It's fair warning. Like I said, you can sort it out among yourselves or I can sort it out for you. Anything you want to add, Smeaton? Thought not. You're not getting too many laughs now, are you? And do you know why that is? I'll tell you, shall I? Because you're a waste of space and because you've got no real responsibilities. No wife or kids. Not like some.' He looked around at the men with those responsibilities. 'All you ever think about is what's in it for Smeaton. It's why you're Jack the Lad one minute, and the next no one's ever heard of you.'

The men still standing close to Smeaton shuffled their feet and avoided Thompson's gaze.

'And if any of you lot want to take your chances with him, then feel free. Shout out now and I'll cross your names off the list. Make my job a lot easier. Honestly, you don't know you're born, some of you.' He folded his arms. 'I'm waiting. What, none of you? Nobody want to pick up his cards when brother Smeaton here goes to collect his?' He pretended to think. 'Oh, that's right – what cards? Most of the rest of you are on the casual list, aren't you?'

Devlin on three counts.

'He's sent a list of names already,' the man beside Devlin whispered. 'All this is just for show. We had enough of his sort in the Army. You'd think things would change, but they seldom do.

People like Smeaton shouting his mouth off, that just plays into his hands.' He walked away from Devlin towards the sluice gate they had all been working on before being called together.

Devlin followed him. The wind off the sea, which had started to blow earlier in the day, caught both men at the lip of the earthworks and caused them to lean forward slightly to carry on walking.

11

DEVLIN VISITED HIS SISTER. ELLEN. HE WENT BECAUSE that, he imagined, was what proper families did: they visited. Christmas, Easter, every other Thursday, first Monday of every month. Illness, birthdays, misfortune, good fortune. Obligation, duty, endurance. To Devlin's mind, they were all just old and worthless rituals pointlessly playing out into the future.

He couldn't remember the last time he'd seen the woman. Three years? Probably nearer four. She'd been married for the past six years to a man called Morris, who considered himself a cut above, and who thought he was doing Devlin's sister the biggest favour of her life by being her husband. Devlin and Morris had almost come to blows – Devlin had raised his fists and shouted at the man the day after the wedding. No honeymoon – waste of money, better things to do, money better spent elsewhere. The world according to Morris. Night classes two nights a week. Certificates in this, that and the other. Morris was going places. First Morris told everyone this, and then it was Ellen's turn to repeat, endorse and embellish whatever he'd said.

At the wedding, a distant uncle – himself never seen or heard of since – had whispered in Devlin's ear that Morris had something of the Yid about him. It was something Devlin was happy to believe, and so the more he had looked at the man, the more he had seen it.

He hadn't spoken to Morris since his last unhappy visit three or four years ago. His mother had always spoken very highly of her son-in-law. There were always comparisons to be made. She believed all that stuff about Morris going places. Not like the rest of them. And not just any old places, places worth going, mark her words.

He knocked on the door and stood back.

His sister unlocked the door, opened it a few inches and looked out at him.

'Hello,' Devlin said.

'What is it this time?' Ellen said.

'Can't a man visit his own family? You're getting very suspicious in your old age.' She was thirty, a year older than Devlin.

'"Family"? We're only ever that when it suits.' She looked along the road behind him. Morris didn't appreciate her having visitors when he wasn't present.

'Aren't you going to invite me in?'

He'd walked from Duggan's to Holbeach and from there he'd caught the bus, walking again from the stop to the house, another mile. Best part of two hours with all the waiting.

'How long are you staying?' she asked him as he stood with her in the narrow corridor Morris insisted they call the hallway.

'Charming. You make it sound as though I've already out-stayed my welcome.' He wanted her to laugh at the remark. He wondered if anyone in their unravelled, evaporated family had ever held out their arms to anyone, let alone embraced them with anything close to affection, fondness even.

'I was passing,' he said, reducing his obligation to stay.

'Hardly,' she said. She lived in a terrace of houses beyond Terrington, towards the coast, not the kind of place anyone ever passed. Back of beyond as far as Devlin was concerned.

'Nearby, then,' he said. 'I'm living over towards Sutterton. Got a good job on the drainage work. Day off, see.'

'It's Saturday.'

It had always been the same, these tired, suspicious, zig-zagging conversations.

'Morris at home, is he?' He knew the man was out, having seen him go half an hour earlier.

'He's got better things to do than lie in bed all day,' she said.

'Never doubted it. Never doubted it for a second. Haven't we all?' He looked around him. Embossed wallpaper, a runner along the boards of the corridor. 'He's done you proud,' he said.

'It's important to make the effort, that's what counts.'

'You want me to take my shoes off?'

She looked down at them.

'I will anyway. It's a nice house. I can see the pair of you are making a go of things.'

'We've done our best.' She led him past the small parlour into the smaller kitchen at the rear. There was no other building between the back of the house and the sea, three miles away.

A year after the wedding, she'd given birth to a baby boy three months early and the child had lived less than a day. 'Premature' was the word she had used, as though this somehow eased her pain and her anxiety for the future. According to Morris, a family wasn't complete without children, and then *their* children, chasing each other into that hopeful future. Two further miscarriages had followed.

Devlin had visited her after the first calamity, not afterwards. He'd arrived to find her in bed, where she stayed for a month, her husband waiting on her hand and foot. Complete rest. Morris had made up a bed on the settee in the parlour. Consideration.

'You're looking well,' he said to her now.

'I'm looking older,' she said. She was. Older than her years. She made them tea and sat at the table opposite him. 'Formica,' she said, lifting his cup and saucer and wiping a cloth over the surface.

Devlin watched to see how she held her own crockery before starting to drink.

'What sort of work is it, then?' she asked him.

Making conversation.

He told her about the Drainage Board and all its grand projects. He said nothing about the clinging mud and the cold water. He told her about Sullivan, and referred to himself as a supervisor.

'Borstal boys?' she said, pulling a face. 'You don't want that lot rubbing off on you.'

'Not likely to happen,' he said. He looked around him again. A place for everything and everything in its place.

Before the loss of the first child, he'd taken her a cot, second-hand but good as new. A few scratches here and there, but only if you looked close. He learned later that Morris had chopped it up for firewood. But the baby was dead by then, so sleeping dogs and all that.

'We've got sugar,' she said. 'Morris knows a man in Yarmouth.' Sacks of the stuff going begging, apparently. Not that Morris himself would ever be involved in anything shady, underhand. Not like some men; most men, come to think of it.

'Sweet enough as it is, thanks,' Devlin said. He liked his tea as sweet as he could get it. Probably from his soldiering days, when most of the tea was piss.

It was piss now, but he drank it and smiled.

'You see much of anybody all this way out here?' he asked her. He mentioned a few old names.

'We have different friends now,' she said. 'Work colleagues, mostly, a few casual acquaintances.'

'I'm still stuck with the usual oppos and mates,' he said, hoping it was a joke, and then wishing he'd kept silent. 'I'm surprised you're not in Peterborough or Norwich by now,' he said. Morris had mentioned it during his last visit.

'Morris says the time's not quite right. He needs to get a few more things under his belt and then we'll be in a better position to consider all our options.'

'Anything on the horizon?'

'Morris says the world's a changing place. Technology, finance, all that. I leave that side of things to him. You know Morris, he likes to keep himself abreast.'

Devlin wondered if she practised saying all this when no one was listening. He began to wonder why he'd even come.

He told her about Duggan and left out more than he made up.

'Does Duggan work for the Drainage Board?' she said. She'd hardly listened to a word of it.

'Something like that.'

'Morris says he'll be running his own department by the time he's thirty-five.'

Two years. 'I'm surprised he's not there already.'

'What's that supposed to mean?'

'All I meant—'

'Don't,' she said, turning to look across those three empty miles towards the invisible sea. 'I know what you meant. This is what you do. This is what you always do.'

'I only meant that if anybody was going to make it in this world, then it would be Morris. He's got his head screwed on, that's all I'm saying. He knows what's what and how to get it.' He hated himself more with every lie, every concession to the man. But it was what she wanted to hear, and besides, it was only like stroking someone's dog when you couldn't stand the fucking things.

'Cambridge,' she said eventually, having allowed herself to be convinced by him. 'We thought Cambridge. More opportunities than either Peterborough or Norwich, see?'

Devlin had spent a long cold night on Cambridge station waiting for a train to Colchester that had finally pulled in four hours late.

'Nice spot,' he said. 'Know it well. You've got everything you'd ever want in Cambridge.'

'One of Morris's colleagues has a brother who teaches there.'

Of course he does. 'Nice little number.'

'Or perhaps he lectures, not teaches. That's it – he lectures there.'

'Better still.'

'It's the kind of place you can make the most of yourself.'

'I can imagine. I can see the pair of you there,' he said. 'No, honestly, I can.'

She lifted a hand to her throat. 'That's what Morris said – that he could see us living there and fitting right in.'

'There you go, then.'

'He said it was time to try and put the past behind us and to move on, to get on with our lives.'

Not in a million years.

'He's right. You've had enough on your plate already to last a lifetime.'

'He says we'd meet a lot of new people there.'

'Of course you would.' And people not the remotest bit like the people round here: savages standing up to their knees in muck and shit and water for half the year and forever talking about things that had happened twenty years ago as though it were yesterday. 'You ought to meet Duggan's wife,' he said. 'You and her got a lot in common. Duggan's father was once the mayor of Lynn.'

'The mayor?'

Big lies, small lies; it mattered.

'And Duggan himself is a big noise in the funny-handshake mob.'

'You shouldn't call them that,' she said sharply. 'Morris says they do a lot of good work, that they're' – she closed her eyes for a moment in an effort of remembering – 'community spirited.'

'Thinking of joining up himself, is he?'

She was reluctant to answer him.

And just when they'd started to get on so well, see eye to eye on things.

'He says it's all about like-minded people giving each other a helping hand. Fellow men and all that.'

'That's exactly what Duggan says. Perhaps I should get him to invite the pair of you over.' Christ, perhaps there were some things you shouldn't even think about, let alone actually say. How many lies was that?

'I'm not sure,' she said.

Devlin caught the sudden tremor of her fingers on the cup and saucer. Besides, suppose Morris *was* what that distant uncle had suggested. Were they even *allowed* into that particular little world?

'Perhaps not,' he said. 'I know Duggan likes to keep that side of things on the q.t., if you catch my drift.' He even tapped the side of his nose as he said it.

'Exactly,' she said. She put down the cup and saucer and locked her fingers together.

For four years she'd kept a brand-new cot and a brand-new pram in the house, in the small second bedroom, under sheets. Tempting fate, some would have said. Common sense, Morris said. Ghosts.

After an hour, Devlin said he ought to be going. He was going to tell her that he'd arranged to meet up with some of his own colleagues, associates, really, men from the Board – engineers, planners, architects, men like that – to discuss the coming work now that the summer was practically over, but he let it pass. Instead, he told her he'd try to come again. Perhaps Morris would be there next time. It all depended on where he was sent to work next. You never knew in that line of business. The sea had risen and come beyond Terrington last winter, but she had been spared.

'It sounds like you've finally found the right line,' she said.

'They tell me I've got a feel for it.'

'Aptitude,' she said, and for the first time she actually smiled at him.

'Tell Morris I'm sorry to have missed him.'

'I'll do that.'

Not very likely. First thing she'd do, she'd go back into the kitchen and wash the cups and saucers, rinse out the teapot and slide the chairs back beneath the Formica table. Then she'd sniff the air and check the floor for dirt from his shoes.

'How about you?' he asked her when they were back at the door.

'How about me, what?'

'Got much on?'

'Not really. Get things ready for when Morris comes home.'

'Real lady of leisure.'

'Chance would be a fine thing.'

He wondered again about holding out his arms to her. 'I suppose that's all any of us ever really needs – a chance in life,' he said.

He went ahead of her through the door and stood under the small porch. The lane stretched away on either side of him, as straight and as empty as when he'd arrived.

He'd been keeping an eye on the time. Half an hour to walk the long mile to the bus.

'I won't come out,' she said.

'Very wise. Rain later.'

The door was closed and locked on him before he'd even started walking.

12

TWO DAYS LATER, AS HE WALKED THE LAST MILE TO WORK, Devlin saw the fairground trailers, lorries and dismantled machines parked beyond the Gosberton road. He left the path he was following and went to them. Other smaller vehicles and pieces of machinery were scattered in the field beyond.

At his approach, a chained dog ran barking towards him, straining to reach him at the end of its tether. A caravan door opened and a woman came out.

'What you want?' she called to him. 'You got no good reason to be here.'

'I was just looking,' Devlin shouted back.

She shouted at the dog, which paid her no attention. It was only a few feet from Devlin, snarling and jumping in the air in an effort to reach him.

'I was looking for the McGuires,' Devlin said. 'I've got some business with them.'

'At this hour?' After a moment, the woman pointed to a nearby caravan. 'They won't thank you,' she said. 'Sun's hardly up.'

'Been up an hour at least,' Devlin said.

She shook her head at this and went back inside.

Devlin walked in a wide curve around the dog and went to the caravan.

He knocked and heard the sound repeat inside the tin box. After a minute, someone shouted to ask who was there.

'It's me, Devlin,' Devlin shouted, wondering if this meant anything whatsoever to the men.

Several more minutes passed before Patrick finally opened the door. He was naked from the waist up and rubbed his arms against the cold. He told Devlin to come inside.

'Duggan send you, did he?'

Devlin looked around the crowded interior. The space was divided by a blanket hanging from the curved roof. A sheet and pillow lay on the floor beside one of the benches.

'I saw you parked up,' Devlin said. 'That's all.'

'A social call, then? What time is it?'

Devlin told him and Patrick swore.

'I was on my way to work,' Devlin said.

'Heard they were moving you all on.'

It was the start of October. Devlin had been kept on at the Welland Channel. The workforce there had been cut by half. Further reductions were imminent. He was starting to wish he'd gone to Sutton Bridge, where the work would at least last into the spring.

'They shift everybody around,' Devlin said. 'That's all, whatever's required.'

Patrick laughed. 'They get rid of you, is what they do. Hire and fire, that's the name of that little game.'

Devlin sat on a narrow seat beneath the curtained window while Patrick searched for a shirt. Any delay would make him late for the morning's roll call. With so few of them still employed at the channel, it was getting harder to go unnoticed. Two and a half months he'd stuck at the work. It seemed more like two and a half years.

'You and Duggan fallen out yet?' Patrick said.

'Why would we?'

'Give it time. I bet he hardly gives you ten per cent of what he makes.'

Patrick searched amid the clutter of bottles and cans until he found something to drink. He poured the flat beer into two cups.

Devlin cleared a space on the table.

'I keep telling her to clear the place up' – Patrick nodded at the hanging blanket – 'but she says what's the point?'

'Your sister?'

'Who else?'

And as though summoned by the remark, Maria's face appeared at the edge of the blanket. 'What's *he* want?' she said. Her black hair fell in disarray across her face and she pushed it back. Then she rubbed at her teeth with a finger.

'Not said yet.' Patrick went to the stove and struck match after match, trying to light it.

'No gas,' Maria said. 'Ran out last night.' She went back behind the blanket for a few minutes, dressed and then returned to them, pulling down the blanket as she came to reveal her makeshift bed beneath the caravan's solitary large window. She was bare-legged and had nothing on her feet. She sat beside Devlin and pressed herself close to him, putting her arm around his shoulders. 'He came to see me,' she said, her mouth close to his ear. 'That's right, isn't it, lover boy?'

Devlin looked at Patrick and wondered what to say.

'Look, he's gone all red,' Maria said. She withdrew her arm. 'Got anything to eat?'

Devlin took out the sandwiches he had made. Unbuttered

bread, cheese and onion. And seeing these, Patrick came back to the table.

'Why are you here?' Devlin asked him. 'Setting up?'

'Like I said at the airfield,' Patrick said, 'we're here for the winter. Most of the heavier stuff's gone off to Nottingham and Lincoln. We got a few local bookings with the smaller shies and stalls, but the rest of the gear gets parked up here until March, Easter time. Maintenance, repairs, painting, that sort of thing. We used to take most of the stuff up to Hull, but we knocked that on the head a few years back. Hardly worth the effort these days.'

'And you stay here all winter?'

'A few bits and pieces here and there, but mostly we sit tight and wait to see what turns up.'

'In the shape of Duggan?'

'And others. He's not all he likes to think he is, tends to get stuck in his ways. He's an old man compared to some of them these days.'

'Do the animals come?' Devlin said.

'Some. The horses go to the stables over Surfleet way. Every year there are new rules and regulations. That's who I thought you were – the police. The minute we show up they come knocking and shouting the odds to let us know what's what. We show them our licences and leases and everything, but they still like to show up and give us all the usual warnings.'

Maria took the last of the sandwiches, picked out the onion and ate what remained. Patrick picked the onion off the table and ate that.

'It's all a bit hand-to-mouth, this time of year,' he said.

'Is there much to do – with the rides and stalls?'

Patrick shrugged. 'We strip down the generators and overhaul the rides. Everything turns to rust and rot at the drop of a hat in this neck of the woods.'

'You still at Duggan's?' Maria asked him.

'It's only temporary. Until something better turns up.' When work on the Welland Channel ended, he would be miles away from the nearest drainage work. He'd wait and see.

'Always something better round the next corner,' Patrick said. 'And then the corner after that.'

'You got anything saved?' Maria asked him.

'Not really. A bit.'

'Enough to see you through?'

Devlin had nothing. Everything he'd earned in those two and a half months, he'd spent. He paid Duggan his rent, and then the rest just blew away on the wind. Some of it blew back during his excursions with Duggan, but then even that blew away eventually.

Most of the new work had been dreamed up by the Ministry of Transport. And their rates of pay were lower than those of the Drainage Board. And some said that the Ministry wouldn't even look at you until you'd filled in at least a dozen forms. Taxes, pension contributions, National Insurance, everything. Cash in hand? No chance. So you could forget it with that mob.

Maria put her hand on Devlin's arm.

'You want to get yourself a caravan and come and stay here for the winter,' she said.

With her?

'I suppose I could,' he said. Ten a penny, caravans. Death traps hauled off the holiday camps up around Skegness every year and sold mostly for scrap or chicken houses. Duggan had always done a good trade in caravans. Perhaps he would even sell him one cheap.

95

'What you got to lose?' Maria said.

'I suppose.'

Patrick attracted his attention. 'You tell Duggan we only got half what he told us we'd get for those cisterns.' It wasn't a genuine complaint, more a reflex.

'None of my business,' Devlin said. Sold on and sold on and sold on. Where did it all end?

'You tell him, all the same. Tell him we're not happy. Times are going to get hard over the coming months. We don't need rubbish from Duggan to make things even harder.'

In the distance, beyond the road, Devlin heard the machine whistles calling the remaining workers to their labours.

'You ought to get moving,' Maria said to him, but making no move to release him from where he sat in the tight seat.

'Might give it a miss,' he said, surprising himself.

'They'll dock you.'

'So? What's the point if they're just waiting to lay us off anyway?'

'You ought to stick at it as long as it's there,' Patrick said. Duggan had already told him the same.

What difference would half a day make? He could always think of some excuse. And the water certainly wasn't getting any warmer.

'Ignore him,' Maria said to him, her face back close to his own. 'Perhaps you've got hidden talents. What else are you good at?'

He tried hard to think. 'This and that,' he said.

Patrick laughed. 'We're *all* good at that.'

Devlin knew she was playing with him, passing a few minutes of another empty day, an empty month, perhaps, and he understood that. But it was something. Everything came apart in the end, everything floated adrift and everything was eventually carried away on that same cold and uncaring wind which took his money.

At the pumping station, a second whistle sounded. He would be an hour late, that's all.

Patrick found another half-filled bottle of beer and poured it out. 'It's not a bad life,' he said, 'if you don't weaken.' He held his cup towards Devlin and Devlin tapped it with his own.

13

HE LEFT THE CULVERT WHERE HE'D BEEN HIDDEN WITH Sullivan for the past few hours and made his way towards the others. At the same time, the borstal boys came back to the bus and Sullivan counted them off as they climbed aboard. The field drain on which they'd started work twenty days earlier was still only half cleared, and Sullivan shouted his complaints and accusations at each of the boys as they passed him in the doorway. As elsewhere on the site, now that its workforce was depleted, there was little urgency.

Devlin handed in the shovel he carried, which he had pushed for the first time into the mud of the culvert as he'd risen to return. Despite his late arrival a week earlier, no action had been taken against him and he had been kept on as part of the workforce. Most of the men he had become acquainted with over the summer had been sent to work elsewhere, and as a result he'd spent more of his time with Sullivan.

A horn sounded in the distance, and Devlin saw Duggan's lorry on the hard-standing beside the pumping station.

'I've got a lift,' he said to Sullivan, who had taken to diverting the borstal bus to give Devlin a ride home.

'Good for you.'

Devlin left the gathering boys and went to Duggan.

'This where you're working then, is it?' Duggan sat with his arm outside the cab, his fingers drumming a tune on the door. He'd known exactly where Devlin was working. Sizing up his opportunities, as usual. 'You got some good stuff just lying about over there.'

'Don't even think of it,' Devlin said.

Duggan laughed at him. 'Don't look so serious. You know me – I never shit in my own back yard. I was just passing, that's all. Thought I'd do the decent thing and give you a lift home.'

'And the rest,' Devlin said. He climbed up and sat beside Duggan.

'They borstal boys?' Duggan said, shielding his eyes. 'From the camp?'

They both watched as the bus came towards them and then passed them on the narrow road. Sullivan raised his hand from the wheel and Devlin returned the gesture.

'You don't want to be tying yourself in with that little lot,' Duggan said. He watched the departing bus in his wing mirror. 'Evil little runts. Beats me why the Drainage Board lets them anywhere near.'

'So what is it?' Devlin asked him.

Duggan rubbed his palms together. 'Had a nice little tip-off. Sleaford depot.' It was at the edge of the territory Duggan usually roamed. 'Apparently, they've been unloading tons – and I mean *tons* – of stuff over the past week. Stockpiling for the winter work. Ministry, Board, the lot. Gear's been arriving all hours of the day and night, and the word is that nobody's done anything like a proper inventory of it yet. I thought we might have a drive over for a shufti before anybody else gets a sniff.'

'It's a long way,' Devlin said.

'All to our advantage. They'd point a finger at the Newark or Grantham boys for anything that did come to light. Me and you, we'd be long gone by the time anyone came looking in our particular direction. Word is, it's all good stuff, brand-new. It'll fetch a good price. You could at least show a bit of enthusiasm.'

'What sort of stuff?'

Exasperated, Duggan banged his hands on the wheel and then leaned past Devlin and pushed his door open. 'I get it,' he said. 'You want to go back to the farm, have a chat with the old man about the state of the economy or the Queen's Commonwealth visit and then put your feet up and listen to the Light Programme until bedtime.'

Devlin pulled the door shut.

'Right,' Duggan said, and started the engine.

They drove beyond Heckington and pulled up close to the reservoir there. The light was half gone by then, and Duggan had already calculated the remaining distance against the onset of night.

It was eight when they arrived at the makeshift, unfenced depot.

Duggan parked up and turned off their lights.

The depot was another disused airfield, and from where they sat on a slight rise they could see the mounded stores and equipment spread along what was left of the runway. Parked vehicles lined both sides, many with tarpaulins roped over them. A few lights shone in the distance, but there was no sign of any activity amid the stores.

'What do you think?' Duggan said.

'There'll be somebody left to watch it,' Devlin said.

'Not according to my tip-off. Not yet, at least. They couldn't use their original site because the hard-standing had already gone and nobody had thought to tell them. This is all a bit last-minute. Apart from which, apparently, they hadn't expected so much to come so soon.' He continued looking around him as he spoke, falling silent as a car passed by. 'Let's wait and see,' he said. 'No urgency.'

'We could come back another night when we know for certain,' Devlin said. Despite having done little all day, he was tired. Duggan would have been in his bed until noon.

Duggan shook his head. 'Sometimes I wonder if you listen to a single word I say. This time tomorrow, the Grantham mob will have got wind and they'll be out here with every lorry they've got. This is our one big chance. And let's face it, after that little outing to Tattershall, I could do with something to top up the coffers.'

An hour later they drove into the depot itself. There were no barriers, no one stopped them, no lights came on, no one appeared out of the darkness, there were no warning signs, no barking dogs. It was every invitation Duggan ever needed. An open door: they'd be mugs to ignore it.

Duggan climbed down and walked among the stores, lifting tarpaulins and using his lighter to read the stencilled writing on countless cases.

Devlin watched him from the lorry.

Eventually, Duggan came back to him. 'It's a fucking goldmine,' he said, unable to contain his excitement. Devlin had never seen Duggan like this before and it made him wary.

They drove closer to the furthest stack Duggan had examined, and they began to load up the lorry with small cases of machine parts, tools, including several industrial drills and jackhammers, nuts and bolts, and canisters of good-quality lubricating oil Duggan said were worth their weight in gold. They filled what space remained with copper piping and fittings.

After an hour, the lorry was loaded fuller and higher than Devlin had ever seen it and was low on its axles. He pointed this out to Duggan, who told him to stop worrying. During that hour, they'd stopped at every distant noise and had waited for silence to return.

When they'd finished and were both back in the cab, Duggan said that the haul had exceeded his expectations and then started to speculate on where best to sell on its various parts. Devlin knew some of the men he mentioned, but many were new to him.

They drove away from the depot on the back roads. Duggan kept the speed down on account of all the extra weight.

At midnight, Duggan pulled up at a farm on the edge of the Mareham Fen and drove into an open barn.

'Where are we?' Devlin asked him, looking round at the cavernous space.

Duggan tapped his nose. 'Don't you worry about things like that. Foresight, that's the name of this game. I was here before I came to the drainage, opened the doors. The only problem with a load as good as this is, first, that I won't be able to unload it in one place to get the top prices; and second, that I can't bring it anywhere near the farm. There might not be any proper docketing or inventory yet, but everything in this little lot will be traceable one way or another. I'm not *that* stupid. This place has been empty for years. I slip the land agent a few quid now and then for the occasional use of the barn, no questions asked. Don't worry, he knows the score.'

'So we have to unload everything?'

'Since when were you bothered about a bit of hard work?'

Nineteen hours Devlin had been out of his bed.

'Winter's coming on,' Duggan said. 'This lot should see us

pretty for a fair few months. Don't worry – you'll get your fair share.'

Devlin doubted this. And whatever he did make from the night's haul, he wouldn't get it until the money was warm in Duggan's own pocket.

'With this little lot, it's worth our while to leave it sitting for a bit until things cool off. Chop-chop, let's get moving. Hardly going to unload itself, is it? Sooner we start, sooner we're done. And the sooner we're done, the sooner and further away we are from this place. We'll be home in an hour, all tucked up and sleeping the sleep of the righteous, dreaming of all that lovely money coming our way.' He left the cab and started unsheeting the load.

Duggan threw, Devlin caught. And then they both stacked everything they'd stolen at the far side of the barn and concealed it beneath a pile of disintegrating hay bales, long since desiccated and turned grey.

When they'd done, there was no sign of the cases or piping, or even of anyone having been there.

They left the place, waiting where the overgrown farm lane met the public road. A sign pointed back to the buildings, already invisible in the darkness. Dovecote Farm. It seemed a mockery of the place.

They continued driving, faster now they were without their load and following wider roads.

'Place has been empty since the war,' Duggan told Devlin. 'The old man who farmed there lost two sons. It went back to some estate holding. A lot of places did. Landlords sit on the land. To be honest, the buildings become a bit of a nuisance. That's where the money is, in the land – if you learn nothing else in this sorry life, at least learn that much. The tenants lose their homes and livelihoods and the landlords just sit on their fat arses getting richer by the day. Always somebody ready and waiting and willing to take advantage of somebody else's misfortune in this world.'

And all this from Duggan.

'And you're sure nobody will come here?'

'Stop worrying. Nobody's been within a mile of that barn for the past year. Yours truly excepted, of course. Besides, suppose somebody *did* come. In the first place they're not necessarily going to jump to the conclusion that the stuff's been nicked, and in the second, it'll never be laid at my door.'

Devlin doubted both of these supposed reassurances.

It was almost two in the morning and it took them a further forty minutes to reach home.

The place was in complete darkness, and Duggan's father and wife were long in their beds. Duggan took a bottle of whisky from a cupboard and poured them each a large drink. 'We had a good night,' he said. 'Perhaps now you can stop worrying and leave things to me.' He tapped his forehead. 'It's all up here – what we got, where it will be best appreciated, and where it'll fetch the best price. All *you* need to do now is sit back and start thinking about how you're going to spend your share.' He drained his glass in a single swallow.

Devlin couldn't deny that he felt some excitement at the prospect of having some decent money in his pocket for a change.

The clock on the mantel struck the half-hour. It was a cooler night than usual – autumn moving towards winter – and after draining his own glass, Devlin followed Duggan up the stairs to his own hard bed.

14

FOUR DAYS LATER, DEVLIN RETURNED TO THE FARM TO see Duggan standing in the doorway and watching him come. It was rare for Duggan to be home at that time and, looking more closely at the man as he came to him, Devlin knew something was wrong. His first thought was that the hidden crates had been found and taken.

'What is it?' Only then did Devlin see the hessian sack on the floor behind Duggan.

'We've had visitors,' Duggan said.

'Oh?'

'Go on – ask me what kind of visitors.'

Devlin stopped walking.

'I said, ask me what kind of visitors,' Duggan shouted.

'What kind?' Devlin said, and continued to where Duggan waited.

Without warning, Duggan punched him hard in the stomach, causing Devlin to fold over and then stumble backwards and fall to the ground. He remained where he sat for a moment, trying to make sense of what had just happened.

Duggan came to him and pulled him upright. He held on to Devlin's arm and steered him into the house.

The old man sat at the table. One of his eyes was swollen and bruised and closed. Another mark spread across his mouth and cheek, and dried blood ran in a line from his lips to his chin. Duggan's wife sat beside him, a bowl of pink water and a cloth on the table. The torn pages of the old man's Bible lay scattered across the table and the floor.

Duggan held the back of Devlin's head and turned it from side to side to take in everything the room contained. '*That* kind of visitor,' he said. 'Now ask me why you only got the one punch and not the proper going-over you deserve.'

'I don't—'

Duggan punched him again, this time in his side.

'Why?' Devlin said, unable to breathe.

'Because most of this, I put down to me. I should have read things better and left you at the Tattershall fucking airfield after your little run-in with that bastard Harrap. I listened to your lies and I let it go. I should have kicked you out of the cab there and then and left you to get all that was coming to you. You *swore* to me that nothing would follow you back here.' He was panting now, spraying Devlin with spittle. 'You don't seem all that surprised,' he said. 'Expecting a little visit all along, were you?'

'No,' Devlin said, still struggling to free himself. 'Who was it?'

Duggan turned him until their two faces were inches apart. 'You know exactly who it was. Someone saying you owed another man money, and now that they knew where you were they were coming to get it. You can't run from owed money, and a bad debt is always on your back. You never even listened to a single word of what I told you about settling at least something on Harrap.'

Duggan finally released his grip on Devlin and pushed him towards the table.

'I can get you a new Bible,' Devlin said to the old man.

'What?' Alison Duggan said. 'One that's a hundred years old and with every birth, christening, marriage and death in the family marked up in it?'

There was nothing Devlin could say.

''Course he can't,' Duggan said, still close behind Devlin. 'He's fucking useless. I should have left him to take his chances with Harrap, but instead I gave him the benefit of the doubt and this is what happens.'

'How many were there?' Devlin said.

'Two of them,' Alison Duggan said. 'Man my age, another yours. The older man said he had an outstanding court order on you.'

Skelton.

And after all Duggan had said about greedy landlords the other night.

'It isn't even—' Devlin began to say.

Duggan cuffed the back of his head. 'I don't care what it is or isn't. You could have nicked the Crown Jewels for all I care. What I *do* care about is that you brought *your* mess to *my* door.' He motioned to his wife. 'Tell him.'

'They came a few hours ago,' she said. 'Just me and him were in. They were convinced you were hiding somewhere. When I told them you were off working they just laughed in my face.' She held out her arm to show him her own livid bruises. 'I told them where you were, but they said they weren't leaving until they'd got what they'd come for.'

'Harrap must have asked round about the lorry,' Duggan said.

'I swear—'

'What, that he'd cut his losses and let you go on your merry way? You know as well as I do that it doesn't work like that. Swear whatever you like, but as far as I'm concerned, it isn't worth the breath it comes out on. Look at him. He's an old man. You and me – we're finished. That sack in the doorway? That's everything you brought with you.'

'They went round all the outbuildings,' Alison Duggan said. 'And when they couldn't find you, they came back here and did that to him. Then they pulled the Bible out of his hands and tore it to pieces. He tried to stop them. Then he told them where *we* had some money.'

'It just gets worse,' Duggan said. 'Thirty quid I keep on hand for unexpected business. They took the lot.'

Devlin saw where the cupboards had been emptied, tins and jars scattered and smashed, where crockery lay in pieces against the wall.

'And so now, in addition to what you still owe Harrap, you owe *me* for everything here.'

'I'll pay you back,' Devlin said. 'Every penny.'

'You sound as though you're doing me a favour,' Duggan said. 'I *know* you're going to pay me back every penny. So what do you think that swollen eye's worth, eh? Those bruises? Hers? That cut lip? He might even lose the sight of that eye. What then? How much do you reckon *that* would be worth?'

Devlin considered all his useless answers and stayed silent.

'The older of the two . . .' Alison Duggan said, and then hesitated and looked at her husband.

'Tell him,' Duggan said.

Devlin felt himself tense at what she might be about to say, this new turn in all this debt-reckoning.

'He said you shot him.'

'Not really,' Devlin said, wishing he'd remained silent again.

'Don't get smart,' Duggan said. 'He showed her where. Though personally I wouldn't have thought you had it in you.'

Devlin considered what to say. 'He had it coming,' he said eventually, sounding braver than he felt.

Duggan laughed at this. 'Now he's starting to sound like Alan Ladd. Punch a man, kick him, that's one thing. But to point a gun at him, let alone to actually pull the trigger, that's a different thing completely. You're the only man I know who ever did it, straight up. I don't know what that makes you, exactly, but I know how I feel about having a man like that under my own roof.'

'I'll go,' Devlin said.

Duggan laughed again. 'Nothing so certain, sunshine. But you and I both know that that's hardly likely to be an end to this particular problem for any of us.'

'I'll find Harrap and give him what I can,' Devlin said.

The previous day they had all been given warning of further lay-offs at the drainage work. Devlin's luck wouldn't last for ever.

'No you won't,' Duggan said, his hand close to Devlin's face. 'You'll get out of sight of this place and never look back. You'll do what men like you always do – you'll look after Number One, as per, and leave all your mess and stink behind you for others to clear up. Well, not this time. This time, it's *me* you're dealing with.'

Men like you?

'You know where I work,' Devlin said. 'You could always find me.'

'Now you're laughing at me,' Duggan said.

Alison Duggan took the bowl to the sink and emptied it. She refilled it from the kettle on the range and then cooled this with water from the tap. She wrung out the cloth beneath the tap.

Devlin looked at Duggan's father. Fresh blood was starting to flow from his lip. Not much. The old man clutched several of the

109

torn-out pages and the thin paper flicked back and forth in his dark, bony hands.

'I'm sorry about the Bible,' Devlin said to him. It was the truth. His mother possessed something similar. His own birth and christening were recorded in the thing, unknown ancestors pushing him forward into a new world they would never inhabit, and in which he himself had always struggled to exist. Or so it seemed to him now.

Alison Duggan came back to the table and dabbed at her father-in-law's face. It was beyond Devlin to ask her if she had considered taking him to a doctor, the hospital even.

As if reading these thoughts, Duggan said, 'She wanted him to go to the quack's, but he has a morbid fear of that lot. They told him ten years ago that my mother was just exhausted and needed a few days in bed. She was dead a week later. Burst ulcer. Besides, he's survived the worst of it. He just heals up slower these days, that's all.'

The bruises on the old man's eye and cheek seemed darker than when Devlin had first seen them.

Duggan finally left Devlin and went to the table to sit beside his father. 'Skelton,' he said. 'I'm assuming it's him. How come he never reported you to the law for it in the first place?'

'Perhaps he did,' Devlin said, realizing immediately that it was the wrong thing to say.

'Can't have. Besides, it's weeks since Harrap saw you at Tattershall. Another day or two to find out about the lorry. The law would have been here then if you'd got that kind of thing hanging over you. You see what I'm saying? My thinking now is that what's happened here today might just give him cause to think again. What if he went from here straight to the station house over in Donington or Kirton?'

'He won't,' Devlin said, but with little conviction. 'Besides, even if he did, I doubt—'

'Not the point, not the point,' Duggan shouted at him, causing both Devlin and the old man to flinch. 'The point now is that he knows you were here. And the last thing I want, especially with so much hanging in the balance, so to speak, is coppers sniffing around on whatever pretext, let alone a shooting. I'm telling you now – they come knocking on my door and I'll tell them everything I know about you, everything you've told me, including the bit about the gun.' He pointed to his father. 'You see that eye, that lip, those bruises? Well, they just brought you more trouble than you could ever imagine. None of this is my doing, and none of it's going to be my undoing either. Are we both clear on that much, at least?'

When Devlin didn't respond, Duggan slapped him again.

'Clear,' Devlin said. He picked at the dry clay on his forearms. The stuff was forever there. He spread his feet and felt the torn pages of the Bible rustle and tear beneath his boots. He watched Alison Duggan wipe the old man's face again and saw him flinch when she touched his swollen eye. The flesh there looked almost transparent; the liquid beneath the surface made it smooth and free of the wrinkles and deeper lines that covered the rest of his face.

'Tell me what I owe you,' he said to Duggan without turning.

'Just the money,' Duggan said. 'Anything else you do to try and put this right would only leave a bad taste. *You* might not see where all this is headed, but *I* do.'

It was the kind of thing Devlin's mother had been fond of saying.

'I'll get it to you.'

'Oh, I know you will. The last thing you want now is someone else following you down that empty lane in the middle of nowhere one dark night.' Duggan lit a cigarette and blew the smoke over Devlin's head and across the paper-strewn table. 'I think you'd better go,' he said. 'Before I come to my senses and do something I regret.'

'Can I at least wash?' Devlin said.

He was answered by another hard slap to the side of his head. His ear stung and it was all he could do not to cry out.

Duggan rose from the table and took a step away. 'I ever hear you've been sniffing round within five miles of this place . . .'

Devlin stood up. The blows to his head had unbalanced him and he paused unsteadily for a moment before walking to the door, Duggan close behind him. He picked up the sack.

'Everything's there,' Duggan said. 'Such as it is. Not much to show, granted, but it's all yours. I'll be in touch about the money.' He flicked the final inch of his cigarette into the yard ahead of Devlin. 'Just tell me one thing – did you mean to do it?'

'Did I mean to do what?'

'Shoot the bastard. You even aim the thing before you pulled the trigger? Or was it all like *he* probably wants to think it was?'

'It wasn't even a proper gun,' Devlin said.

'I guessed that much. But the fact is, in my book, you've done it once, you'll do it again, only next time worse.'

His mother's voice again.

Devlin walked several paces ahead of Duggan and then turned to face him. The doorway behind the man was dark, the room beyond and the people inside no longer visible to him.

15

HE WALKED UNTIL HE COULD NOT BE SEEN FROM THE FARM and then he sat for a while on the verge to consider his options. Even calling them that made them more than they were. He resented how Duggan had treated him and remembered all the warnings he'd been given about the man. He was exhausted after his day's work.

Rising, he circled the farm until he arrived at the outermost of Duggan's dilapidated sheds. It stood on the seaward side of the farm, and all the time Devlin had been staying there, no one had ever gone to the building. There was no lock, and the weathered timbers that hung from the shed's frame swung aside at his touch.

Inside, every panel of the corrugated roof showed the evening sky above. An abandoned, stripped-down tractor stood to one side, an inch of bird shit covering its open seat and seized engine.

A drift of old straw lay piled against one wall and Devlin pushed enough of this together to form a makeshift bed. The straw smelled of dust and the same dry shit. What he ought to do was to spend the night there and then in the morning set light to all that waiting kindling and burn the place down. But what would that achieve? What sort of revenge would that be? A disused, collapsing barn and an unworkable tractor. Duggan would only profit from the loss and then be even more determined to collect whatever he now considered he was owed. The best plan now, Devlin knew, was to get as far away as possible and then to keep his head down.

Pushing his sack of belongings into a corner, he searched the small building. A few empty drums, folded seed and grain sacks, wooden fence posts as grey and light as planking, two rolls of fence wire bound in solid red circles. Something and nothing, but mostly nothing.

He went to the wall facing the distant farm and peered through a knothole towards the light of the place. Pale smoke rose from the chimney. Dim lights at two of the windows.

He went back to his straw bed and lit a cigarette. He held the match to a handful of the straw and was surprised by how quickly it caught light, causing him to drop the bundle he held and then stamp out the sudden blaze. He was hungry and thirsty. He hadn't eaten since noon and now it was pitch dark. He went to the doorway and watched the open land. The noise of the road was little more than a distant hiss.

After an hour, he fell asleep and then woke again to the noise of Duggan's lorry leaving the yard. He watched it go, waiting until it had turned on to the road and all sight and sound of it was lost. Birds called across the darkness; he could only imagine the time.

Leaving the shed, he went back across the fallow fields to the farm. He crept to the lighted windows and looked in. Duggan's father slept in his chair. Someone had gathered up the scattered pages of the Bible and these were now pressed beneath a plate on the table. There was no sign of Alison Duggan.

Devlin let himself in and went to the food cupboard. A radio played somewhere upstairs – Alison Duggan listening to one of her programmes, or most likely asleep with the thing still on. The old man sat with his chin on his chest and snored occasionally.

Devlin took another sack from a hook by the door and put food into this. Bread from the bin and tins from the cupboard. A piece of cooked meat sat on a board by the sink and he took this too. Then he quietly drew open the cutlery drawer and took out a bone-handled carving knife and added this to his load.

Duggan, he remembered, had once wielded the knife and called it a family heirloom. He'd shown Devlin how its blade had been worn to a thin crescent of steel by a century of sharpening and use. After using the knife, Duggan had flicked it in the air so that it fell point first to the table and stuck there quivering. Devlin had tried to repeat the trick and Duggan and his father had laughed at his countless failures.

The old man shifted in his chair and Devlin froze. The clock on the mantel chimed midnight. Another so-called heirloom. Devlin considered taking that too. Or pushing it to the stone hearth below. The old man settled again, his breathing softer than the ticking of the clock.

Devlin went to where Duggan kept money, but the tin was empty. Duggan would know immediately who had taken the food and the knife, but so what?

He left the house and looked up at the bedroom windows. There was no light. The radio still played. Who broadcast music at that time of the night? Who listened?

Quickly enveloped by the surrounding darkness, he made his way back to the shed.

115

16

EARLY THE NEXT DAY, SEEING THAT DUGGAN HAD NOT YET returned, Devlin walked to the road and left the farm.

Before leaving the shed, he'd kicked apart his bed and brushed the remains of his cigarettes and the food he'd eaten under the straw.

Once at the road, his first thought was to return to the drainage work and wait there with the others for the bad news that was coming to them all. But as he approached the pumping station gathering point, he saw in the distance the wintering fairground and went there instead. It was not yet seven and none of the other workers had arrived. Wherever he went in that small world he would leave a trail for Duggan to follow, so what difference did it make where he went?

Walking beyond the pumping house, he came to the scattered caravans and trailers, and arriving at the compound he was surprised to see Maria McGuire at the gateway surrounded by a dozen horses. He looked around for any sign of her brothers, but there was no one. It was the first time he had encountered her alone. He attracted her attention and she left the horses and came to him. He told her that he'd finally left Duggan's and that he was on his way to work.

'So?' she said. She searched the road along which he'd come.

One of the horses approached and butted his arm with its head.

He asked her what she was doing out so early.

'Waiting for the slaughterman from Boston,' she told him.

'What, he's coming for the horses?'

Maria continued looking behind him. 'No, he's coming for the lions and tigers. Perhaps he might even take one of the elephants.'

Devlin had seen a solitary lion and two small, deflated-looking elephants at the fairground. The lion looked diseased, its skin bare in patches. The elephants had always seemed to be restless, shuffling back and forth in their shackles.

'I never saw the tiger,' he said.

'That's because we never had one. The lion's on its last legs.'

'What's wrong with the horses?' Another of the creatures pushed towards him. They were mostly brown and stocky, all with untidy manes and tails, and all showed their ribs.

'Nothing wrong with them. It just makes more sense to get rid of half of them each winter and use the money to feed the other animals. We buy new ones each spring at the Lynn fair. The slaughterman likes to come early and I usually draw the short straw. He should be here by now.'

'Where are your brothers?'

'Where do you think? They were out most of the night.'

Devlin went closer to her in the gateway. 'Duggan kicked me out,' he said.

She laughed at the words. 'Poor you.'

'He still owes me.'

'That won't be how he sees it. Besides, whatever it is you *think* you're owed, you might as well start whistling for it now.

Duggan owes everybody money. It's how he operates. It's why people keep on dealing with him. Because most of the time they've got more to lose than he has.'

Devlin knew all this, and if he hadn't known it for certain, then it was what he would have guessed.

'What's in the sack?' she said.

Devlin dropped the bag to the ground. 'All my worldly goods.'

She hardly looked. 'You've done well for yourself,' she said. 'You're going to be late.' She nodded towards the pumping station, where other men were now starting to gather. Vehicles already stood with their engines running in the cold air.

'They're laying most of us off in a few days,' he said. 'Not much point in going.'

'Horses, men, it's all the same,' she said. 'You get through the summer and then you do whatever you have to do to get through to the start of the next one. Everything's uphill for people like us.'

There was already talk among the remaining workers of the drainage projects being planned for the following year. It was something, but for the months ahead that's all it would ever be – talk.

'Most things look better when they're in the future,' Maria said, looking back at the road as she spoke.

'You could always try your hand at something different,' he said.

'Such as? I'm a traveller. What else do you think there is for us? You might as well tell a rat to try living as a swan. Besides, let's face it, it's hardly any better for people like you. Like they say, you might have started out with nothing, but at least you've managed to hold on to most of it.'

Devlin offered her a cigarette, which she took.

'Said he'd be here at seven.' She picked at the matted mane of one of the horses.

'Where does the meat go?' he asked her.

She shrugged. 'None of my business. Animal food, I expect. We always keep one or two back for the lion, though I doubt if the poor bloody thing will see out another winter.'

'Is it here?'

'Skegness. Indoors, with most of the other animals. One of the empty camps. Some of the men get work there. Perhaps you could try your luck. There's always some kind of maintenance or building going on in the closed season, the better months at least. Patrick and Colm will know a few names. You could ask them. The camps are getting bigger every year, very popular, fully catered, happy families, all that.' It was another long, tired breath of disappointment.

'I suppose so,' Devlin said. It was a way forward, a vague, unknown path through the dark months ahead of him. He started to explain to her what had happened at Duggan's with Skelton.

'Save your breath,' she said. 'I don't care for the man and I never heard of the other. Everything round here ends up with somebody or other getting knocked down or cheated out of something. Besides, that's all some people ever do, moan and complain about how unfair everything is.'

Devlin said nothing.

'You're probably no different from anybody else,' she said. 'Men like Duggan can't help but take advantage, it's in their nature. In fact, men like Duggan think it's their *right* to behave how they behave because the world provides the men for them to do it to, otherwise why would all these others exist?'

And again, Devlin knew this already. There was no malice

or pleasure in her voice as she said all this, but instead something almost comforting, reassuring to him.

'I suppose so,' he said again.

'No "suppose" about it.'

He wanted to ask her what she believed gave Duggan the edge over all these other men, but said nothing because he already knew what her answer might be.

'They *eat* horses in France,' he said.

'I heard that. I went to France once. Calais, if you can call that France. Went with my father when I was a girl to buy an old carousel. Took a transporter over on the ferry. We were only there two hours. A piece of wasteland a quarter of a mile from the terminal. My father was coughing blood even then. He died a few months later.'

'I was in Germany,' he said. 'In the war. Towards the end.' As soon as the lie was out of his mouth he wished he could suck it back in. It was getting harder to remember all those non-existent facts and details. Besides, she was different.

'You and a million others,' she said.

'It wasn't anything special,' he said, a retraction of sorts. 'Ruins mostly.' Newsreel footage.

'My father's funeral lasted a week,' she said. 'Longer. When we were in Calais he had his first ever glass of wine, we both did. First and last. Both of us.' She stopped abruptly at the sudden fond memory.

'Never got the taste for it,' he said. Ellen's wedding to Morris. For the toasts, everybody sipping at the unfamiliar drink, Morris making another of his points.

'My father said afterwards that it was the worst muck he'd ever tasted.' She smiled at the recollection. 'But he said that drinking it with the Frogs saved him a few hundred quid. I can see the French eating horses.'

'And snails and frogs,' Devlin said.

'You know a lot about the French all of a sudden.'

'Not really. Just stuff I picked up.'

'During the war?'

'I suppose so. Afterwards, mostly.' More edge chipped off the lie. He looked beyond her to the caravans and trailers, booths and covered rides. Most of the caravans would be empty for the winter.

'I know what you're going to say,' she said. 'Nothing to do with me. You'd need to pay your way.'

'You could ask for me,' he said.

'What difference do you think that would make? They're a law unto themselves, that pair, especially Patrick. Besides, he'd probably say no just because it had come from me.'

'You'd be doing me a favour,' Devlin said.

Before she could answer him she was distracted by the arrival of the slaughterman, whose high, slat-sided lorry came noisily towards them.

The vehicle drew up and the man climbed out and went immediately to look at the gathered horses. He slapped their bony flanks and held their heads to examine their yellow teeth.

'He's going through the motions,' Maria said behind her hand to Devlin.

'I thought they'd have a bit more meat on their bones when I made my offer,' the man said as he came to them.

'Change the record,' Maria said.

'Who's this – your lover boy? Brought him along for a bit of clout?'

'I've been running rings round you for the past five years,' Maria said. 'No need to stop now.'

The man laughed and took out a roll of money.

'Give me what you offered or you've had a wasted trip,' Maria told him.

The man made a point of looking back along the road. 'Got others queuing up desperate to take them off your hands, have you?'

'Pay her what you said,' Devlin said to the man, coming closer to the pair of them.

Both the slaughterman and Maria shook their heads at hearing this.

'He's eager, I'll give him that,' the man said to her.

'He was in the war,' Maria said, winking at Devlin. She knew.

'Was he now? Well, in that case . . .' He held up his arms in surrender and then laughed at Devlin. 'Keep your hair on, son. She knows the rules as well as any of them. Besides, when did she or her lot ever pay a fair price for anything?' He looked back to the horses. 'Not too bad, I don't suppose,' he said. 'For circus nags. I've seen worse.' He offered her ten pounds less than she'd been expecting and Maria accepted it. The pair of them shook hands.

'He thinks you're going to butcher them and send the meat to France,' she said.

'The Frogs? Perhaps I should look into it. I daresay they got enough of their own.' He turned back to Devlin. 'Supply and demand, see? That's what this game's all about. What anything's all about, really, when you come to think about it. Supply and demand and all those so-called market forces we keep hearing so much about these days.' He peeled several notes from the wad he held and gave the rest to Maria. 'You going to count it?' he asked her.

'No need,' she told him. 'You know who I am and I know where to come looking for you.'

'I suppose so,' the man said. 'You going to give me a hand getting them loaded?'

'What do you think?' Maria said.

17

'SHOULDN'T THEY AT LEAST BE DOING SOMETHING?' DEVLIN motioned beyond Sullivan to where the borstal boys sat gathered at the back of the bus.

'No point,' Sullivan said, unconcerned, his eyes fixed on the paper he was reading. 'You know it, I know it, and they know it.' He wiped his hand across the condensation which coated the inside of the window to reveal the falling rain and the dark, sodden fields beyond.

'Nothing's certain yet,' Devlin said.

'Who are you kidding? By this time tomorrow nobody will ever know we were even here. All the heavy plant's being taken off this afternoon and won't be back until next March. Anything still here this time next month will be stuck fast. Job's only half done, if that, but that's how things work where water and the seasons are concerned. Besides, our contract finishes today – you don't get more certain than that.' He looked up, wiping his hand on his sleeve. 'How about you? Off to the new culvert work over at the Washway road?'

'Word is, they're laying the last of us off for the winter.'

'Makes sense to the money men, I suppose,' Sullivan said. 'It's the machinery gets most of the work done these days.'

Devlin looked along the line of parked lorries waiting for their final loads of clay. The dredgers had already been pulled away from the new embankment. Men cleared the buckets and treads with shovels.

Most of the borstal boys played cards or read the pages of a dismantled paper. A few sat apart from the others and looked back along the length of the bus.

'So what will we do?' Devlin said. 'Sit here all day?' He already knew the answer.

'I don't see why not. Unless you'd prefer to be outside, up to your arse in freezing water. I know where I'd rather be.'

Devlin considered the day ahead, and the day after that, and the day after that.

'I've got wet all over the paper now,' Sullivan said, pushing it into the seat beside him. 'We're set to get a lot more of this sort of contract work over at the camp, and most of it will involve days like this. Repaying their debt to society? Christ, I wouldn't want any of this little lot anywhere near me or my society, whatever that is when it's at home. See that little bugger sitting by himself? Messed with his own little sister. Twelve, she was. Half a dozen mothers in the neighbourhood came forward when he was arrested, said he'd tried to do the same to their kids.'

Devlin looked at the boy. He sat with his eyes closed, his hands twisting in his lap.

'Twelve,' Sullivan said. 'Christ. How on earth is he going to repay *that* particular debt to society?'

'What'll happen to him?'

'He's on a Transfer Notice. When he's old enough he'll be off to the prison in Lincoln or Norwich. *Then* he'll find out all about that debt to society. We've got relatives of some of those other girls – brothers, cousins – at the camp. This is the first time I've seen the little bastard without a black eye, cut lip or a swollen mouth in a month. Ask me, he gets all he deserves.'

Devlin looked harder at the boy, who finally opened his eyes and let his hands fall still. He saw Devlin looking at him and stared back, grinning and mouthing something Devlin couldn't decipher.

'Ignore him,' Sullivan said. 'He's like a wild fucking dog that's been pushed into a corner. I told them not to put him on the work list. He's the sort who'll one day fancy his chances and set off running, and you wouldn't believe how much trouble and extra work that brings down on all our heads. You can't do what he did and *not* have ideas about doing it all again.'

The boy closed his eyes again and resumed wringing his hands.

'Besides,' Sullivan went on, 'you ought to be more concerned about your own prospects now that your number's nearly up. Last in, first out, is it? Another stupid bloody rule, you ask me.'

Devlin had been away from the site for the past three days. He had only come today to collect what was owed to him. Others had done the same, looking for alternative work before the queues suddenly got much longer.

'I said it's a stupid bloody rule,' Sullivan repeated when Devlin didn't respond.

'You're right,' Devlin said. The man was starting to annoy him.

'Course I'm right. What good's a man who sticks at something he's no good at? You got any prospects?'

'I'm going to ask round the holiday camps,' Devlin said. In truth, he'd done little and achieved less during the past few days, and the caravan park work was still only a vague idea.

'Need to get your skates on. They're building a new camp

from scratch over Hunstanton way. Young man like you, no family, no commitments, suit you down to the ground. And if all else fails, you might even want to consider this little game.'

'The prison?'

'Don't sound so surprised. You could do a lot worse. Cushy little number if your face fits and you get your feet under the table. Nowhere near as hard as it looks.'

Devlin wondered if this was a joke, but suppressed his laughter.

'Look at them,' Sullivan said, again indicating the boys. 'Any two or three of them could overpower me and scarper. Do some real damage, some of them. But look at them. They just sit there, throwing me dirty looks and doing nothing. Know why that is?'

Devlin shook his head. Any *one* of the boys could probably overpower Sullivan.

'Because they know they'd get what's coming to them if they so much as lifted a finger to me. Perhaps not straight away, or here, or when they were expecting it, but they'd get it all the same, one way or another, and they all know that. I'm serious. You should look into it. I could put a word in if you like.'

'I don't think they'd look at me,' Devlin said. He turned in his seat to look back out of the window. The narrow road stretched ahead of him into the rain and cloud. He could see neither its ending nor the road it eventually joined. A solitary tree rose out of the grey.

'Why's that, then?' Sullivan said cautiously.

'I've been inside myself.'

Sullivan considered this. 'Local?'

'Colchester.'

Sullivan laughed. 'Colchester? Military? That won't count against you. If anything, it might even work in your favour. Half the blokes at the camp are ex-military. And half of *them* will have been on the dodgy side of things, if you catch my drift. Wartime regulations, was it?'

'I suppose so.'

'There you go, then. Wartime. It makes all the difference. They'll have wiped the slate on whatever you did or didn't do. And I'm guessing you were only ever charged with half of what you got up to in the first place.'

'Less,' Devlin said.

'Then on top of everything else, you'll know how to look after yourself. You and this lot, you're out of the same mould. So-called experts are ten a penny in this racket. What *we* need are men on the ground who know what's what. I won't deny you look as though you could do with a bit more meat on your bones and a decent wash and brush up, but you strike me as a man who knows how to look after himself under the circumstances.'

Everything Sullivan said sounded good to Devlin. It sounded true and right. Honest. 'I suppose it's worth thinking about,' he said.

"Course it is. In addition to which, most of the men at the camp are sitting on a prison pension the rest of the world can only dream about. Security – that's what it's all about these days. Looking ahead, planning for the future. If you don't plan for things you're going to end up like this lot here. You'd think they'd learn something after coming to us, but they never do. Not a single one of them. Never. They'll all be back up to some sort of mischief or other the minute we kick them out of the gates and wave them off.'

As Devlin watched, the cloud around them grew thicker, swallowing up more of the narrow road and the tree.

'You think about it,' Sullivan said. 'That's all I'm saying, you give it some thought. You know where I am.'

18

HE SAW THE FIGURE HALF A MILE AHEAD OF HIM, COMING
towards him on the bank above the Lynn Channel. Earlier, he'd
watched a Sunderland flying boat moving slowly over the sea,
east to west, a few hundred yards offshore. At the start of the
war he'd gone with the other boys to watch the planes coming
and going from the Wash. North Sea patrols. A series of jetties
had been built between Ongar Hill and Admiralty Point, a barracks and a clubhouse. A month after the war's end, everything
had been demolished or dismantled and removed. Now only a
few concrete slabs and brick foundations remained. There had
been talk of a passenger service using the Sunderlands, but this
had come to nothing. He'd watched the plane earlier until it
had disappeared over the horizon.

As the figure came closer he finally recognized the old shepherd he'd encountered three months earlier in the tin chapel.
He continued towards the man. The path at his feet was soft
and stuck to his boots. Coils of rusted barbed wire trailed down
the slope into the water on both sides.

Eventually, the two men met. Devlin wondered if the old
man remembered him.

'You look better than when I last saw you,' the shepherd said.

'Been doing all right for myself,' Devlin said. He remembered the man's name. Samuel.

'I can see that. See the flying boat?'

'Hardly miss it.'

'They scare the sheep.'

Everything scared sheep. 'I suppose so.'

'So what you up to? Not still sleeping rough, I imagine.'

'Been staying with a man called Duggan.' A month had passed since then, and afterwards he'd hardly spent two nights in the same place. He was still hoping to rent one of the empty caravans at the fair's winter quarters.

'*Him?*' Samuel turned away from him and scanned the horizon.

'Just moved on,' Devlin said.

'Best thing to do where that man's concerned.'

Devlin gave him a cigarette and the old man broke it in half and put an inch of it behind his ear. His fingers and nails were brown with smoke.

Devlin saw that the man stood stiffly, that his legs seemed swollen.

Samuel saw him looking. 'Newspapers,' he said. 'I push them in for warmth. I embarrass my daughter. She said as much. To my face.'

'Does it work?' Devlin said.

'Wouldn't do it otherwise.'

'I suppose not.'

There was a moment of silence between them.

'They were hare coursing over Sutton way last night,' Samuel said eventually. 'Lampers. Some sharp-looking dogs.'

'This time of year?' He'd done it himself, but mostly in the spring.

'What difference do you think that makes? They come out from Spalding and Holbeach. Anything that moves, they'll set a dog on it. And when there's nothing to chase, they'll set the dogs on each other for a bet.'

Devlin had heard about the fights, the money supposedly made and lost.

'There was a man up Clenchwarton way,' Samuel said, 'fisherman, kept a boat in Lynn, who was cautioned by the Lynn magistrates for killing seals. Took an axe to twenty of them, mothers and pups, back around April time. Said he was defending his livelihood. Thirty others turned up at the court to shout at the magistrate. The police said he'd get Norwich gaol for a few months, but it never came to that. They had a photo in the *Gazette* of the bodies on the beach. Chopped the heads off some of them.' He paused. 'Some people used to swear by seal meat during the war.'

Devlin wondered where all this was leading. 'You on your way to the chapel?' he asked him. The building was at least five miles distant.

'I might take a quick look. Just walking, mostly. You working?'

'Drainage work.' Which had finally ended ten days ago, after which he'd received only half of what he'd been expecting in his final pay packet.

'Labouring?'

'Mostly.'

'Saw a lorry yesterday piled with Nissen huts over towards the Nene Outfall. All stacked like ridge tiles one atop the other. Temporary accommodation, the driver said. He got caught fast on that sharp bend. The lorries aren't suited. Will you stick at it, the work?'

Devlin told him about the lay-offs.

'Done more than my share in that line,' Samuel said. 'Thirty years back. It's a young man's game. If there's one thing certain in this neck of the woods, it's that the water's always going to be there and either want moving somewhere else or getting rid of completely. What will you do to get through?'

'See what turns up, I suppose.'

'It doesn't sound like much of a plan,' Samuel said.

Another of those evaporated conversations. Passing the time of day, most would call it.

Devlin wanted to leave the man.

'I ought to be making tracks,' Samuel said eventually, finishing the half cigarette. He shielded his eyes and looked directly up into the sky above them.

'Me, too,' Devlin said.

'Right.'

They moved apart, slowly at first, as though held together by the simple presence of one another in such an empty place, but then Devlin started walking faster. He'd seen the photograph of the decapitated seals and their recently born pups. The men he'd been with at the time said it served the greedy little bastards right, that a seal would take a single bite out of a fish and leave the rest of it to rot. According to them, the only mistake the man who'd killed the animals had made was to have left the bodies and heads out in the open on the mudflats for everybody to see. These days, some people would see the injustice in every little thing. Greedy, thieving little bastards, and vicious with it.

19

DEVLIN AND THE MCGUIRE BROTHERS SAT IN THE BACK
room of the Oak at Sutton Bridge. They had been there since
noon and it was now close to four. Few other drinkers had come
and gone in that time.

The brothers were there on business, but the man they had
been expecting to meet hadn't shown up. Devlin paid for most
of their drinks out of the last of his pay. He'd spent the past
three nights in an empty trailer close to the brothers' own
caravan. The drink was a sort of rent. Devlin was hoping for
something better, something more permanent. Nothing seemed
straightforward any more; there were no proper paths, no
squares on a calendar waiting to be crossed off. He was drifting
again, weightless, everything beyond his control.

He'd been as drunk as he'd ever been by two o'clock and the
McGuires had laughed at everything he'd said.

Now, getting to his feet, he immediately lost his balance
and fell back to his seat. The two men pushed him from side to
side between them. They seldom showed signs of their own
drunkenness – even on those days when they did little else but
drink – until much later in the day. Rising before noon was still
a rarity for them.

Patrick pushed a hand into Devlin's pocket and pulled out the last of his change. He went to the bar and returned with three more glasses. He and Colm drained theirs quickly, but Devlin left his where it sat on the table. He held the edge of his seat. He felt sick.

An old man came into the room and pulled a stool to the bar, where he sat with his back to them. He ordered a whisky and sat with the glass, hardly sipping at it. Much of the time he folded his arms on the polished wooden surface and sat with his head on them.

At five, the brothers told Devlin that they were going out for a few minutes and that he was to stay where he was in case the man they'd been expecting showed up late. They described the man to Devlin, but little of what they said registered.

Alone, Devlin straightened his back, released his grip on the chair and sat with the back of his head against the wall.

After a minute, the old man at the bar came across to him. He sat opposite Devlin and studied him.

'You're Jimmy Devlin's boy,' he said.

'So?' It was as much as Devlin could attempt.

'Have it your own way. I know him, that's all.'

'Good for you.'

'You're the spit of him when he was younger.' The man looked around the empty room. 'Gone, have they, the gyppos?'

Even in that state, Devlin heard the change of note in the man's voice.

'Not for long,' he said. He tasted vomit deep in his throat.

'Everybody round here's had dealings with that pair. Known, they are.'

'So?' Devlin took a deep breath. 'Get lost. Leave me alone.'

The old man drew back from the table, beyond Devlin's reach.

'No need to be like that. I was only trying to offer you a piece of friendly advice. He's a good man, your father.'

'Not to me, he wasn't.' Not to anybody.

'Yes, well, there's still some round here won't hear a bad word against Jimmy Devlin.'

'Not interested,' Devlin said. The taste in his mouth cleared. He even thought about picking up his glass and drinking from it. 'So if you think all this is going to get you another drink, you're wasting your time.' His head felt suddenly clear. Perhaps his drunkenness had passed. Perhaps he was on the other side of it. He'd heard of men drinking themselves sober. It made a sort of sense, but probably only to a drunken man.

'I was only trying to be friendly,' the man said.

'Then you're wasting your time.' Testing himself with everything he said.

'I can see that now. Besides, I heard about you. You taking up with the gyppos is the least of things. I know more about you than—'

'Than what? More about me than what? I've never even seen you before.'

'What's that got to do with anything?' The man seemed genuinely surprised.

'Just get lost,' Devlin said. 'The gyppos will be back soon. I doubt you'll want to stick your nose into *their* business.'

'Don't worry, I'm going. Seen all I need to see. You don't know the half of it, son.'

Devlin laughed at him. The taste was back in his mouth.

The man rose and picked up his empty glass, sucking at it as he went first to the bar and then to the door. As he left, he turned to Devlin and said, 'Pass on your regards, shall I?'

'Do whatever you like,' Devlin told him. 'Or you could try

keeping your fucking nose out of other people's fucking business.'
He finally picked up his glass and drank from it. He wondered
how long the McGuires would be gone. They talked about hours
and minutes, dates and appointments, but none of it meant
anything.

'He said you'd got a mouth on you,' the man said, and then
he left.

Devlin sat breathing deeply for a while. This time when he
rose to his feet the room stayed in place. He went to the toilet and
returned. The brothers might leave him sitting there for hours.
They might even forget he was with them. The man they were
there to see wasn't going to show. Three hours late? They might
even meet him somewhere else now and then spend what was left
of the day with him. He'd give it another hour, two at the most,
and then he would leave and make his own way back to the
trailer. He tried to remember if he'd heard the brothers' van leaving the small car park when they'd gone out. Two hours. It would
be dark by then and they were different men in the dark.

As he considered all this, the door opened again and Devlin
turned to look, expecting the McGuires to enter and to come
and sit beside him.

But instead of the brothers or the man they were there to
meet, the same old man who knew his father came back into
the room and stood in front of Devlin with a grin on his face.
He was followed a moment later by a man Devlin's age. He was
tall and heavy. Perhaps he was the old man's son.

The old man came even closer to Devlin and then pointed
directly at him.

'Told you it was him,' he said triumphantly to the man behind him. 'Recognized him the instant I clapped eyes on him.'
He turned to the younger man and held out his hand.

The younger man took out a wallet and gave him a single note.

'Is that all?' the man said.

The younger man pushed him to one side and took his place directly in front of Devlin.

'You Jimmy Devlin?' he said.

'What, just because he says I am?'

'You're him,' the man said, grinning.

Devlin smelled the drink on his breath. The man's hands were dirty, as though he'd come to the bar from wherever he'd been working.

'I don't know what you think I'm supposed to have done,' Devlin said, wondering if the words had come out right. It sounded much less of a threat than he'd intended.

'I couldn't have put it better myself,' the man said. 'My name's Sewell. George Sewell. Ring any bells?'

It didn't.

'Never heard of you,' Devlin said.

'Perhaps this will jog your memory,' Sewell said, and before Devlin could prepare himself, the man formed a heavy fist and swung it hard into Devlin's face, catching his nose and cheek and lip and forcing him back in his seat, banging his head against the wall and causing him to swing his own arm and knock over his glass and the two empty ones still beside it, all three of them falling to the stone floor where they smashed. He struggled to pull himself upright, and as he did this Sewell hit him again, on the other side of his head. This time Devlin shouted out in surprise and pain, and at the same time Sewell grabbed him by the front of his shirt and pushed him even harder back against the wall. Devlin tried to hold his hands in front of his face. Blood ran from his nose into his mouth and then from his mouth down his wet chin.

Sewell finally let go of him, his fist still clenched, his arm drawn back.

'I don't know you,' Devlin shouted at him, causing himself more pain and seeing his hands flecked with red spittle. 'I never knew any Sewell. I'm telling you, whoever you are, you've got this wrong.' He struggled to make sense of what was happening to him. Perhaps the man had been sent by Duggan. Or perhaps he was working for Harrap now that the court and Skelton had failed him?

George Sewell stood panting for a moment. He lowered his arm and uncurled his fingers. 'You know Barbara Collet?' he said, and in that instant everything began to make sense to Devlin. Painful sense.

'Whatever she's saying—' he began to say, then stopped and considered his words more carefully. 'No, not her – that old bitch of a mother of hers. Whatever *she's* saying, it's not true.'

'You calling her a liar, then? You calling the pair of them liars?'

Devlin touched a finger to his lips. 'I'm bleeding,' he said. 'That's what I'm doing.'

'Good. Because this is only half of what you deserve. Plenty more where that came from.'

'What's she been saying?' He remembered Skelton's wife on the morning of his eviction. 'Because whatever you've heard, it's not—'

'So you keep saying. What I've heard,' George Sewell said slowly, 'is that you're playing the big man and going round telling everybody that it's your kid.'

Devlin wondered why the landlord hadn't come to see what was happening, or at least come to demand payment for the smashed glasses. He looked down at the new drops of blood appearing on the wet table. He held the edge again, but all that achieved was to betray the shaking of his hands.

'Me and Barbara, we're engaged to be wed,' George Sewell said.

'So what?' Everything became clear to Devlin. As clear as it would ever be.

Sewell smiled at the words. 'And the last thing either of us wants now is some pathetic little toe-rag like you going round shooting his mouth off about the kid.'

'I never said anything,' Devlin said. He watched the viscous blood pooling in his palm.

'Not what I heard,' Sewell said.

Was that a note of uncertainty in his voice?

Devlin seized his advantage. 'I had a bit of a run-in with Skelton, that's all, got the better of him. His fat, blousy tart of a wife has obviously decided to get even on his behalf. *She's* the one going round shooting her mouth off about me and the kid, not me.' It was mostly the truth. Truth plus a bit of guesswork, but who was counting? Sewell was beginning to swallow it. 'I used to see Barbara Collet,' Devlin said. 'It's common knowledge, I won't lie to you. But the kid's nothing to do with me.'

George Sewell looked as though he was going to sit down. Perhaps it was all starting to make better sense to him than whatever he might have heard from either Barbara Collet's mother or Skelton's wife. All he wanted to be told now, Devlin guessed, was that the child was his, Sewell's, and that nothing to the contrary was being put about by the only other person who might have had something to say on the matter. That only other person being him, Devlin, Jimmy Devlin.

'We're going to be wed,' Sewell said again.

'So you keep telling me.'

'In Lowestoft, and then we'll live there. I've got a half-decent job there, and once we're married we'll set up home there and as far as everybody's concerned the kid is mine.'

'The kid *is* yours,' Devlin said. 'There was no need for any of this. By rights, I should have the law on you for assault.' It sounded like a legitimate threat.

Lowestoft. The arsehole of beyond. The pair of them were welcome to it; them and the kid.

'Nice place, Lowestoft,' he said.

'Who cares? The point is, it's not here. Am I making myself clear?'

'Crystal,' Devlin said. He held up his bloody hand. 'I'm bleeding,' he said again. Red strings fell to the table.

'What, and you want an apology?'

'I can see why you might be put out,' Devlin said, causing Sewell to bang both his heavy fists on the table. There might even have been some of Devlin's blood on one of them.

'The kid's mine, and that's all there is to it,' Sewell said. Melodrama.

Not once had he said 'daughter', let alone whatever name they had given her.

Devlin considered asking, but didn't.

'Who was the old man?' he said.

'Just somebody I knew who said he knew you and would let me know when he spotted you.'

'He knows my father,' Devlin said. 'Not me.'

'I doubt there's much to choose between the pair of you from what I hear,' Sewell said. It was another blow to Devlin, but again he said nothing. 'So have I made myself clear enough for you?'

'Crystal,' Devlin said. 'I already said.'

'Just don't give me cause to come looking for you again, that's all I'm saying.'

George Sewell turned and went to the door.

As he left, the landlord finally appeared at the bar and shouted in to ask who was going to clear up all the mess and then pay for everything that had been broken.

Devlin wondered how much money was still in his pocket. He cursed the McGuire brothers. He wondered if it was already dark outside, or if the light of a dull day had yet to die. He felt sick again. He held a hand to his chest and when he looked he saw a vague red print there. The taste was stronger in his mouth. He tried to remember when any of his clothes had last been washed.

20

HE OPENED AN EYE AND WATCHED MARIA WHERE SHE slept fully clothed on the bench opposite him. A solitary shaft of weak light crossed the caravan from back to front. Blankets hung at the windows. The same stale smell filled the air.

He pushed himself upright and struck his arm against the metal edge of the flimsy table, crying out at the sudden pain. One more to add to all his others.

'What time is it?' Maria said, her eyes still closed.

'Eleven, half past?' Devlin said, rubbing his arm.

He remembered Maria coming to him an hour after Patrick and Colm had brought him to the caravan the previous night.

He remembered the brothers telling her everything that had happened in the Oak, and he remembered them laughing at everything they said. Maria had washed his face and bleeding mouth. She told him there was no real damage, just cuts and bruises. Devlin had practised opening and closing his mouth, sucking air through his nose. The brothers had said he just had to give the word and they'd go in search of Sewell. Devlin told them not to, that it was an ending of sorts, a tie finally severed.

The empty caravan stood a hundred yards from the brothers'

own. They'd told Devlin he could have it for the winter. The rent was negotiable, they said, and laughed again.

'This the best you got?' he'd asked them.

'Who said you were getting best?' Patrick had answered him.

And, just as at Duggan's, Devlin had understood immediately and precisely where he stood.

His mother used to say that some men lived their lives like leaves in the wind.

'You pay us, one way or another, at the end of every week,' Patrick had said. 'Yes or no?'

Yes.

His mother used to say that some men never knew what choices they had until not a single one of those choices remained.

When Patrick and Colm had gone, and he was alone with Maria, she had warned him about paying her brothers on time. There had been others, she'd said, her warning clear.

Rising now from where she'd slept on the opposite bench, she showed him how to light the paraffin heater at the centre of the caravan. There was a can of fuel under the doorstep. The burning wick added its own sudden sharp aroma to the room.

'It stinks,' Devlin said.

'It's paraffin. What did you expect? I can sell you a lucky lavender bag if you like.'

Devlin started to laugh. It hurt him to open his mouth more than a slit.

Maria went to the sink. A foot pump did nothing to bring water to the tap, just a dry rasping sound.

'Something else you've not got,' she said. 'Beggars and choosers and all that.'

If he was begging, he'd hardly be paying rent, would he? But he kept the thought to himself.

Maria left him after that and returned an hour later to say that her brothers had gone. She brought the cold remains of a meal with her – even after testing it, Devlin was none the wiser – and a bottle of clear spirit, which she poured into cups.

Gone where?

Usually better not to ask.

Like that, was it? Stupid question. It was *always* like that.

They shared a bitter toast to his new home. She showed him where small tables appeared and how seating was turned into beds. She told him not to get any funny ideas. 'Such as?' Devlin wanted to say, but didn't. Their breath clouded the cold air.

'Colder in here than outside,' she said. 'No, seriously.'

Devlin finally managed to get the heater burning, strewing the floor with spent matches. Fumes rippled to the tin ceiling, where they left a faint sheen. The place was a death trap, but no one had ever spent a night in a caravan without that particular understanding. He sat with his palms held close to the top of the heater.

Maria pulled a blanket over her shoulders and came to sit beside him, her hands close to his.

'You should have got out while you had the chance,' she said to him.

The remark surprised him. 'I'm hardly—' he began to say.

'Everything catches up with you one way or another in this place.'

Devlin touched his lip. 'It already did.' He wanted to laugh again.

'Trouble is, this place, you can usually see that trouble coming from a long way off. Or if it isn't coming directly at you, then it's still out there, going round and round in circles and waiting its chance.'

He wanted to tell her she was wrong. His tongue felt swollen in his mouth. He began to wonder if one of his teeth had come loose.

'Does it still hurt?' she asked him.

'I'll survive.'

'You keep telling yourself that.' She looked around her. 'They'll sell off some of the other vans when money gets tight. They gave you this one because it would fetch next to nothing, even for scrap.' Every farm for twenty miles in every direction had either a wheel-less railway carriage or a sagging caravan sitting at the corner of one of its fields. In some parts, they were all that broke the never-ending watery flatness of the place.

'When do they start the maintenance work, repairing the rides and machinery?' he asked her.

'Not for months yet. No point doing anything too early. There's a lot of winter to come.' It was the middle of November.

Devlin was about to suggest going in search of more food when Patrick returned, pulling open the door without knocking and coming straight in to them. He was surprised to see that his sister had spent the night there and did nothing to disguise this.

Devlin wondered what to say to him.

Patrick laughed at his discomfort. 'You're a fast worker,' he said. He looked from Devlin to Maria to the bottle on the table.

'When did you get back?' Maria asked him.

'Just this minute.'

'From?'

Patrick looked back to Devlin and smiled. 'From where I went,' he said.

Then he went to Devlin at the heater, held him by his shoulders and laughed in his face. 'I'm joking with you, boy. You and her. Bit of a laugh, that's all. You should see your face. She's her own woman.'

Patrick went to the sink. 'You got any water running yet?' He stamped on the pump, making the same rasping noise. He reached for the door and pulled it shut. It made no difference to the temperature. Then he went to the table, sat down and finally drank from the bottle.

'Busy night?' Devlin asked him, bracing himself against Patrick's answer.

'That lip's bleeding again,' Patrick said. 'So-so. Scrap, mostly, already sold on. He must have hit you harder than you're letting on. Didn't you even get one shot back at him?'

'A bit of one, in the gut.'

'Gut's no good. You need to get straight to the face every time. Eyes first, mouth, then nose. Let the bastard know you're there. We saw Duggan earlier. Hit a man in the gut and all you do is give him time to work out what's coming next. A bit of blood in his eyes or down his shirt lets him know *exactly* what's happening. Gut? Jesus.'

Devlin felt suddenly warm. 'Duggan?' he said.

'He'd been at the scrap yard over Gosberton way. Don't worry, we didn't let on that we'd seen you. And it surely wouldn't be in our interest to let him know that we're keeping you here in the lap of luxury. Your name came up, but only because he mentioned it.'

'Oh?'

'You never said anything to us about robbing him blind when he kicked you out.' He looked from Devlin to Maria and smiled as he said it.

'That's because I didn't,' Devlin said, his mouth dry.

'Not according to him. According to him, you waited until he'd gone out and then, like the coward that you are, you crept back when only his defenceless wife and poor old father were in the house and helped yourself to whatever you could find.'

'A bit of food,' Devlin said. 'That's all.' It wasn't even stealing.

'And the rest. He said something about a knife. Seemed a bit put out about that, he did.'

Devlin wondered whether to laugh at the remark.

'He said that if I came across you I was to let you know that he wanted it back. What's it made of, solid silver?' He watched Devlin closely as he said this. 'Christ, perhaps it is.'

'It's cheap plate,' Devlin said.

'Whatever it is, if I were you I'd do exactly as he says. There's some things not worth arguing the toss over. He said that whatever the outcome, he's adding a few quid to what you owe him until he gets it back. Seems to me, you could do yourself a favour in that direction by doing what he says.'

'What I owe him?' Devlin said.

'Where is it, the knife?'

Devlin reached under the table and pulled it from his bag.

Patrick examined it and then dropped it on the table, disappointed. 'It wouldn't fetch five bob in Lynn market on a good day. He said he was still looking to see what else you might have taken.'

'He knows there's nothing else. In fact—'

Patrick held up his palms. 'Only passing on what he told me.' He looked hard at Devlin. 'Go on – "in fact" what?'

'Nothing,' Devlin said. He picked up the knife, the first time he'd held it since leaving Duggan's. 'I should have stuck it into the old man where he was sleeping,' he said.

'Even you're not that stupid.'

'No, but it would have taught Duggan a lesson.'

'Would it really? He'd have been at your throat within the hour and you'd have been six foot under somewhere no one ever went ten minutes after that. Everybody knows what a bastard Ray Duggan is. I'm telling you again – if you owe him, pay him. Give me the knife, I'll get it back to him without him knowing where you are.'

'He'll already know,' Devlin said.

'Perhaps. But the fact that he's keeping his distance counts for something. We do a fair bit of business with the man. I doubt he'd want to put the kybosh on that.'

Devlin doubted this. In fact, he knew precisely why Duggan was keeping his head down and keeping him, Devlin, exactly where he wanted him.

'I could get the knife back to him and tell him that makes you even,' Patrick said, but with little conviction. 'Besides, Duggan's old man's been more dead than alive these past ten years. It's why he goes on and on about all that Bible stuff.'

Maria came to sit beside Devlin and helped herself to another drink. Both men held out their cups to her.

'The knife would be a start,' she said to Devlin.

He knew that. But why was *he* always the one making concessions, always the one bending, giving way, telling people what they wanted to hear, falling silent?

Patrick picked up the knife again and ran his finger along the length of its blunt blade. The metal was tarnished from tip to handle. He pointed it at Devlin's mouth. 'You healing?'

'Probably.'

'At least that little bit of business is over and done with. Bad debts and grievances you know about are one thing, but something like that – blood, family – is a different nest of vipers entirely.'

'What's he talking about?' Maria asked Devlin.

But before Devlin could answer her, Patrick said, 'Romeo

here knocked up somebody else's woman. There's a kid. Fiancé, no less.'

'It wasn't like that,' Devlin said. 'It was before she even met the man.'

'Not the way *she*'s telling it, apparently.'

'She's saving face, that's all – her and her interfering mother. All she wants now is to wash everything clean and make a new start for herself. Who's stopping her? Not me.'

'What was it?' Maria said.

'A girl,' Devlin said. 'I never knew.'

'What would you have done if you had?'

Devlin shrugged.

It was an honest response and she saw that.

'They're going to live in Lowestoft,' he said.

'The place stinks of fish,' Patrick said, causing all three of them to smile.

The smell of paraffin grew even stronger.

Devlin told Patrick to take the knife and to get it back to Duggan.

'Consider it done,' Patrick said. He picked the thing up and then he rose and left them as suddenly as he'd come.

'Did you once think it might come to something, you and the girl?' Maria asked him when they were alone.

'Once,' he said. 'Perhaps.' He'd never even known she was pregnant, let alone had had the baby, until Skelton's wife had turned up shouting the odds.

'I see,' Maria said, and then she too left him.

He stood at the window and watched her through the yellow lace curtain. The fumes from the heater were starting to catch in his throat.

21

HE WORKED WITH THE BROTHERS FOR A WEEK. EACH MORNING they were picked up at six at the compound gate and driven with twenty or thirty others to various holiday camps along the coast and then dropped off in groups according to where the work was. The furthest any of them went was north of Skegness, where the camps were growing fastest.

Mostly they laid foundations, and it was the hardest work Devlin had done in the past five years. The ten-by-twenty plots were already staked out and waiting for them and the pay was by sites completed. Usually, the brothers warned him, it was the kind of work they avoided like the fucking plague. Suckers' work. But needs must and all that.

They showed him how to dig shallower bases than specified. They shovelled hard core – brick and concrete rubble from the torn-up airfields mostly – and then barely compacted it. They mixed wet concrete and poured it to depths also shallower than specified. Patrick showed him the impossibility of checking any of these specifications once the concrete was mixed and poured and already going off. It would become obvious in a year or two, he said, when it started to break up or subside, but a year or two was a lifetime in that game. Besides, no one would ever remember who had worked on which particular sites, let alone camps. It was a job that cried out for short cuts. You could hardly blame a man for taking whatever small advantage presented itself to him. At the end of each week, the brothers arranged for a man to come and collect the sacks of cement they had hidden away. The man paid almost nothing for these, and to Devlin, as with much else where the McGuires were concerned, the theft seemed more of an irresistible impulse than a considered act.

They poured concrete when it rained and altered the amount of cement required for each mix to steal even more of this. Someone would eventually come to inspect the bases, but in all likelihood this wouldn't happen until the start of the following season when the caravans were pulled on to them and the chalets erected.

The next week, they laboured at the excavation of an outdoor swimming pool and then dug the ten-foot-deep foundations for a raised cable-car track. The McGuires stole tiles from the pool, and steel, rivets and cables from the cable-car. And for everything they took, there was always someone waiting to take it off their hands at the end of the day.

Mechanical diggers scooped out the rough shape of the pool and Devlin, the McGuires and a dozen others worked behind the machines, preparing the hole for its concrete lining. There were more labourers and overseers on this job and so the opportunity for thieving was restricted. In fairness, everything the brothers earned, they gave Devlin his share. And then Patrick took back whatever he considered Devlin to owe them in rent. This varied, and though Devlin knew he was being charged more than the caravan was worth, he was in no position to argue.

During their frequent breaks, Patrick and Colm searched the

closed arcades, scouring the store rooms and repair shops and shaking every dormant machine in the hope of hearing a few forgotten coins rattle in its innards. It was like breathing and eating to the men, all this scavenging and stealing.

Colm showed him how to swing a sledgehammer so the action looked effective from a distance but took little out of the man doing the swinging, and Patrick showed him how to shovel the same load of soil back and forth to appear as though he was actually achieving something. Devlin learned from everyone else at the sites how to appear twice as industrious when someone was watching you and then how to do nothing whatsoever when you were left to your own devices. It was all about appearances, Colm told him, and if not that, then it was about pieces of paper being ticked and signed; work undertaken, work delivered, specifications set and met, allowances, alterations, exceptions. It was all one big game to the brothers, and one they had long since mastered. But whatever he learned during those early winter weeks, at the end of each day Devlin was usually exhausted.

After the second week, having been dropped off at the unnamed pub close to the Clay drain, Patrick took Devlin's rent and then gave him a pound back and told him to get their drinks.

The bar was full of other working men. Friday. Most would be there until closing time. Devlin felt uncomfortable, his face and hands still covered in the day's grime.

Returning to the brothers with their drinks, Devlin said to Patrick, 'Did you get it back to him?'

'Come again?' Patrick was preoccupied, searching the room around him.

'Duggan. The knife.'

'That? Ages since. I said I would. What you still going on about that for?'

'What did he say?'

'About what?'

'I don't know. About how things stood between us.'

Patrick considered his answer. 'He said that the knife changed nothing – that you shouldn't have taken it in the first place, so don't expect him to be grateful on that particular score – and that he wasn't likely to forget what you still owed him.' He raised his hand to a man at the far side of the room.

'What else were you expecting?' Colm asked him.

Devlin shook his head and then drained the glass he held.

'That's more like it,' Patrick said. 'You were beginning to sound like a stuck record.' He emptied his own glass and then left them to talk to the man he had greeted.

Devlin and Colm discussed the likelihood of work in the weeks ahead. The labouring at the holiday camps would last through most of the closed season, Colm said, but he and Patrick were finished with it. It was the first Devlin had heard of this.

'Have you got something else lined up?' he asked Colm.

'Nothing specific. A few bits and pieces.'

Devlin felt suddenly vulnerable. With Duggan, he'd at least been half of a pair. Now, with the McGuires, he was the mostly unnecessary member of a three-way split which was hardly enough for two most of the time. And he would still have the rent to find.

Patrick came back to them as he considered all this. The brothers shared a whispered conversation. Devlin knew better than to ask them what it was about.

Eventually, Patrick said to Devlin, 'You and Maria.'

'What about me and Maria?'

'You got eyes for her, that's what. You going to deny it?'

There was nothing Devlin could say. 'I like her,' he said.

'He likes her,' Patrick said, nudging Colm. Whatever bit of business he had just conducted had put him in a good mood. 'Stop worrying. We got cousins married at fourteen. Not married officially, but to all intents and purposes. It's how things work. We're not the same as most people in that line of things.'

'It'll hardly come to that,' Devlin said.

'Oh, we know that already,' Colm said. 'You're an outsider, always will be.'

'You're not even Catholic,' Patrick said. He dipped a finger into his drink and flicked it at Devlin. 'Consider yourself converted.'

Devlin hadn't the first idea what they were talking about. From feeling abandoned by the men only a moment ago, he now felt as close to them as he had ever done.

Patrick dipped his finger again and drew a cross on his shirt.

'When we were little,' Colm said, 'back in Ireland, our mother used to tell us that if we ever drew a cross over a black heart, it would turn to flames on our chest and burn right through our clothes to our flesh.'

'And did it?'

'Once or twice. Some things are easier to get used to than others.'

And again, Devlin had no idea what they were talking about.

After two more hours in the bar, on the point of leaving, and on the edge of his rising drunkenness and with most of what had been left in his pocket now gone, Devlin said to Patrick, 'Next time you see Duggan, tell him from me that unless he settles what *he* owes *me*, then I'll take it for myself and he can see how he likes that.' He clenched his fist and banged it on the table, causing the drinkers nearby to turn and look at the three of them.

Patrick and Colm exchanged a glance.

'What *he* owes *you*?' Patrick said. 'Not *that* again. He's already putting it about that you were never in Germany. According to him, you did most of your Army time in Colchester nick. I doubt he'd be saying it if there wasn't some truth in it.'

'Besides,' Colm said, 'whatever you think you're owed by Duggan, it will never amount to a fraction of what *he* reckons he's owed by you. Believe me, not many people ever got one over on Ray Duggan.'

If he'd been sober, Devlin would have understood the nature of all these probing remarks better, but he wasn't sober, he was drunk, and angry, and resentful.

'Duggan was in Army Transport,' Devlin said. 'Not even a proper soldier.' As though this amounted to any sort of counter-argument.

'So?' Patrick said. 'And all this rubbish about him owing you something – you're just angry, that's all. Duggan did what he always does and this time you were the one on the sharp end of things. Look at the knife business; what good did that do you?'

The brothers waited for him to say something.

'I suppose so,' Devlin said.

'Go on then, while we're here and listening,' Patrick said eventually. 'You can tell us. Nobody else would believe you, but we might. We're on your side, remember? We don't owe Duggan any favours – far from it. And, believe me, if you *did* ever manage to get one over on the bastard, then I'd be the first to congratulate you.' He put his arm firmly around Devlin's shoulders and helped him to stand upright.

Devlin reached down to the table, picked up his glass and drank what little remained in it.

'You want another?' Patrick asked him. Another shared glance with Colm.

'You ever come across a farm on the Mareham Fen road?' Devlin said. 'Dovecote Farm?'

'Know *of* it,' Patrick said. He squeezed Devlin harder. 'Been empty since the war. Most of it was under water last year. What about it?'

In truth, it was all he needed to hear.

'You'd be surprised,' Devlin said.

Patrick told his brother to fetch them more drinks.

22

LATER THAT NIGHT, HOURS AFTER HIS RETURN TO THE
caravan, Devlin saw Maria crossing the open ground towards
the paddock where the few remaining horses grazed. He sat in
the darkness and watched her. He'd been asleep most of the
time since his return.

Outside, Maria saw him watching her and came to him.

'Invite me in,' she mouthed to him, pulling open the door as
she said it.

Inside, Devlin had laid salvaged rugs and offcuts of carpet on
the floor. He'd threaded curtains on the wires above the windows.
He'd cleaned everything, and the van no longer smelled as stale.

It was the first time Maria had been there since the night
she'd fallen asleep on the bench.

'You've been busy,' she said, looking around her. 'Never had
you down as a home-maker. I was on my way to look at the
horses. Chances are, we'll get rid of the rest of them before too
long. The owners are talking about cutting back in the spring.'

'The owners?'

'The fair. The business is falling off.' She seemed unconcerned.

Devlin told her about the holiday caravans and the swimming pool. 'I suppose you've heard about everything already.'

'Not really,' Maria said.

Ever since his return with Patrick and Colm he'd been trying to remember what he'd said to them. He intended to go to see them when he was sober and thinking straight, but it had been late when he'd woken, and he'd decided to wait until the next morning.

'They tend not to dwell on things,' Maria said. 'They might have the gift of the gab when it suits, but they're neither of them what you'd call conversationalists.'

The word made them both smile.

'No,' he said.

He offered her a cup of tea and she accepted.

'I still remember the first time I met you,' he said.

First she shrugged, and then she said, 'I should hope so.'

'You and your brothers. I was with Duggan.' He wished he didn't have to keep using the man's name. 'You had a shawl on,' he said. 'A blanket. You let it fall.' It was as much as he could say to her.

'Did I? Perhaps it was an accident.'

'It looked deliberate.'

'Then perhaps it was. Whatever you say . . .'

'It was only for a few seconds, if that.'

'I was probably just playing with you. It was the middle of the night – it usually is where Duggan's concerned – so perhaps I'd just woken up, perhaps I was still half asleep.'

'Perhaps,' Devlin said.

She pulled shut the curtains where they sat.

'Or perhaps I just liked the look of you,' she said.

He tried to remember when he'd last had a conversation like this. Never.

After a silence in which only the sound of a distant radio could be heard, he said, 'They'll be waiting for you.'

She held an empty bottle up to the gas mantle. 'Hardly,' she said. 'They both went out hours ago. Apparently, something unexpected turned up that couldn't wait.'

He tried again to remember all he'd said to the brothers and felt suddenly cold.

'I never heard them go,' he said.

'So? They've only gone down the road a few miles. Something about a lock-keeper wanting a couple of vans for his livestock. Chickens. They'll be hours yet. They do a fair bit of business with him. I wouldn't be surprised if the man didn't have a still somewhere.'

He'd heard the brothers talk about the man and the spirit he distilled.

'That's good,' he said.

'If you say so. Where'd you get the carpet?'

'One of the other empty vans.' He'd gathered up crockery and glassware, whatever packets and tins of food had been left behind. He'd taken two additional heaters and whatever fuel he could find. He'd be long gone before anyone turned up to complain about the thefts.

At the far end of the caravan the bed was extended and propped on its legs. There was little point in folding it away each day.

'I could get you a better mattress,' Maria said. She left the table and went to sit on the edge of the bed. Devlin followed her.

'I couldn't stop thinking about you for days afterwards,' he told her, bracing himself against her response.

'Only days?' she said. 'I must be losing my touch.'

'Longer, then.'

She took hold of his hand and pressed it to her breast. He could feel the shape and weight of it beneath her clothing.

'Bring back any memories?' she said, catching her breath.

He moved closer to her and kissed her awkwardly, first on the side of her mouth and then on her lips, careful not to draw away from her and give her the chance to do the same and tell him she'd made a mistake. They both still held their cups and so sat awkwardly on the low bed. Eventually, Devlin drew back from her, took the cup from her and put them both on the floor.

'I was drinking that,' she said. Her eyes searched back and forth across his face and then she kissed him again.

A moment later she pulled away from him and unfastened the buttons at her throat.

Devlin watched her, convinced and uncertain in equal measure about what to do next.

'You know this is all it is?' she said to him, her eyes fixed now.

Devlin nodded.

'What I'm saying is – you don't need to go getting any more of those big ideas of yours.'

'I won't,' Devlin said, still uncertain what she was telling him.

'I make you no promises and you make none of your own.'

'Deal,' Devlin said, and then watched her as she unfastened the rest of her buttons and pulled her blouse apart to reveal the darker flesh beneath.

23

THE THREE OF THEM SAT IN THE LORRY AT THE END OF the track leading to Dovecote Farm. It was two in the morning, and for the past two hours there had been no other traffic on the narrow road.

Devlin had worked it out: it had been almost six weeks since he'd been there with Duggan. He pointed out the distant outlines to the McGuires.

Without switching on the headlights, Patrick drove off the road and along the track until they came within fifty yards of the farm's outermost buildings. Devlin showed them the barn where he and Duggan had been.

'You wait here,' Colm told him, and he and Patrick climbed down from the lorry and stood waiting in the darkness.

'I should come with you,' Devlin said. 'It's my—'

'Your what, exactly?' Patrick said in a loud whisper. 'We could just as easily have done this without a word to you. You sure what Duggan told you?'

That he'd stay well clear of the place and everything it contained for as long as possible.

'You keep an eye on the road and flash the lights if anyone comes,' Colm said to Devlin. It was how the brothers worked: a veiled threat from Patrick followed by reassurance from Colm, until whoever was on the receiving end of their double act had little idea of where he truly stood.

Before he could answer them, the two men walked away from the lorry into the darkness, casting occasional fleeting shadows where the near-full moon caught them against the buildings.

Patrick went to the empty farmhouse and pushed open the door. Colm joined him and they went inside, emerging five minutes later with a sack, which they dropped noisily in the yard. Only then did they go to where Devlin had directed them.

Devlin heard a loud banging and then the crack of breaking timber. They had prised the padlock off the barn door. He scanned the track and the road far behind him. Nothing showed through the darkness. An early frost had been forecast beneath the clear night sky and Devlin saw the first bloom of this across the empty ground.

Colm came back to him.

'You were right. Patrick wants you to come and see if Duggan's been back already.'

'What does it matter?'

'It matters. It means he might be coming back regularly instead of waiting to pick the stuff up later in one visit. He's not stupid. He knows you're still out there somewhere, nursing a grudge. It stands to reason that he'd come himself and not let on to anyone else what he's got stashed here. It's a proper little treasure trove. Unlikely he'll be able to unload everything at once.'

'I know all that,' Devlin said.

What he also knew, what he'd known the instant he'd

opened his drunken mouth and told them the name of the place, was that Duggan would know immediately who had talked. When he'd suggested this to Patrick, Patrick had laughed and then told him that anyone could have stumbled across the place and all it held. Finders keepers and all that. The brave part of Devlin wanted to believe that Duggan was getting everything he deserved, and that he, Devlin, was still owed his fair share of everything they'd brought there. The other, larger part of him understood that he had now set in motion a train of likely events that could not end well for any of them, especially himself. It was still a small world, and it was still mostly Duggan's world.

'We're waiting,' Colm said angrily.

'He won't have been,' Devlin said.

'You're guessing. We need to know, to be sure.'

Colm walked back into the darkness and Devlin followed him.

In the barn he went from pile to pile, pulling away the dried straw. He remembered stacking most of what the three of them uncovered.

'It's all here,' he said eventually.

'Probably means Duggan's still working solo,' Patrick said. 'Which gives us a bit of an advantage. Show us what's what and we'll get the best of it out first.'

'What you reckon?' Colm said. 'Two or three trips?'

'Hardly matters. All that matters now is that we're long gone by the time Duggan gets wind. We'll play the same game: stash everything somewhere else and then sit on our hands for a few months. Leave a trail involving others and he'll be on to us like that.' He clicked his fingers.

He'll be on to us anyway, Devlin thought, but said nothing.

'Stands to reason, he'll come looking,' Patrick said. 'And he'll know where you are by now,' he said to Devlin. He shared one of his glances with Colm.

Meaning what?

'Don't look so worried,' Colm said. 'You're with us now. Duggan can go on putting two and two together for as long as he likes. Like Patrick says, all *we* have to do is keep everything hidden and then keep playing the innocent.'

'He's hardly likely to go running to the police, is he?' Patrick said, causing his brother to laugh.

'You're not laughing,' Colm said to Devlin.

'I wonder why.'

Patrick pushed him hard in the chest. 'What, you think *we*'re out to cheat you like Duggan did? There's enough here for all of us. You watch our back, we watch yours. Besides, what does Duggan really stand to lose? Easy come, easy go, that's the trick. Not as though it cost him in the first place, is it? And I'm betting *you* did most of the grafting, am I right?'

Devlin nodded, unconvinced.

'So, by rights, half of it's yours anyway. Like Colm says, stop worrying – any grief Duggan feels the need to hand out will come to us. *We*'re the ones stealing his half of things. All you're doing is taking back what's already yours.'

It was one way of looking at it.

'You arrive at a point in life,' Colm said, pushing Patrick away from Devlin, 'when you decide to stop being walked all over. Especially by men like Ray Duggan, who think they've got a God-given right to do it. You've got to stand up for yourself eventually and push back every now and again. Besides' – another glance, the start of a smile on his lips – 'you and Maria. Just imagine how she's going to look at all this when we tell her

what you've done for us. Three-way split, this lot. Equal meas-
ures. Wait until she works out how much of that will eventually
come her way. She was always the one for numbers. You think
Duggan was ever going to cut you in for even a tiny part of that?
You think money doesn't matter to Maria? You think she doesn't
deserve a few of the – what they called? – the finer things in life?'

They were manipulating him, playing on all these new and
uncertain connections, and he saw that.

'If it was me,' Patrick said, 'I'd wait until we'd got our hands
on the lot and then I'd paint a message on the wall telling
Duggan exactly who it was who'd got the better of him.'

Devlin waited to make sure he wasn't being serious.

'He's joking,' Colm said. 'You know us – since when did we
ever bring that kind of trouble to our door? Never have, never
will. Think about it. It's why you're safe with us. Chances are,
Duggan doesn't credit you with being smart or brave enough to
come up with something like this.'

'And if he does?' Devlin said.

'Then we'll tell him it was all on us. It's probably what he'd
rather think, anyway.'

'We're wasting time,' Patrick said. 'We're here now and the
lock's smashed. What are we going to do – pretend we never saw
it and leave it all for somebody else?'

It was the kind of thin, fractured reasoning that worked well
for the brothers. It was starting to work for Devlin.

'Go and get the lorry,' Colm told him, and he and Patrick
started sorting out what they would take that night.

Devlin went back to the lorry and manoeuvred it closer to
the barn, reversing it through the open doorway. He studied the
empty farmhouse, wondering how long it had been abandoned –
since long before the flood, judging by the state of it – and he

wondered too about the farmer and his family who had once lived there. Perhaps it would one day be a thriving farm again, the land properly drained and improved. Perhaps another man and his wife and family would make a good and dependable future for themselves there. It was exactly the kind of opportunity Devlin himself would once have appreciated.

He was distracted from these thoughts by the noise of crates being thrown and stacked on the lorry's bed. The boxes sounded like falling masonry in the darkness. He shouted for Patrick and Colm not to make so much noise, but they only laughed at his concern.

'Who do you think is going to hear us?' Patrick said. 'And what if someone does hear? You think they're going to come running at this time of night? Duggan's twenty miles away, so *he's* not going to hear a thing. There's always somebody ready to whisper in his ear, I'll give you that, but he's not as popular as he likes to think he is. He's crossed a lot of people in his time; not everybody is happy to forever go on begging for scraps from his table.'

'Meaning . . .' Devlin began to say.

'Meaning that perhaps the reign of Mister High and Mighty Duggan is finally coming to an end.' Patrick seemed to surprise even himself with the remark and all it implied. 'We're still wasting time,' he said, and turned his attention back to the cases.

Less than an hour later they were on the road approaching the wintering ground, the lorry loaded and everything hidden from view beneath a tarpaulin. The plan was for Devlin and Colm to be dropped off at the compound and for Patrick to then leave the lorry and its load somewhere safe a mile away. They would unload and hide the cases the following day.

'Lucky we found you,' Colm said to Devlin as they approached the vans and trailers.

Found him?

'You're like a lucky charm,' Patrick added. They sat on either side of Devlin, looking neither at him nor at one another.

It was almost four in the morning before Devlin climbed into the warm bed beside Maria.

Part II
Winter

24

THE FIRST SNOW CAME EARLY AND SETTLED ON THE COLD fields. Eight days of a cloud-filled sky with no sun. On the few days the ground warmed above freezing, the snow melted and then refroze to ice, building in layers. The water in troughs and water butts froze and stayed frozen. When the wind rose from the sea it blew fresh loose snow horizontally across the open land. And each day spanning the end of November into December fresh falls came, mostly during the afternoons as darkness fell, and then lasting into the night.

People spoke of another hard winter. Only five or six years since the last one. Longer, perhaps, but it seemed more recent, especially with memories of the flood so fresh in people's minds. Dykes froze, and then the slow and stagnant lengths of some of the drains. Culverts were cleared and locks secured, but to little effect. The wind came from the east, from Russia, from Siberia. And when it turned occasionally, from the north, from the Arctic. People spoke as though there were a strategy to the coming winter, battles and war, and as though they were the unforgiven, unmissable target.

At the wintering ground everything was sheeted and roped, stalls finally dismantled and laid flat. Grease was put in handfuls on the generators and over axles and all other working parts. Strips of lights were dismantled and repairs made. Some of the flimsier caravans and trailers were secured to the ground with ropes and stakes.

Devlin helped the McGuire brothers and others in all this. The weather closing in like that made him feel secure. There was fuel for the heaters, and water could always be stored inside, although even there it frequently froze overnight. He got used to his lungs aching in the cold air and feeling his warm breath cauled over his face whenever he was outside for any length of time.

The sheets, blankets and eiderdowns on the bed he shared with Maria were mounded two feet deep. There was always some warmth to be found or created. Some said the early bad weather would be gone by the middle of the month. Some said it would last well into the New Year. Some said March, like the last lot.

After a fortnight, Devlin stopped thinking and worrying about Duggan. And if the brothers had given the man a second thought, then nothing was revealed to him. Devlin knew that he remained a threat to the others while he was at the compound; he also knew that his relationship with Maria coloured everything he now did and said in their company.

The three of them had cleared the barn over four successive nights and had then unloaded everything at a disused boatyard on the Welland, where a boat builder hid the stuff for a price. He was a close friend of the McGuires and grimaced every time Duggan's name was mentioned. There was neither sight nor sound of Duggan himself while all this happened. And then the bad weather had come.

The boatyard was filled with timber and half a dozen dismantled barges. A forge stood at its centre, where the boat builder hammered out bands and pins of metal for what little work still remained to him. Mounds of resin-scented sawdust and puddles of solid pitch lay scattered across every part of the bare earth of the place. Devlin had asked the man if there was enough work for an extra pair of hands and the boat builder had said there was hardly enough for one man, and that most of what he now did would show no profit whatsoever.

Outside, in the first of the sharp air, on a rare day when the cloud over the sea thinned and blue showed through, Devlin sat on a baulk of timber overlooking the dark course of the channel. He searched its straightened length, watching flotsam snag and then float free along its banks. Boats sat moored for a hundred yards in each direction, pale smoke rising from some of their stacks. Other yards, mostly disused or empty of work, stretched along the waterway towards the open sea.

Patrick and Colm had come to him where he sat. The plan now, they told him, was to leave what they had stolen for the whole winter and to wait until the drainage work started up again before selling everything on. They said it as though the winter would wipe everything clean, make people forget, create new chances and opportunities. And Devlin had gone along with all this. Mostly because there was nothing else he could do under the circumstances, but partly, and with a growing conviction, because it was what he too was starting to believe. He had asked them if he could have some money on account. 'On account of what?' Patrick had said. To see him through. 'To see you through what?' Why was he suddenly becoming so demanding? What, really, was there for him to worry about apart from keeping warm? It was all a joke to the brothers. Stop worrying, they told him; something would turn up – it always did. Whatever happened, they wouldn't let him starve, and even if they did go hungry on occasion there would always be a bottle of something on the table to help him forget his hunger. Seriously, what more could he ask for? And anything he did want, he only had to ask. Where the brothers and their demands and concessions were concerned, Devlin sometimes felt as though he were in one of those kids' mazes where the walls rose only a foot off the ground.

Patrick said once that it seemed to him that the McGuires had already done more for Devlin than everyone else in his life put together. It was another of the man's vague but clever arguments that Devlin could not counter. Why behave so ungratefully when all he owed them was his gratitude?

He'd sat on the bank of the Welland and watched a barge move towards the sea. The whole vessel was black from prow to stern and rose barely a yard out of the water. Sooty smoke trailed behind it like a scarf in the cold air, hanging for a moment and then slowly falling to settle on the river. A solitary man stood at the helm and he, too, was black from head to foot.

'Coal,' Patrick had said, guessing at the cargo's start and finish. He warned Devlin to stay clear of this work, however desperate he became. Their uncle had worked on the coalers for twenty years and had died before he was forty, having coughed up his blackened lungs. Even the man's flesh had turned black. Even his blood. Both Patrick and Colm had risen to their feet to spit into the barge's churning wake. The vessel cleared the low pipe bridge and then continued towards the open sea and blue sky. The man at the tiller raised his hand to them as he passed. Buckets of coal lined the deck and stood at the doorway to the small cabin. It looked a cushy number to Devlin and he said so, and so Patrick told him about their eleven fatherless cousins and their wrung-out mother, old before her time, living in a council house – a fucking *council* house – in Peterborough. *Peterborough.* He made it sound as though the woman were living in her own coffin.

They eventually left the boatyard and returned to the compound. The day's first flakes of thin snow drifted and melted on the windscreen. Only the offside wiper worked, and then only intermittently.

When they arrived home, Maria was waiting for them.

Patrick asked her if anyone had been there during their long absences over the previous few days. No one, she told him.

Devlin examined the few tracks in the barely settling snow. Only the dark lines of their own departure and return stretched to the gateway. In the sky above the road, a flock of starlings drifted like smoke, darkening and thinning as they twisted and turned in the cold air.

The evening forecast on the radio was for a drier, brighter spell. But after that, the wind would come back from the east and bring more bad weather with it.

25

'WHAT YOU DOING HERE?'

Devlin had turned a corner in Lynn and walked into his sister. The woman stood at a bus stop with two full bags of shopping at her feet.

'Nice to see you too,' he said.

She looked him up and down. 'That jacket looks as though it's been slept in,' she said. 'And that shirt.'

'There's a good reason for that.'

'Don't tell me,' she said. 'I don't want to know. You're back on your uppers.' She held out her hand, palm up. The sky, which had started dark, had darkened even further in the past hour.

'It'll pass,' Devlin said to her.

'Most things do. I wanted to get home, that's all. And now this.' She made him sound like a wall blocking her way.

Devlin was in Lynn on an errand for Patrick. A man owed Patrick money and had arranged to meet him to pay him, but then something had come up at the last minute and Patrick had been unable to go. It was at times like this that Devlin came in useful, earned his keep, pulled his weight, did his bit. Devlin had come to the town because there was nothing else he could do. He had hoped to meet the man, collect everything Patrick was owed and then return to Maria before the weather took its predicted turn for the worse.

'You not working, then?' Ellen said.

'Not today. Here on a bit of business.'

'I don't want to hear about that, either,' she said.

'Why not? Not everything I do is' – he couldn't think of the word – 'you know.'

'Oh, I *do* know,' she said. 'That's half the problem.'

It seemed in her nature now to behave like this towards him. Or perhaps it wasn't just him, perhaps it was everybody. With the notable exception of Morris.

'What about you?' he said.

She tapped the two bags with her feet. 'Guess,' she said.

'You here with Morris?'

She shook her head. 'It's the middle of the day. Morris is where most hard-working, law-abiding, decent men are at this time of day.'

Devlin thought of a cruel and funny answer, but kept it to himself.

'I daresay,' he said. He could spend a year throwing rocks at the impregnable Morris and not a single one would chip him.

'You could at least wear a tie,' she said.

A tie?

'What I mean is – you could at least *try* to appear respectable.'

'To what end?'

'What end? I should have thought it was what most men wanted. Especially men—'

'Like me?'

'If you'd let me finish, I was going to say men who were hoping for a bit of an upturn in things.'

'I've been hearing about that "upturn in things" ever since I came back from doing my bit for King and country,' he said, immediately wondering how much she knew for certain.

Duggan wore a shirt and tie, Skelton wore a shirt and tie, Harrap wore a shirt and tie.

'Yes, well,' she said. 'I suppose all good things come to those who wait.'

'I hope so. Patience being its own reward and all that.'

'Exactly.'

Every conversation with the woman flowed into the same soggy ground of her marriage. At least Morris would probably argue with him.

A light sleet started to fall and Ellen shuffled the bags closer to her feet.

'What you got?' Devlin asked her. He was hungry. When the man paid him, Patrick had said, bring some food back. Watch what you spend, but get something.

'Just the usual. He's a creature of habit, Morris. He likes to know what he's got coming, and when.'

'I can imagine.'

'He says routine is important. He tells me he spends all day looking forward to whatever it is he's got waiting for him when he comes home.' She smiled at the thought of her husband and his compliments.

'I can imagine that too,' Devlin said.

'No need to make everything sound so . . . so . . . Besides, you know where you are with a routine.'

'A place for everything and everything in its place.'

'Exactly. See – you do have some half-sensible ideas in your head.'

'What is it tonight then?'

'Thursday. Liver and onions.' She smiled again at the thought of putting the plate of food in front of her husband. 'Never been particularly keen myself.'

'I could eat it seven days a week,' Devlin said. The last hot meal he'd eaten had been four days earlier. Rabbit. Left at the field gate. Friend of Colm's. Rabbit. He'd thought those days were long gone. Rabbit and potatoes, cooked by Maria. There were always potatoes. Some days there were only potatoes.

His sister looked alarmed at the remark, as though he might be expecting to be invited to share the meal.

'Don't worry,' Devlin told her. 'I've already got plans for tonight.'

She smiled at the word. 'What sort of plans?'

'Seeing a few friends, that's all.'

'Oh, those sort of plans. I can imagine. So what is it, this bit of business you're here to do – to transact?' She was pleased with the swift revision.

'A man owes one of those friends of mine some money, and I'm here to meet said party and recoup the wherewithal for the other said party.'

She shook her head at this. 'You want to be careful. You're so sharp you'll cut yourself one of these days.'

'I'm only as sharp as I need to be,' he said.

'I doubt that very much. Look at you. People take advantage – they always did. Everybody you meet, everybody you ever knew, they all just look at you and try to work out how to get one over on you, what's in it for them.'

The blunt remark surprised Devlin and he could think of nothing to rebut it.

'You don't know what you're talking about,' he said eventually. 'Besides, it's dog eat dog in this world. Always has been, always will be.'

She smiled again. 'You should listen to yourself. The things you come out with. King and country. Honestly.' She looked over his shoulder and her smile spread. 'My bus is here,' she said. 'I'd like to say it's been nice bumping into you like this.'

There was no need for the punchline.

He could imagine her telling Morris everything that had happened. And he could imagine Morris chewing carefully on his liver and onions – would there even be bacon in it? – and then telling her he was proud of her.

She picked up her bags and held out her hand. 'It's the same driver,' she said. 'He lives close to us. Lovely man. His wife's a trained touch typist, you should see her fingers. They're going to promote him to inspector soon. She has manicures, in a salon, to keep her nails trimmed and her fingertips smooth.'

She waved to the driver, the handle of her bag at her elbow. 'I'll help you on,' Devlin said.

'No need.'

He wondered if he should kiss her cheek. She was much happier back in her own world, finally rid of this open door letting in the cold wind.

She climbed aboard and stood in the doorway for a moment, telling the driver how pleased she was to see him. Then she went to the closest seat and sat at the window, her bags beside her. Three or four other women sat further back on the bus.

Devlin waited where he stood.

She looked out at him, wiping the damp from the window with her fingers. She held them there briefly; she might even have been waving at him.

When the bus finally moved off he raised his hand and waved at her.

She watched him but made no further response. Exhaust fumes spread in a cloud across the road in the cold air. He waited until the bus turned a corner and then walked back in the direction he'd come. Another hour to kill until he was due to meet the man who might or might not turn up with some, all, or none of Patrick's money.

26

A LOUD BANGING ON THE CARAVAN DOOR WOKE DEVLIN
where he lay on one of the seats. Maria stood crouched at the
sink, pumping water and drinking from the tap. The banging
continued and then someone called in for Devlin. Sullivan.

Maria opened the door and looked around the deserted site
over Sullivan's shoulders.

'What time is it?' she said.

'You going to invite me in or what?' Sullivan said. 'It's brass
monkeys out here.' He came inside, screwing up his face, first at
the aroma and then at everything he saw. He went to Devlin on
the bench. Gesturing at Maria, he said, 'I didn't know you
were – you know.'

'Know what?'

'That you had a lady friend, a bit on the side. You kept that
quiet.' He held out his hand to Maria and she took it. 'Wake you
up, did I?' he said to Devlin. 'You need to get yourself up, old
chum. Bit of the old spit and polish. This could just turn out to
be your lucky day.'

Maria filled the kettle and waited at the sink.

The two men sat at the table.

'How did you know where to find me?' Devlin said.

'I asked about. Why, no big secret, is it?'

'Not particularly.'

'I asked in the Oak. Landlord said you hadn't been back there since a bit of bother you had. He mentioned the gyp— the boys at the fairground and so I took a chance and here I am. A woman in one of the other vans told me which one was yours. This where you been living since the drainage, then?'

Maria came to the table with mugs of tea.

'Why are you here?' Devlin said. It was one thing sitting in the bus with the man, avoiding the rain and the sun and the work and enduring his endless moaning at the world, another thing completely having him turn up like this. He wanted to say all this to Maria. Perhaps even to Sullivan.

'Like I said – it's your lucky day, old son. They're recruiting up at the borstal. Three vacancies. I already put in a good word for you. Trouble is, they're interviewing later today. I've been off for a week – bit of a chest. Must be all that outdoor work.' He slapped his chest and laughed.

'What sort of a job?' Maria said.

Sullivan resented this intrusion and he continued looking at Devlin as he spoke.

'Sort that would suit him down to the ground. He knows what I'm talking about. You got something to wear? Two o'clock kick-off for the interviews. Just the Governor, in all likelihood. You wouldn't believe the trouble we have filling vacancies in this God-forsaken neck of the woods. Got to keep up numbers, see – *ratios*, they call it. Believe me, after all I've spoon-fed the old man, you're a shoo-in.'

'What time is it?' Devlin asked Maria.

'Nearly twelve.'

'Ten to,' Sullivan said, tapping his watch. He finally sipped at his tea and pulled a face.

183

'No sugar,' Maria said.

'I can see that. Anyhow, like I said, it's a two o'clock start and I've put your name down. Are we on?'

Devlin exchanged a glance with Maria, who shrugged.

'What are we waiting for?' Sullivan said, angry now at Devlin's lack of enthusiasm or gratitude.

'It's just a lot to take in,' Devlin said.

'Perhaps you've been offered a job running the Bank of England,' Sullivan said. 'Thing to remember about the prison work this time of year, it's mostly indoors, sitting with your feet up, the odd roll call, the odd hour of supervision here and there. It's not exactly what you'd call hard labour. Not for the likes of you and me, at least.' He laughed again and this time Devlin smiled. 'So?'

'Patrick's got a funeral suit that would fit,' Maria said.

'There you go, then,' Sullivan said. 'I came in the motor. Parked up on the road. Didn't want to risk getting bogged down. Look at the state of my shoes as it is.'

'Nobody else ever complains,' Maria said.

'That's them,' Sullivan said. 'Not me. Besides, your lot – all I'm saying is that some people get used to things quicker than others. No offence.' He rose from where he sat and clapped his hands together. 'Come on then, chop chop. No time like the present. *Tempus fugit* and all that.'

Two hours later, wearing Patrick's dark brown suit, a clean shirt that felt uncomfortable at his throat, and a tie borrowed from Sullivan, Devlin sat in the Governor's office and waited for the interview to begin. The last time he'd sat in any office – another prison, as it happened – had been when he was in the Army.

The Governor was overweight and sweated in the warm

room. A cast-iron radiator stood at each wall and the heat these gave out was almost visible. It was the warmest Devlin had been for months. The Governor wiped his brow and chins with a handkerchief and every now and again gave a nod to Devlin, who was starting to wonder at the delay.

'We're just waiting,' the man said to him. 'New rules. We are nowadays obliged to have someone from the Department for Prisons sit in at the interviews. A formality, that's all. These people come and go. They seldom actually involve themselves in the thing itself. Between you and me, it does them good to imagine they're keeping their hand in. You're in luck today – they've sent a woman. A Miss' – he scanned the sheet in front of him – 'Scott-Dyer. Double-barrelled. I ask you. She arrived just before you. Late train, apparently, and then no taxi. If I'd known when the train was in, I could have sent a car. Expenses, I suppose. She'll be here any moment. She's just doing whatever it is women do. Nothing to concern yourself over. I've already had the low-down from Officer Sullivan. Said you and him were at the drainage work together. Good man, Sullivan. He tends to get landed with some of our more wayward customers. Firm hand, they appreciate that, and that's what Sullivan gives them. Some of our newer officers have funny ideas about the place. Most of them are looking to move on from the day they arrive. Not Sullivan.' He paused, waiting for Devlin to speak.

Devlin wondered at the man's nervousness.

'We worked together most of the summer,' he said.

'And the fact that your own superiors appointed you liaison officer already speaks volumes in your favour,' the man said.

It was the first time Devlin had heard the title.

'I suppose so,' he said. He was considering what more he

might add when the door opened and a woman in a pale grey jacket and skirt and carrying a briefcase came into the room.

Devlin caught a glimpse of the half-dozen other men sitting along the corridor outside, all of them waiting.

The Governor rose and Devlin copied him.

'Mr Devlin,' the woman said, holding out her hand to him. 'I'm Janet Scott-Dyer. I'm here as a representative of the Juvenile Prisoner Licensing Authority. The Governor here will be conducting the interview. I might throw in a few questions of my own, but essentially I'm here to observe due process, and perhaps, should the need arise, though I think it unlikely, to consider any arising matters of regulatory procedure.'

Everything she said knocked Devlin even further off his guard.

She went on, 'I don't know if you are aware – and why should you be? – but there are big changes coming in the prison service, and you might say that some of us stuck away in our offices are beginning to feel the need to get our hands dirty, so to speak, to see how things actually work at the sharp end of things.' Her tight smile was gone as quickly as it had come.

'I see,' Devlin said. Already it was much more than Sullivan had led him to believe it would be. Process. Licensing. Regulatory. It was a foreign language to Devlin. More than that – it was the foreign language of a hostile country.

Before Devlin could say more, Janet Scott-Dyer went and sat beside the Governor. She opened her briefcase and took out several files and laid them on the desk in front of her. The Governor pushed away some of the desk's clutter to make way for these.

'Shall we start?' she said. Another quick smile. 'As I say, please ignore me.' She opened the uppermost file and Devlin was relieved to see that it contained only blank paper. She took a fountain pen from her inside pocket, unscrewed its cap and sat ready to write.

'Mr Devlin comes highly recommended by one of my own officers,' the Governor said. 'Been with us almost twenty years.'

'And he is . . . ?' Janet Scott-Dyer said.

'Dan – Daniel Sullivan.'

She wrote the name on the empty sheet and both Devlin and the Governor watched and waited.

'Go on,' she said.

'Perhaps you might care to tell us something about yourself,' the Governor said to Devlin. 'A bit of background, say, what it is that makes you think you'd be suitable for the work.'

Sullivan had told him what to say during their drive to the camp. *Mention the flood.*

'I was trying to set up as a farmer before the drainage work,' Devlin said. 'The flooding put paid to that.'

'You were a farm labourer?' Janet Scott-Dyer said.

'I rented a farm.'

'I see.' More writing.

'I was trying to make a go of things, but with one thing and another . . .'

'Sorry. Such as?'

Hadn't she been listening? 'Like I said – the flood.'

'Ah, yes, the flood. I understand it was quite severe hereabouts.'

And, according to Sullivan, it was another one of those things that was supposed to wipe the slate clean.

'It must have been very difficult for you,' the Governor said, his eyes flicking from Devlin to the woman.

'Under water for weeks,' Devlin said. 'Lost all my crop. All the livestock gone.'

187

'Killed?' Janet Scott-Dyer said. 'How awful.'

'A few. I lost the grazing. Mostly I had to sell them off at a loss.'

'And afterwards?' the Governor said, dabbing again at his cheeks.

Devlin started to calculate how thin the lie was already stretched.

'I was going to be married,' he said. 'But the flooding was a hard thing. My fiancée had a kind of breakdown, couldn't cope – very house proud, she was. It made her – I don't know . . . Sorry, I don't suppose this is the kind of thing you want to hear about.'

Lay the foundations, Sullivan had said. *Lay it on a bit thick. Just watch the military stuff – they have a tendency to check up on things like that.*

'I tried to hold everything together, but I failed,' Devlin said. He was starting to like the sound of himself.

Blame yourself. The old man's a sucker for that kind of thing.

'And so then you worked on the drainage and reclamation work?' Janet Scott-Dyer said.

'I did.'

Drainage and reclamation work. Standing up to your knees in a muddy channel, soaked to the skin and lobbing shovelfuls of muck to some other poor bugger who cursed you and every load he either caught or missed.

'And before that – before your venture into farming – you were in the Army, I believe.'

'I was,' Devlin said, stiffening slightly.

'As indeed were a great many of our current employees,' the Governor said.

'It's a considerable gap,' Janet Scott-Dyer said. She opened another of the files and read from it.

'What is?' Devlin said.

'A decade almost. Sorry – between your discharge and your attempts at farming.'

'Times were hard,' Devlin said, wishing he hadn't.

'As we keep hearing,' Janet Scott-Dyer said.

Outside, along the corridor filled with other waiting men, a door slammed loudly and the noise echoed along the painted brick walls.

Devlin looked from his lap to the Governor, hoping for more help from him, but knowing the instant the man avoided his eyes that it wasn't coming. If she had the date of his discharge, then what else did she have? And if she had the word 'discharge', did she also have 'dishonourable'?

'I was Army of Occupation,' he said. It still sounded good, solid, even if it was a lie. What did the woman want him to say?

Say you want to start making something of yourself, Sullivan had said. *Say you want a better life for your children than you had yourself. A bit of humility never hurt.*

Had Sullivan even known the woman was going to be there? Everything felt unbalanced.

'Very commendable,' Janet Scott-Dyer said when Devlin finished telling her all this.

'Of course it is,' the Governor said. 'Very commendable indeed.'

Devlin wanted to tell the man to shut up.

No one spoke for a moment.

Both Devlin and the Governor watched Janet Scott-Dyer as she continued writing.

'Shall we carry on?' she said.

'I thought you were only here to observe,' Devlin said.

'Technically speaking, that's all I am doing,' the woman said.

She looked hard at Devlin, laying down her precious pen for a few seconds.

'So what are you writing?' Devlin asked her.

'This? Nothing, really. Call it an *aide-memoire*. We're seeing eight or nine others today. After a point, you all begin to merge. Please, carry on.'

In the car, Sullivan had said that in the past the Governor had invited *him* to sit in on the interviews.

You just get the feel of a bloke, he'd said. *You often learn more by what he doesn't tell you than by what he's all too keen to tell everybody at every opportunity. You know the sort.*

Devlin had said that he did know the sort, but had remained confused about what this might mean regarding himself.

'I understand you submitted no formal application,' Janet Scott-Dyer said.

'Possibly my fault, I'm afraid,' the Governor said. 'All a bit short notice. We advertised, of course, all the usual places, but when you said you wanted to sit in on the interviews, everything became a little rushed. It's not necessarily how we're used to working in this part of the world, if you get my meaning.'

'I see,' she said.

Devlin waited for her to close the file, sit back in her seat and look at him. She might even shake her head to make it all the more clear to him where he now stood.

'Still, we have a good batch of men for interview. Four or five of them ex-Army. I daresay we shall fill our vacancies, and that's the main thing,' the Governor said.

Ask her where she lives, Devlin wanted to say to him. *And then ask her how quickly she'll be getting herself back there when all this is over and done with. Ask her where else she's been to stick her fucking nose in. Ask her how long your job will be safe when all these fucking changes and new regulations she's only too fucking keen to keep on mentioning are put in place. Ask her that.*

'Of course,' Janet Scott-Dyer said. She screwed the cap back on her pen and then laid this carefully across the closed file.

Now it was the Governor's turn to stare out at the trackless terrain ahead of him. 'Perhaps if, as I say, things hadn't all been somewhat rushed, then we might all have been better—'

'You,' Janet Scott-Dyer said sharply, interrupting him.

'Sorry?'

'*You* might have been better prepared,' she said. 'I consider myself to be perfectly well prepared, under the circumstances, for everything taking place today.'

'I see,' the Governor said, and then repeated this four or five times.

The wind blew, the wind changed direction, the wind blew again.

Devlin loosened his tie and then unfastened a button. The jacket still felt tight across his shoulders, the trousers tight at his waist.

Janet Scott-Dyer looked at her watch.

They were finished with him.

She would already be thinking about her journey from the borstal back to the railway station all those long miles away, and from there back to London.

'When will I hear?' Devlin said to the Governor.

'I'm sorry. Hear what?'

'Whether or not I've been successful in my application,' Devlin said. 'I'll need to start thinking about somewhere closer to live. Mister Sullivan said you had accommodation at very reasonable rates. And then there's my uniform to consider – presumably I'll need to come in for a fitting.'

'First things first,' the Governor said.

'Exactly,' Devlin said. He rose, stretched his arms and yawned. 'Looks like more snow later,' he said. 'No trains for a month this time last year.' He waited for the sudden worried look to cross Janet Scott-Dyer's face and then he turned and left the room.

27

'YOU COMING?' PATRICK PUSHED OPEN THE DOOR AND stood holding the frame. It was early evening, already dark for three hours, and with a skim of ice and snow still filling the ruts and hollows of the ground.

'Where to?' Devlin said. He was alone. Maria had spent the day with the few other women sitting out the winter in the compound.

'Fishing,' Patrick said, grinning.

'I'll need to let Maria know.'

'Why? Leave her a note. Tell her you're with us. We won't let any harm come to you.' He grinned again.

'What time will we be back?'

'When we get here.' He was already walking away, drawing Devlin in his wake.

Colm was waiting for them in the lorry at the field entrance.

'He going to be warm enough?' Colm said as Devlin climbed in and sat between the brothers. 'You going to be warm enough?' Another freezing night was forecast.

'It's Friday,' Devlin said. 'The weekend. You don't normally—'

'We don't normally what?' Patrick said. 'Besides, it's the best time of the week for some kinds of work.'

They drove towards Boston, along the Cowbridge drain, and then turned away from the town where this joined the Witham, following the Haven along a track which passed beside the Toft jetty at the Cut End road. The dim lights of the borstal shone in the flat distance. A week had passed since Devlin's so-called interview.

They left the path and turned inland for a hundred yards, then Colm drew up the lorry and parked beside a sluice platform.

Patrick pulled a mound of empty sacks from the bed of the lorry and gave them to Devlin. The three men stood for a moment listening to the night's silence all around them. The hot engine cracked in the darkness. The lights of Boston were scarcely visible behind them, only a glow in the sky above the place.

Without speaking, Patrick and Colm walked back to the river, climbed its embankment and walked along this a further fifty yards towards the sea. Devlin followed them. The ground there was less frozen than further inland and the thinner ice of the puddles shattered beneath his feet.

Eventually, the brothers stopped and then slid down the levee towards the water. They called for Devlin to do the same.

Devlin dug his heels into the grass slope to prevent himself from sliding too far.

Halfway down the levee he reached a line of wooden stakes driven firmly into the ground. The remains of a jetty gave the three men a small platform upon which to stand. Attached to the stakes, Devlin saw, were a number of heavy ropes which trailed down into the channel below.

It was where the fishermen of Boston secured their sacks of live shellfish before returning to the town. The shellfish sat there for days, sometimes weeks, flushed by the tide, awaiting any small increase in its value in the market. Midwinter always meant scarcity and higher prices.

Patrick started to haul on one of the ropes, calling for Colm and Devlin to help him. The three men pulled and a hundred-weight of mussels or whelks or cockles came slowly up out of the channel, rattling against the slope and growing lighter as the water drained quickly away. The rope was coarse and crusted with salt, and it scoured Devlin's palms as he pulled. Both brothers were wearing gauntlets, and he cursed Patrick for not warning him about the nature of the work.

Colm and Devlin alone pulled a second sack from the water and laid it beside the first.

After that, Colm returned to the lorry and came back with a pair of gauntlets for Devlin.

'I forgot to mention you'd be needing them,' Patrick said, laughing.

They continued hauling the sacks from the water until a dozen lay draining across the slope.

'Don't want to get too greedy,' Patrick said, as though a dozen missing sacks might go unnoticed by the men who had worked hard to fill them.

All three men stopped speaking at the sound of a distant whistle.

'Is it a boat?' Devlin said. There was nowhere for them to hide, and the hauled-out sacks would be clearly visible to anyone passing either above on the embankment or below on the water.

'It's the borstal,' Colm said eventually. 'Whistles, bells, alarms, you name it. They just enjoy letting everyone know how slow the hours and days and weeks are passing.' The camp was no longer visible from where they stood.

The dozen drained sacks were then dragged to the rim of the slope and Devlin saw for the first time the numbers and letters crudely stencilled on their sides denoting ownership.

'It's why we bring the empty, unmarked sacks,' Colm told him. He took out a knife and slit open one of the sacks. Together he and Patrick transferred the load of whelks it contained. Devlin was told to gather up any spilled shellfish.

After half an hour all the newly filled sacks were ready and waiting at the top of the embankment.

'Gather up the empty ones,' Patrick told Devlin. 'We'll burn them. No point alerting anyone to what's happened before they come back on Monday morning and pull on the ropes.'

Devlin did this.

After a short rest, during which a succession of further whistles sounded at the distant camp, the three men each took up a sack, balanced them on their backs and shoulders and carried them to the waiting lorry.

The loads were heavy and all three of them grunted and panted and stopped frequently to drop their sacks to the ground. It took them another hour to carry everything they had stolen to the lorry, where Patrick covered and roped the haul.

On their return they avoided Boston by turning along the Fishtoft road and then towards Sibsey. Devlin said little as Colm again drove.

'Cat got your tongue?' Patrick asked him. Cigarette smoke filled the crowded cab.

'I just don't like the idea of stealing from the fishermen, that's all,' Devlin said.

'You never said anything earlier.' It was another joke to the brothers.

Devlin had known some of the fishermen in the years since

his return from Colchester. He had worked through four winters on the boats, cash in hand, and afterwards on the Boston and Lynn quays. For all he knew, he might have just stolen from the men who had employed and befriended him.

'I knew some of them,' he said eventually. 'It's hard work.'

'*Everything*'s hard work,' Patrick said. 'Unless you got that silver spoon in your mouth. And so what that you knew them, so what?'

'I just don't like the idea of it,' Devlin said.

'What's that supposed to mean?'

'He'll get over it,' Colm said. He dug his elbow into Devlin's side.

They arrived at the drain corner at Northlands and Colm pulled into the lay-by there and switched off the engine and lights.

'Now what?' Devlin said, already guessing.

'You think we're going to take a load like this back to the compound?' Patrick said. 'You know us better than that. Besides, it has to shift fast, this kind of stuff. Buyers know what they're looking at. Two days – not even that in the summer – and everything starts to get a bit iffy.'

'They'll find out,' Devlin said. 'Shellfish – they'll find out who's buying and then find a way back to you.'

'To *us*,' Patrick said. 'Besides, that's not going to happen. In a few hours this lot'll be in Yarmouth or Lowestoft, fresh out of the sea on one of the boats there. Now shut it and keep your eyes peeled.'

Ten minutes later, a pair of headlights showed in the distance, coming towards them from the direction of Hackerley Bridge.

'This is our man,' Colm said and flashed their lights once.

Patrick and Colm climbed out to await the arrival of the buyer. Devlin edged along the seat to follow them, but Patrick told him to stay where he was and keep his eyes open for other lights. 'Less you know, less you've got to worry about,' he said.

At the far end of the lay-by a small van pulled in off the road and a man came to them.

It always surprised and reassured Devlin to see how easily all this endless wheeling and dealing worked for the brothers, and how well-timed it was. And he saw too how little he was actually told about it all.

The shellfish were inspected, the man brought his van alongside and the sacks were thrown down.

When Patrick and Colm finally returned to the lorry, Devlin expected Patrick to be waving money about, and to be paid his own lesser share of the night's profits.

But there was nothing. 'All in good time,' Patrick told him. 'The shellfish game doesn't work like that.'

'He thinks we're out to cheat him,' Colm said.

'What, us?' Patrick said. He put his arm around Devlin's shoulder. 'What you need, my friend, is to have a bit more faith in your fellow man. Am I right or am I right?'

'You're right,' Devlin said.

''Course I am. Right as rain.' He withdrew his arm and slapped both hands on the dashboard. 'Time to get going,' he said. 'What we hanging round here for?'

28

A WEEK LATER DEVLIN WAITED FOR THE BROTHERS IN THE pub on the Nene Outfall outside Sutton Bridge. Patrick and Colm had gone into Long Sutton to see a contact there with the intention of selling on the first part of Duggan's haul. They would have preferred to wait longer, but this opportunity had arisen and they'd snatched it.

Devlin watched out for Ray Duggan whenever they went near his usual haunts. Even the mention of his name still unsettled Devlin. Duggan must surely have discovered his loss by now, put two and two together, and be deciding what to do next. The fact that he hadn't shown his face yet meant nothing.

Devlin was alone in the small bar. The wait would be at least two hours. A fire burned in the grate, but did little to heat more than the closest part of the room. He sat with his feet on the fender. Spilled ash and small pieces of coke and charred wood filled the hearth. The room's only window overlooked the Outfall and Devlin turned to watch each time a small boat went by. There was no lock or jetty between there and the Wash and so none of the few vessels stopped.

After two hours, with most of his money gone, he went out

to the toilet, and when he returned he saw that a bag had been placed on his empty table and that a woman stood at the hatch waiting to be served.

Devlin went back to the fire and the woman turned at the scrape of his chair.

He identified her immediately as Skelton's wife. But the woman seemed not to recognize him and she turned her back on him.

Coming to the table a moment later, she too sat close to the fire. She took the bag and slid it beneath her chair, watching Devlin closely.

'You don't recognize me,' he said to her.

She sipped her drink. 'Don't flatter yourself. I knew who you were the minute you walked through the door. The only reason I might not have known you is because you look ten times worse than when I last saw you. Getting everything that's coming to you, I hope.' She sniffed deeply. 'Or perhaps I recognized the smell. Besides, what are you doing in this neck of the woods? Long way from home, aren't you? Where you living these days?'

'Here and there,' Devlin said.

'I'll bet. More "there" than "here", I hope. Barbara Collet was well rid of you.' Another sip of her drink. 'Oh, that's right: I hear George Sewell finally caught up with you. I heard all about that, we all did. Celebrations all round at that particular little bit of good news. You'll not go bothering either of that pair again, not if you know what's good for you, that is.'

'He caught me off guard,' Devlin said. 'That's all.' It was half true.

The woman laughed at him. 'What, meaning you were drunk? He said. Either way, drunk or sober, a man like him would always get the better of a runt and a coward like you.'

Devlin clenched his fists and she saw this.

'What you going to do?' she said. 'Hit *me*? Try it and see how far that gets you. You think Ray Duggan coming looking for you is a problem? Hit me and you won't know the half of it, or what hit you back.'

There was Duggan again. Of course her husband knew the man, heard the same whispering voices.

'They gone off to Lowestoft yet, the happy couple?' Devlin said.

'All three of them have gone. Well out of harm's way. They worship that kid, the pair of them.'

Devlin tried to calculate how much money he still had in his pocket. Then a thought occurred to him.

'They'll never be entirely certain though, will they?' he said.

'Now what you talking about?'

He knew from her voice that she understood him perfectly.

'The kid,' he said. 'They'll never rest easy, the pair of them, thinking there's a chance it might not be his. There'll always be something niggling away in his head, a funny little taste in his mouth every time he looks at her, especially as she gets older and looks less and less like him.'

'You don't know what you're talking about,' she said. She held her glass between them.

'It's what you believed the last time we met.'

'Yes, well, things change.'

'Not things like that. Things like that stay as they are for ever.'

'I can change my mind, can't I? Besides, you want to consider yourself lucky my husband didn't report you for shooting him.'

Changing the subject.

'It's still on the cards, mind. If he ever sets eyes on you he'll be straight over to the police station at Boston.'

'No he won't,' Devlin said, wishing he had a full glass to raise to his own lips. 'He'd be a laughing stock. Already is, probably.'

She could think of nothing to say to this and Devlin knew he was right.

There was a long silence.

Devlin finally rose and went to the hatch, sorting the change in his palm. He had enough. The McGuires had been gone almost three hours. Then it occurred to him that either he needed to leave or the woman needed to go before they returned and she saw him with them. Or perhaps old man Harrap had already spread the word. All those connections, possibilities, paths closed to him.

He expected her to leave when she'd finished her drink, but she didn't. The pub was in the middle of nowhere, barely surviving. Why was she even there? Perhaps she was waiting for Skelton. Perhaps the landlord had recognized him and made a telephone call. Did the place even have a telephone? He struggled to contain this sudden explosion of thought. Or perhaps the woman was staying put simply because she understood all of this as well as he did and she relished the advantage it now gave her. Perhaps *this* – her sitting in front of him – was her husband's revenge.

'Why are you here?' she said eventually.

Devlin shrugged. 'Good a place as any.'

'You look to cause trouble wherever you are.'

'I wouldn't be causing trouble anywhere if I was still at Harrap's,' he said.

'What, and my husband's to blame for that, is he? You want to listen to yourself. Pathetic. You were never going to make a go

of that place, not in a million years. Besides, once Harrap had
made his mind up to sell, your days there were numbered.'

It was the first he'd heard of Harrap wanting to sell the place.

'It was only a few quid,' Devlin said. He'd forgotten the
amount.

'Nearer four hundred, more like. I saw the eviction notice,
remember? And my husband was in for ten per cent of the total
value recovered.'

'Pity,' Devlin said.

'Don't get too smug. Harrap gave him what he was owed out
of his own pockets. Just glad to see the back of you so he could
get on with selling the place.' She watched his reaction. 'You
didn't know, did you? That's the trouble with people like you –
you never see beyond the end of your own greedy nose. You never
look beyond what it is *you* want, what it is *you* can get out of
something.' She rubbed her thumb and forefinger together.

'The place was soured,' Devlin said. 'The flood saw to that.
Who'd want to buy a place like that?'

'What's that got to do with anything? Ancient history, that
is. All land can be made to pay. All you need is a bit of money
and the know-how. Harrap sold up to a corporation in Lincoln.
They might consider themselves to have got everything cheap,
but it was still three times what Harrap thought it was worth. At
least, what it was worth without the inconvenience of a sitting
tenant, that is. They've already stripped out most of the hedges
and filled in the dykes. Potatoes. They don't even need a new
tenant on the place. Not even one that pays the going rate and
on time. The house was bulldozed flat, reduced to rubble and
carted away less than a week after you were turfed out. Truth be
told, Harrap was probably only too happy for you to give him
every reason to kick you out. He's retired on what he got for the

place. Life of Reilly, you ask me. Land, see? There's been machinery on it ever since you went. By all accounts, it's going to be a goldmine come the spring. In fact it's the only reason—' She stopped abruptly.

'What?' Devlin said.

She couldn't resist. 'It's the only reason my husband didn't bring wounding charges against you. It would have held everything up for Harrap. We got paid a nice little bonus on that score.' She raised her glass to him. 'So cheers for that.'

It was all Devlin could do to stop himself from swiping the drink from her hand.

Here it was again – all profit and success on one side and all loss and denial and uncertainty on the other.

'He'd still have been a laughing stock,' Devlin said.

'Who cares, when it turned out better than any of us could have expected?' She rubbed her finger and thumb together again. 'Like I said – that's the difference between people like you and people like us.'

'You seem to know a lot about me all of a sudden.'

'I know your sort. It's enough.'

'Go on, then.'

'Go on, what?'

'The difference between people like me and people like you and your greedy little bastard of a husband profiteering out of other people's misfortune and hardship.'

She laughed at the words. 'Touch a nerve, did I? Hardship and misfortune? You don't know the meaning of the words. Self, self, self – that's all it is with people like you.'

And without warning, she rose and pulled the bag from beneath her seat. She looked out of the window, took several steps away from Devlin and then turned to look back at him.

'I'm serious,' she said. 'Go and make a nuisance of yourself somewhere else. Nobody wants you and your sort round
here.'

'If you say so.'

'Oh, I do. You got any mirrors wherever it is you're staying?
Because you need to have a long hard look in one and see what
you've become. A good wash wouldn't go amiss, either. And rest
assured, I'll be telling my husband that I bumped into you. I
might even get word to George Sewell over in Lowestoft – tell
him what you've been saying about *his* kid. Perhaps he could
come back with one or two of Barbara Collet's brothers next
time. The only place *you're* a big man is in your dreams. To the
rest of us you're nothing but what you are. Believe me, nobody's
taken in by the likes of you.'

She left him then and Devlin sat thinking about all she'd
said. At least the McGuires hadn't shown their faces.

Then he had an idea.

He took an old envelope out of his pocket and went to the
serving hatch. 'That woman,' he said to the landlord. 'She
dropped this. Looks important.'

'Skelton's wife,' the man said. 'She's two houses down. Out
the front, turn left, directly opposite the water.'

Devlin went outside and walked along the rear of the houses.
That was why she'd been in the pub in the first place, because
she practically lived there.

Waiting beside an outhouse, he watched the second house
until he saw a light come on. Then he saw the woman cross a
window. She drew the curtains against the failing light.

Devlin watched the house for ten minutes longer, until he
was distracted by the noise of the McGuires' lorry coming along
the road. They would want a drink themselves, and if they were

flush, they would buy more for Devlin. He'd seen all he needed to see. He went back to the pub and waited for them.

'Good day?' he said to Colm as he came into the room.

'Good enough.' He pointed at Devlin's empty glass.

Patrick followed his brother into the room. 'You look pleased with yourself,' he said to Devlin.

'Not really,' Devlin said.

29

'THERE'S SOMETHING HAPPENING,' MARIA SAID. SHE SHIELDED her eyes at the window to look out.

From where he sat at the heater, Devlin heard distant shouting. He went to stand beside her.

At the far side of the compound he saw Patrick and Colm and a third, smaller man standing close and shouting at each other. The smaller man then ran away from the brothers, but tripped and fell. Patrick and Colm went to him and pulled him to his feet.

'It's a boy,' Maria said. She rapped on the window to attract her brothers' attention.

A minute later the three of them arrived at the caravan.

The boy was in his mid teens. His face and hands and clothing were dirty and his hair was cropped close to his head.

He looked familiar to Devlin.

'He's been sleeping in the carousel,' Patrick said. He held the boy by his arm and pushed him into the small space ahead of them.

The carousel was mostly dismantled and boarded up in readiness for its spring overhaul; its engine, horses and boards lay stacked at the centre of the giant frame, awaiting their own repair.

The boy looked hungrily at the loaf on the table and Maria cut a slice and gave it to him. He tore at this and ate it quickly, then picked up a mug of cold tea and emptied it in a swallow. The brothers laughed at all this.

'Who is he?' Maria said.

Runaways, waifs and strays were a common feature of the fair and circus during the season.

The boy made a sudden dash for the door, but Patrick blocked his way and pushed him to the floor.

'He won't say. All he wants is for us to let him get on his way.'

'Where you going?' Colm asked the boy.

'London,' he said, causing more laughter. The boy climbed to his feet and sat at the table opposite Devlin. 'I know you,' he said.

Devlin wondered how many more people there were in the world about to turn up, point their fingers and say that same thing to him. Wondered, too, at the trouble that usually followed.

'I doubt it,' he said. He saw the sudden interest in both the brothers' eyes.

'You were at the drainage work,' the boy said. 'With that bastard Sullivan.'

'I knew it,' Patrick said. 'He's on the lam from the camp. That's all we need – a row of coppers and their dogs lined up to search the place.'

Now the boy laughed. 'Search the place? You think they actually come looking for us? All they do is sit on their fat arses and wait for us to turn ourselves in. Half the absconders just walk back in through the gates with their hands up. Search parties? It's a joke. The whole place is a joke.'

'When did you go?' Colm asked him.

'What difference does it make? Nine or ten days back. You

think if they'd actually been looking for me they wouldn't have found me by now?'

Devlin looked hard at the boy and finally recognized the inmate Sullivan had pointed out to him on the bus. The boy sitting apart from the others, the one who had assaulted his own sister.

'What did you run off for?' Colm asked him. 'It sounds a cushy enough number.'

'It is,' the boy said. 'Especially after what I'd been used to.'

'So why run?' Patrick said.

'Because the bastards kept changing my release date, putting it further and further back. Every Juvenile Board I went up for – they just kept on saying I had longer and longer to serve. I just got sick of waiting.'

'What were you in for?' Colm asked him.

The boy cast a glance at Devlin. 'Thieving,' he said.

'Is that right?' Patrick asked Devlin.

Devlin avoided looking at the boy. 'How should I know? All I ever did was watch them while they pretended to work.'

'You and that bastard Sullivan,' the boy said.

'Thieving what?' Patrick said.

'Anything I could get my hands on. I got five brothers and sisters.'

'What about your parents?'

'What about them?' He looked back at the loaf on the table. 'Can I have another slice of that? You could let me stay – I can work.' There was neither hope nor pleading nor conviction in his voice.

'Funnily enough,' Patrick said, 'we got all the spongers and hangers-on we need for now. Besides, you're trouble, anybody can see that. Best thing for you to do is to get as far away from this place as possible.'

'Got a fag?' the boy said. He took the one Maria gave him, lit it and sucked hard on it. He blew the smoke directly at Devlin and then sat looking at him, smiling.

Patrick watched all this carefully. 'You know him,' he said to Devlin. 'You can help him on his way.'

'I don't know him from Adam,' Devlin said. 'He hasn't come here because of *me*.'

The boy took pleasure in this. 'I might have,' he said. 'You and Sullivan looked a cosy little number. Everybody knows how he likes to shout his big mouth off. Half the lads in there reckon that when they get out they'll be going to pay our Mister Sullivan a little visit.'

'Then they're probably all like you,' Patrick said. 'All talk.'

The boy continued looking at Devlin, the same thin sneer on his face.

'What's he looking so smug about?' Colm said. '*Do* you know him?'

'I already told you,' Devlin said. 'What, now you're taking his word over mine?'

'I doubt either would be worth the breath they came out on,' Patrick said.

'If I get to Peterborough, I can catch a train to London,' the boy said.

'And use what for a ticket?'

'Norwich station would be a better bet,' Colm said. 'They'd be keeping an eye on the main line. Your picture will be up somewhere.'

The boy laughed at the suggestion. '*Wanted Dead or Alive*.' He pulled out two imaginary pistols and started shooting.

'You're laughing now,' Patrick said. 'But that won't last.'

The boy blew into the smoking barrels and pushed the guns

back into their holsters. 'I already told you, nobody's looking. I got friends in London, contacts.'

Patrick laughed at the word. "Course you have. You're a big man. They'll all be waiting for you with open arms.' He pulled Colm to the far end of the caravan and the two of them held a whispered conversation.

'This your piece of skirt, is it?' the boy said to Devlin. He tried to put his arm around Maria's waist and she slapped him hard across his face. The boy only laughed. 'Didn't feel a thing,' he said. He nodded to the brothers. 'What do you reckon? Reckon they're planning to do me in and then chuck me into a drain somewhere?'

'It's a possibility,' Devlin said.

The boy shook his head.

'You should have finished your time,' Devlin said to him. 'You're just a kid. You don't know what it's like out there. London? You've been gone a week, longer, and you're still only half a dozen miles from the place.'

'I know better than most what it's like. And you can tell your mate Sullivan that when I'm free and clear, I'll be putting in a written complaint about everything he gets up to.'

'Right,' Devlin said. 'He'll be sweating it already.'

'You think that's funny? Well, his days are numbered. *Everything*'s set to change at that place. Most of the old warders are getting ready to leave. They reckon that compared to what's coming, the place is run like a doss house now. New staff, new fences, the lot.'

'Whatever they do,' Patrick said, coming back to them, 'nasty little runts like you will always be jumping up and down attracting attention. We need you gone.'

The boy turned to him with the same malicious grin on his

face. 'Why's that, then? Got something to hide, have you? It's not *me* you're scared of the coppers finding here.'

Patrick slapped him harder than Maria had slapped him, and again the boy took only a few seconds to recover from the blow.

No one spoke for a moment.

'Can you even write?' Devlin said then.

'What's that got to do with anything?' the boy said.

'You said a written complaint. My bet is, you can't even write, let alone read.'

'So what? I'll get someone to do it for me. A written complaint's more official. Write something down and they take notice. I got the right of appeal against every decision the fucking Juvenile Board have ever made.'

'Of course you have,' Patrick said. 'And look how far that's got you.'

The boy seemed to sag where he sat.

There was a further long silence.

Outside, the light sleet of earlier thickened and turned briefly to snow.

'You going to put me out in this?' the boy said.

'What's your name?' Maria asked him.

'Billy Egan.'

'We don't owe you any favours,' Patrick said. 'Like I already told you, all you are to us is trouble.'

'Put me out in this and the next thing you know the coppers will have pulled me in and then they'll start asking me questions about where I've been, who's been hiding and feeding me.' He picked up the last of the bread and pressed it into pieces with his dirty fingers.

Devlin watched him eat. 'What you said about Sullivan,' he said.

'What about him? Him and his big mouth, or him and the fact that his own days are numbered at the place?'

'That.'

'It's no big secret. They reckon the Governor himself has already had his marching orders. Once he's gone, Sullivan and all the others like him will go too. They might even turn the place into a real prison.'

'They've been saying that ever since the war,' Colm said.

Egan shrugged. 'All I know is what I see and hear.' He looked back at Devlin. 'What, Sullivan reckons he can do you a favour, does he? You want to steer well clear of that. There's even talk of an official inquiry into how the place is being run now. They put up pictures of the new Queen. Anybody who wanted one could have one for their dormitory or cell. You can imagine how that went down.'

Devlin had said little to Maria about his failed, pointless interview, even less to Patrick and Colm.

'You say one word to anybody about being here and you'll need more than your fingers turned into guns to save you,' Patrick said. Then he pulled on Colm's sleeve and the pair of them left.

30

LESS THAN AN HOUR PASSED BEFORE THE POLICE ARRIVED looking for Egan.

Patrick and Colm had gone to their own caravan, returned soon after with extra clothing and blankets, and had taken the boy back to where they'd found him in the dismantled carousel. Patrick had decided that the best thing to do now was to hide him until they could take him out of the compound and deliver him to Norwich station. It was too dangerous to kick him out and then let him wander nearby until he was either found or gave himself up before he froze to death.

The police car stopped at the field entrance and two men got out and went from trailer to trailer asking questions. Most of the trailers were unoccupied and they made swift progress in the failing light.

They came to where Devlin and Maria awaited them.

'We need to have a quick shufti inside,' one of the men said to them.

'Why?'

'Routine. We're looking for a runaway, an absconder. The North Sea Camp. Bane of our bloody existence, that place.'

Maria told them to come in.

214

At the table, Devlin picked up the last of the bread and started eating it. He sat with Egan's mug in his hand.

The two men came in and looked around them. 'To be honest, we're doing you a favour. The last thing you want is that particular nasty little piece of work turning up on your doorstep. William Thomas Egan, he's called.'

William Thomas. Devlin doubted if the boy had ever been called that outside of a courtroom or a police station.

'How long's he been gone?' Devlin said.

The men exchanged a glance. 'Too long. Truth be known, we should have started looking a lot sooner, but word was that he'd gone straight to London. They've been keeping an eye out down there for the past week. But apparently he's still in the neighbourhood.'

The two men made a cursory search.

'Perhaps he's hiding under the sink,' Maria said.

Both men laughed, and then one of them went to check. 'He's definitely not there,' he said. It was clear they considered even this small effort a waste of their time.

Devlin indicated the falling darkness and snow. 'You've got a lot of mud to wade through if you want to make a thorough search of the place.'

'We should have been off duty an hour ago,' one of them said, sitting beside Devlin. 'Been up since five this morning, we both have.'

'Middle of the night round here,' Devlin said.

All the two men wanted to do was to write up their time sheets, work out their overtime, say they'd searched the place and go home.

Maria put a bottle and four glasses on the table and the policemen silently accepted her offer.

'We usually pick them up in one of the nearby pubs,' one of them said. '*That*'s where we should be looking.'

'Somewhere nice and warm.'

'Precisely.'

'What's he in for?' Maria asked them, feigning a lack of concern.

'They never tell us that. Not officially, at least. But take it from me, this little sod's got more than his fair share of black marks against him. "A Danger to the Public", they call it.'

'Meaning?'

'Meaning, like I said, you'd be well advised to steer clear of the slippery little bastard until we pick him up. The Chief Constable's getting angry at the time we're taking. We'll have him before long.' He pulled aside the lace curtain and looked out at the half-drowned, half-frozen compound.

The other man drained his glass and took out his notebook. 'And you are?' he said to Maria.

She told him.

'We just spoke to your brothers, that right?'

'They have the van over there.'

'So that makes you Jimmy Devlin.'

'That's me.' He waited, hardly breathing, for what the policeman might say next, but the name meant nothing to him and he closed his book and slid it back into his pocket.

'What do you think?' the man said to his companion.

And again Devlin waited.

'It makes sense that the little bastard would want to put some distance between the camp and himself,' the other man said. 'We already know that his family won't have anything to do with him. Two and a half years and not a single visit. Makes you wonder.'

'Once he got to Peterborough,' Maria said, 'another hour and a half and he'd be in London.'

'That was the general consensus at the station. The so-called local sighting was bad info. Besides, they're keeping a close watch on Peterborough, so if he does decide to show up there . . .'

Devlin saw what Maria had done.

'And if he doesn't?' he said.

'Who knows? To be honest, we get sick and tired of clearing up after that lot at the borstal. The place is a disgrace, a law unto itself.'

Maria tapped their empty glasses with the bottle she still held.

The two men finally took off their helmets and put them on the table.

'This five o'clock thing,' one of them said. 'New kid, see? Up all night, most nights.'

'I can imagine.'

'And I'm already half asleep before I get back through the door at the end of the day.'

'Change the record,' his colleague said good-naturedly.

The four of them drank a toast to the newborn child.

'It looks like you've had a wasted journey,' Maria said to the men.

'Tell me about it,' the new father said, draining his glass and then stretching his arms and yawning.

31

DEVLIN WENT TO FIND BILLY EGAN THE FOLLOWING morning. Another frozen night had passed and he felt the cold air deep in his chest as he walked.

He found the boy swaddled in blankets behind a stack of pallets inside the sheeted carousel. Devlin nudged him with his foot and then kicked harder. There was still no response, and it occurred to Devlin that the boy might have died in the night.

A further kick and Egan groaned and half turned, rubbed his face on his sleeve and looked up at Devlin.

'What time is it?'

'I've come to hand you over to the police,' Devlin said. 'And then collect the thousand-pound reward on your head.'

Egan laughed. 'You brought anything for me to eat? I'm still starving.'

'You should have stayed where you were, then.'

Egan sat up and pulled the blankets close to him. 'You ever been in a place like that?'

Devlin shook his head.

'Thought not. If you had, you'd know why I'm not going back. Whatever Sullivan might or might not have told you

218

about me, there's worse things happen in there than any of us ever got up to on the outside.'

'I'll take your word for that,' Devlin said.

'You do that.' Egan rose to his feet, rubbing his arms and legs. With his dishevelled hair and clothing he looked younger than his age.

'They want you gone,' Devlin said.

'The gyppos? They made that clear enough. What you listening to them for?'

'The police were here. They could easily have said something. We all could.'

Egan laughed and then started coughing, unable to regain his breath for a full minute. He stood with his hands on his knees for a few seconds and then spat heavily. 'Not that lot,' he said. 'Common knowledge that a gyppo wouldn't give the law the shit off his arse. Turn me in? More trouble than it's worth.'

'Just like you are to them,' Devlin said.

Egan brushed sawdust from his shins, making little difference to his overall appearance. 'Faster I'm out of this dump the better. What's the plan?'

'I'm taking you to Norwich station.'

'Got no money.'

'Not my problem. What were you going to do, walk all the way to Mayfair?'

'I hadn't given it much thought. Where's Mayfair?'

'*Have* you got people in London you can go to?'

'People?'

'Friends, other boys.'

'Not really. I was just going to see what turned up. Something usually does.'

The boy couldn't have been more than thirteen or fourteen when he'd been sentenced.

'Family?' Devlin said.

'Them? First thing they'd do is call the coppers to come and get me. I'd rather take my chances as I am than turn up at any of their doors.' He licked his palm and wiped his face, running his hand through his cropped hair.

'Sullivan told me,' Devlin said. 'What you were in for.'

The boy considered this. 'It wasn't half what they said it was.'

'It was still your sister.'

'So? It was more her than me. She's a proper little tart. Moved to Lynn. It's what she does. Sullivan probably told you she was a kid, did he? Nothing like. People need to get their facts straight. Got any of your own?'

'Any what?'

'Sisters.'

'It's just me,' Devlin said.

'Best way to be,' Egan said. 'Look out for yourself and nobody else, that's my motto. Will they feed me before they kick me out, do you think?'

'I doubt it. Why should they?'

'Same reason I should keep my mouth shut about where I've been if the law ever does catch up with me.'

Devlin shook his head at the boy's bravado. 'I'll see what I can find,' he said. 'You still set on London?'

'Where else is there? You think I'm going to rot in this backward neck of the woods and go nowhere? It's a fresh start, London. So what if I don't know anybody? At least nobody there knows me. I'll probably even change my name.'

Devlin could see the sense of all this in the boy's head.

'Can we get going? Sooner the better, as far as I'm concerned.'

Devlin left him and returned twenty minutes later with bread and ham. Egan ate half of this the moment it was in his hands; the rest he put into a canvas satchel.

'You got any possessions?' Devlin asked him.

'I'm travelling light,' the boy said. He studied Devlin for a moment. 'You know what?' he said.

'What?'

'You should pack your own bag and come with me. London. You and me.'

'I'm twenty-nine,' Devlin said.

'What's that got to do with anything?'

Two hours later, Devlin sat in the car park at Norwich station and watched Egan cross the road and the forecourt and then disappear into the darkness of the entrance. He'd given the boy money for a ticket, but doubted if he'd buy one. It was all the money Devlin had possessed, unable to ask either the brothers or Maria for more. All that mattered to them now was that the boy was gone and that no trails led back to them. The instant Egan disappeared, Devlin wished him luck, but doubted if this was what he needed. The next any of them would hear of him, he imagined, would be another newspaper headline, everything one day, nothing the next.

He was a stranger in the city, and having waited to make sure the boy didn't come back out, he plotted his return along the main road to the west. The lorry was playing up in the cold weather, stalling when he stopped and then either drying up or flooding on him when he tried to get it going again.

32

THE NEXT DAY A MAN SHOUTED FROM THE FAR SIDE OF
the compound, close to where the larger rides stood boarded up,
some already dismantled and scattered over the sodden ground.
The patches of settled snow gave everything an air of abandon-
ment and loss.

Maria went to the window and looked out, careful not to
reveal herself.

A second man appeared and went to the first and both continued shouting, their hands cupped to their mouths.

Devlin went to stand beside her. 'Recognize them?'

Maria shook her head. 'Two guesses who they're looking for,
though.'

Patrick and Colm had left earlier in the day, before
Devlin was awake. As the days passed and the weather wors-
ened, the brothers involved him less and less in their dealings.
There was little enough profit in it for the pair of them, they
insisted.

As they watched unseen, a woman emerged from one of the
trailers and went to the men. When she reached them, one of
them grabbed her arm and shook her and she was forced to pull
herself free, almost falling. The second man gave her something

and the woman pointed to Patrick and Colm's empty caravan. Then she turned and pointed to where Devlin and Maria stood and watched.

The two men crossed the open ground, avoiding the worst of the ruts and mud. Devlin watched them come but recognized neither of them. They were both his own age and both wore overalls.

'Whoever they are, they're not happy,' Maria said.

The men went to the empty caravan and walked around it, banging on its sides and looking in at every window.

'What do you want to do?' Maria asked Devlin. 'They'll know fast enough that we're in here.' A good kick would open even the locked door.

'Act dumb,' Devlin said. 'At least until we know what they want.' He sat back at the table and waited.

The men knocked and shouted and Maria went to the door.

'You McGuire?' one of the men shouted over Maria's shoulder at Devlin, trying to push past her.

'You've got the wrong van. Theirs is over there.'

'We know that much, smart-arse.'

Both men came inside and closed the door behind them.

'Who are you looking for?' Maria said. 'There are lots of McGuires.'

'You must have heard us shouting.'

'We were asleep,' Devlin said. He motioned to the unmade bed.

'The McGuire brothers. That's all we know,' the first man said. He had a damaged lip, split and healed, a waxy scar, and this affected his speech.

'If they're not in their van, then we don't know where they are,' Maria said.

'Don't come the innocent with us.'

'Have it your own way.'

'What do you want with them?' Devlin said, pretending to yawn.

'What we want is to get our hands on the thieving bastards who took our sacks from the river, that's what we want.'

Fishermen.

'What sacks?' Maria said. 'What are you talking about?'

'The sacks that pair hauled out of the storage jetty a fortnight back.'

'How do you know it was the McGuires?' Devlin said.

'Because somebody told us, that's how,' the man with the scarred lip said.

'And we're here to find out one way or another.' The second man looked hard at Devlin as he spoke. 'And if we find out that either of you two had anything to do with it, then you'll get the same as what's coming to them.'

'They're a law unto themselves, that pair,' Maria said. 'They're gone for days on end sometimes.'

'And I'm supposed to take your word for that, am I?' the man said.

'Suit yourself,' Maria told him.

'Gyppos,' the man with the lip said. 'They're all the same. Ray Duggan warned us we'd have to watch our backs with this pair.'

'Who's he when he's at home?' Devlin said, waiting for the smallest sign that he'd said too much.

'He's the one who pointed us in this direction. We thought at first that he was involved himself – he usually is, one way or another – but he swore blind it was nothing to do with him and then suggested a few likely candidates.'

'And so here we are,' the other said, rubbing his hands together.

'Perhaps he was lying to you,' Devlin said. 'Pointing you anywhere except at himself.'

'Not Duggan's game. Besides, why are *you* so interested in him all of a sudden?'

'I'm not. I just don't like being accused of things I've not done.'

'Who's accusing you? It's the gyppos we've come to have words with. Duggan's had plenty of his own dealings with them in the past. He told us to pass on his regards. Said he'd be catching up with them on his own account soon enough, whatever that means.'

Devlin considered the threat and consequences of everything the man had just said. Always Duggan, always there, never gone.

'. . . nothing of the small matter of his slashed tyres,' the man was saying.

Devlin hadn't been listening.

'The what? Whose slashed tyres?'

'Duggan's. Who else? Put him out of action for a week, at least. Someone stuck a knife into all four of them. Cost him a fortune to get new ones. The old ones weren't worth patching up. And to add insult to injury, he reckons they even used one of his own fucking knives to do it. Not well pleased, I can tell you, not well pleased at all.'

'How does he know it was his own knife?' Devlin said.

'Take a guess.'

'So why hasn't he come looking for them himself, this Duggan?' Maria said, diverting the man from Devlin. 'Letting you do his dirty work for him, is he?'

The man smiled at this. 'Something like that. We said we'd sort out our own business and then let him know how everything went. Said we'd get back to him. He insisted on it. Get back to him and tell him everything we'd found, he told us. He said it was hard to know when a gyppo was lying, came that natural to them, but that they were never as clever as they liked to think they were, that they'd give something away, and that whatever that was it might be worth something to him.'

'Sounds like a long shot to me,' Devlin said. 'And, like I said, with you two doing all the leg work. And in this weather. Pair of mugs, you ask me.'

'No one did,' the man with the lip said.

'But feel free to look around,' Maria told them.

Patrick and Colm had burned the stencilled sacks within an hour of their return from the Haven.

'Already have,' the other man said. 'Nothing. But then *they*'re not here, are they? In my book, that makes this unfinished business.' He pointed at Devlin. 'And if I ever find out that you *were* in some way involved . . .'

The threat hung in the air like a bad smell long after the men had gone.

33

PATRICK AND COLM STAYED AWAY FOR THE FOLLOWING three days. They finally returned in the middle of the night and went straight to their own trailer. Maria asleep beside him, Devlin heard the lorry but knew that nothing would be achieved by going out and confronting the brothers.

Later the following morning, he was woken by Maria. She prodded him gently in the chest with a rolled newspaper.

'He's been caught,' she said as he rubbed his eyes. 'Patrick and Colm are back. They've been in Lincoln and Grimsby. Something to do with selling Duggan's stuff.'

'What did they say about his tyres?'

'They just laughed when I told them the fishermen had been here.' She unrolled the paper and held the front page to him.

RUNAWAY CAPTURED.

It came as no surprise to Devlin. 'What did he expect?' he said. 'It was all high hopes and no notion with that one. Where?'

'He was on the train. The police were informed and got on at the next stop. He was back in a cell in Norwich less than an hour after you dropped him off, apparently. Some spree that turned out to be.'

The McGuires. They'd sent him to Norwich with the boy and then called the police to tell them to watch the trains.

Maria took the paper from him.

'Does it say anything about where he was beforehand?' he asked her.

'Nothing. Not yet, anyway.'

The police would be questioning him now. They'd had three days. It was a local weekly paper. Perhaps the nationals had carried the news sooner. What was Egan likely to have said in those three days?

'They'll probably just end up taking him back to the camp and telling him not to do it again,' Devlin said, but with little conviction. Others would also now be considering the likely consequences of whatever Egan might reveal.

'They're not happy,' Maria said. 'Patrick and Colm.' She sat with her back to him, looking out over the empty compound.

Devlin noticed a note in her voice he hadn't heard before. She'd spoken to her brothers before coming to him, and he saw by the way she avoided looking at him now that she'd made up her own mind before she'd woken him.

'They've already decided, haven't they?' he said to her.

'They want you to go.' She turned to face him, but still nothing in her voice spoke in his favour. He'd been there seven weeks and it was beginning to feel like a settled life to Devlin.

'Egan won't say much,' he said. 'Besides, the police were here – they won't want it getting out that *they* didn't do their job properly, that your brothers got one over on them.'

'That *we* got one over on them,' she said. It was more than enough.

'Does Patrick—'

'Patrick thinks they'd be only too happy to come back here

228

and keep looking and looking until they found something, anything.'

It was why the brothers had been away for so long, leaving Devlin and their sister alone to face what might come. Had she, too, understood that much, at least?

'The boy will just be happy to get back to the camp while he's still a juvenile,' he said. Everything now was a failed hope.

'They're waiting to see you,' Maria said eventually, leaving him where he lay and going to stand at the sink.

'And what about you?'

'What about me?' A final rebuttal.

'If I left . . .' He waited, but she said nothing.

'If you left, what?' she said eventually.

'You know what.'

She shook her head. 'This is my home,' she said. 'They're my only family.' It was the simple, blunt and unassailable end to everything he might say to her. 'They told me to tell you to go to them when you woke.'

'If the boy had said anything over the past few days the police would be here by now.'

'Or they could just be biding their time.' Patrick talking.

'They're watching their own backs,' he said. Just like they always did. Just like Egan was now probably doing. 'Where does that leave me?'

She shrugged and the simple gesture was another blow to him. There was nothing left for him to know or to learn or to understand.

He climbed out of bed and got dressed. Maria gave him a mug of tea. There was no food.

After sitting in silence for several minutes, Devlin left her and went to the brothers.

Colm's face appeared at the window as he approached and then the door was pushed open for him.

'She shown you, then?' Patrick said as soon as Devlin was inside. 'Bad news all round, you ask me.' He grinned as he said it.

'You tipped the police off,' Devlin said simply.

'What?' Colm said, looking from Devlin to his brother.

'You got no proof of that,' Patrick said. 'Besides, why would I do that? You know where I stand with the coppers.'

'Save your breath,' Devlin said. 'You just say what suits you and what you want people to hear.'

'So?' Patrick said.

Colm stood between Devlin and his brother.

'The police would have been here already if they were coming,' Devlin said uncertainly.

Patrick pushed him aside, causing him to collide with the wall and then stumble in the tight space. 'Of course the police are coming. The kid will lead them back here one way or another. And if not the kid, then the blokes from Lynn. And if not them, then don't forget that Duggan himself still has a few scores to settle.'

'All of which—' Devlin began to say.

'All of which,' Patrick shouted at him, 'are pointed at us on account of *you* being here.'

It was beyond Devlin to argue the point. Nothing he said now would convince the brothers of anything except what they already believed.

'We've been doing bits and pieces with Ray Duggan for ten years,' Patrick said. 'If he wasn't pissed off at us, then the Lynn men would never have found their way to us. And that little bastard from the borstal probably only came here because he knew you from the drainage work. It all adds up, see? It all adds up and it all points in one single fucking direction – towards you. Let's face it, we've had nothing but trouble since the day you showed up. As far as I'm concerned, Duggan sending the Lynn blokes was the last straw.'

'*You* were the ones who stole the sacks,' Devlin shouted at Patrick. All wasted breath.

'Prove it,' Patrick said. 'All I know is that *you* turned up and showed us where everything was ready for the taking. You'd been nicking the things for years. All you needed from us was a bit of muscle. You'd worked on the boats years ago and so you knew the score.' He smiled again as he said this. Perhaps he was only just working all this out and was surprised by his own cleverness.

'And the guard from the camp,' Colm said. 'Why was he here?'

'That was nothing to do with the boy,' Devlin said.

'Not how it'll look to the police,' Patrick said. 'Perhaps you and him were all part of the kid's plan.'

'How?'

'I'm just saying, that's all. All the police will see is a connection. Let *them* start to work it all out. They're good at putting two and two together and coming up with whatever suits them best.'

'You ought to just go,' Colm said.

'That's exactly what he *is* going to do,' Patrick said. 'Because sooner or later somebody's going to come back here looking and—'

'And you'll point them at me to save your own skins,' Devlin said.

'Do I look worried to you?' Patrick said. 'And, like I already told you, we've had a handy little arrangement with Duggan for years now. Honestly, who do you think he's going to want to listen to, to believe?' He paused, still pleased with himself. 'You know your trouble – you don't listen to people, you don't work things out before you jump in with both feet. You think you're clever, but you're not. Not really. Not *clever* clever.'

'Duggan knows exactly what you are,' Devlin said.

'Of course he does. Just as we know exactly what he is. That's what I'm trying to tell you, but you're still not listening. Besides, last time we saw Duggan he could hardly see beyond those slashed tyres of his.'

'Why did you do that?' Devlin said.

Patrick shrugged. 'Because it was the least the bastard deserved.'

'And because Duggan would think it was me.'

Another shrug. 'He certainly knew you'd got his knife. Look on the bright side – at least he got that back. Probably wondering right now where to stick it next.'

'He'll soon enough—'

'What – work things out for himself? So what? He might work it out, know it was us, and then *still* consider it more worth his while to go on blaming you. You still stole all his stuff, re-member? You think we're scared of an old man like Ray Duggan? Men like Duggan, their time's been and gone.' He paused again. 'A bit like yours, really. You should seriously consider making tracks if you don't want to be caught here when any of this turns up back on your doorstep. All *I'm* doing here is looking out for my brother and sister. All *you're* doing is making things ten times worse for any of us, yourself included. Tell you what, I'll do you a favour – if Duggan does come here I'll tell him you're long gone, been gone for days. I'll tell him you've gone to London. He'll go looking in a lot of places, Duggan, but I doubt he'll go there. And I'll tell the coppers that you and the boy planned to meet up down there, having gone your separate ways to get there.'

It was all starting to sound too plausible to Devlin. He saw what a trap Patrick had laid for him and how easily and blindly he had wandered into it.

He looked around him. The caravan was in disarray as usual; it seemed hardly to have changed since his first visit there.

'You owe me,' he said to Patrick. 'Duggan's stuff. The boatyard.'

'I don't think so,' Patrick said. 'Besides, as far as I'm concerned, you only told us about Duggan's stuff to get your feet under the table here.'

'Leave Maria out of it,' Devlin said.

Patrick held up his palms. 'Glad to. But I can see by your face that you're even starting to have your doubts in that direction now. Perhaps all we ever wanted of her was to keep you happy until everything started to work out in our favour.'

'You're lying,' Devlin said.

'Perhaps, but you'll never know for certain, not now that you're going.' He thought of something. 'A bit like that kid you're supposed to have had and the doting father bringing it up as his own. Chickens coming home to roost, I'd call it.'

Devlin went closer to him, his fists clenched.

Patrick saw this. 'I'd think again, if I were you. Perhaps I got a knife even bigger than Duggan's stuck down my belt. And here's something else you probably never even thought of – perhaps the police were watching Norwich station. Perhaps they saw who dropped the boy off there.'

It was unlikely; the police would have been back long before now if they'd seen Devlin. But it was something else to add to the growing weight of his own lost argument.

Patrick held up his watch. 'Clock's ticking,' he said. 'Perhaps the police have already been tipped off about where you are right now. And perhaps it would suit me and Colm down to the ground to be able to help them make their arrest and then to let everyone know how surprised we are that you're involved in any of this. Especially when all we'd ever done was to extend the hand of friendship to you after Duggan kicked you out and you were down on your luck. If only we'd known what trouble you were bringing to our door.'

It was the last option remaining to Devlin.

'I'll go,' he said. 'But you still owe me.'

'Owe you?' Patrick shouted, a spray of spittle covering Devlin's face. 'What you're owed is Duggan getting tipped off and finding you all alone one cold dark night, *that's* what you're owed.'

'That works both ways,' Devlin said.

Patrick laughed at the empty threat. 'What, you think the stuff's still in the boathouse? It's not been there for weeks. It was there for a few days and then it went somewhere else. First you and Duggan knew where it was, then you and we knew where it was, and now only we know. Like I said, you're not anywhere near as clever as you like to think you are.'

Meaning Patrick would tell Duggan that they had no idea where everything had been taken, that only Devlin knew. There was a trap laid out in every direction he turned.

Patrick tapped the face of his watch again. 'I can see you're struggling to come to terms with all this bad news and that you're probably trying to work out what to do next. Trouble is, you need time for that. Time, and for all these other men to be as far behind you as possible. Keep Duggan and the police guessing – that would be my plan. Get as far away from here as you can and then keep your mouth tight shut. See that little bastard from the borstal – how far was he ever going to get shouting his mouth off to everybody who'd listen? The best thing that was ever going to happen to him was that he'd get to London, have his few minutes in the limelight and then lose the lot – and I mean *everything* – because it was what somebody somewhere decided was best. The sorry little bastard didn't have the first idea what he was letting himself in for.'

Just like me, Devlin thought.

Outside, a car came towards the compound entrance, but then drove on without stopping.

'Go,' Patrick said. 'You've got no choice. Besides, it's a big world out there for a bright spark like you. You got this far, you can get further. The drainage work will start up again in three months. Perhaps they'll want somebody to shovel mud again. Call yourself by a different name, grow a beard, I don't know. Nobody here will be looking for that long. Even Duggan knows his limits. You should consider yourself lucky you aren't already in custody, because then he'd *certainly* know how to get his hands on you.'

Devlin took several paces towards the door. He exchanged a glance with Colm, who bowed his head slightly and then looked back up at him. 'He's right,' he said, and then pushed the door open.

Devlin went outside, pulled the door shut behind him, and looked across to where Maria was watching him from the window of their own caravan. A bag lay on the step. She waited a moment and then let the curtain fall slowly between them.

34

HE STOOD BEHIND SKELTON'S HOUSE OVERLOOKING THE drain and the embankment beyond. He'd been there since dawn, watching and waiting. A small herd of cattle came to the wire of a neighbouring paddock and gathered close to where he stood, made inquisitive and nervous by his presence, steam clouding the air above their mud-caked bodies.

At seven Skelton came out carrying a coal scuttle, went to the outhouse and then returned to the house. Smoke rose from the chimney and lights came on. Devlin heard the woman's voice, a radio, singing. He wore two pairs of gloves and his fingers were still cold, deep in his pockets.

He'd spent the fortnight since leaving the compound in an empty prefab on the outskirts of Kirton. There were eight of the buildings, all empty since the war. The power and water were long gone, but the simple structure was mostly dry and mostly windproof. There was a table, a chair, a bed, and cracked linoleum on most of the floor.

The smell of cooking came to him on the still air.

Thirty minutes later both Skelton and his wife came out and the woman waited, her arms wrapped around herself, while her husband struggled to start his lorry. After ten minutes the engine was finally running and Skelton drove off. His wife watched him go, waving until he was out of sight.

One of the cows came closer to where Devlin stood and butted its head against his arm. Devlin slapped it hard on its bony cheek and the animal snorted and shied away from him, causing all the creatures to run a few paces over the frozen ground before coming to a standstill.

Devlin had no clear plan, other than to break into the house and find whatever was there for him to steal. He'd hoped the woman might have gone with her husband again, taking pleasure in some other poor bastard's sudden misery. He was uncertain now what to do. But as he considered his options, the back door opened and the woman came back out, in her coat and scarf this time and carrying a bag, and stood by the roadside. In the distance, Devlin heard and then saw a small green bus coming towards her. The woman raised her hand to it and crossed the road to the embankment side.

Devlin watched her board and talk to the driver. Other early passengers already sat at the windows and Devlin saw her go and sit beside one of these.

'Bye,' he said. 'Good riddance.'

He checked the few houses further along the road, and, certain he had not been seen, he left the paddock and went into the yard, where he was again hidden from sight.

He peered through the window. A fire burned in the small, cluttered room. Meaning what? That either the woman or the man or both would soon return?

He pushed at the locked door and then picked up a brick and swung it at the lock and handle. The door gave after only two blows and Devlin went inside.

After warming himself at the fire, he went upstairs. The bed was unmade and the wardrobe door open. A dressing table at the window lay spread with the woman's things.

He took an Army-issue kitbag from the top of the wardrobe and tipped her jewellery box into this. He doubted there would be anything of real value, but it was something. A burglary. He took off one of the pairs of gloves he wore.

Back downstairs, he searched drawers and cupboards and took whatever might be of any value: fishing trophies, silver picture frames, a cutlery set, service medals in their cases. He found a tin full of change, and beside it another stuffed tight with pound- and five-pound notes. A glass-fronted cabinet was filled with spirits and crystal glasses. More than he'd hoped for. In one drawer he found Skelton's ledgers and he took these out and threw their torn pages on to the fire, where they burned quickly, a few of them drifting back out into the hearth and settling on the rug there. Serve the pair of them right if he burned the place down. The rug scorched in places, but no fire started. Lucky them.

On the mantel above the fire he saw a photograph of the man and woman standing together, smartly dressed – something formal, a celebration. He took this down and smashed the glass on the edge of the table. There were two plates containing the remains of the couple's cooked breakfast, a third piled with buttered bread. He ate all this and then smashed the plates in the hearth. He took the photograph from its frame and tore it into small pieces, careful to scatter these away from the flames. Another frame held a picture of the couple with their children, and a third showed the woman holding two babies, grandchildren. More smashed glass and scattered pieces. He dropped the silver frames into the kitbag.

He wiped shelves clear of books and cheap porcelain ornaments, stamping on the few bits and pieces which fell but didn't break. He tipped every plate and cup and serving dish from the dresser beside the sink. Everywhere he walked in the house, the ground crunched beneath his feet.

A further ledger, hidden at the back of a cupboard, revealed its treasure of notes, almost ninety pounds. Devlin tore the pages from the book and threw these, too, on to the fire. Where would the man be without his records? Whose bidding and dirty work would he be able to do now? How could he even work without knowing for certain who owed him what and when? Everything now was a bonus to Devlin. There might be a hundred others out there, all living in fear of the man, who would be only too happy to do what he was doing now. Another bonus, he realized, was that Skelton – and perhaps even his wife – would already have plenty of enemies, any one of whom might have broken into their home. So where would the police even start looking? And to cap it all, no one had yet come looking for him, Devlin, not even the police, and so how on God's earth were they ever going to connect him to this?

The kitbag was full and as much as Devlin could carry. A satisfying weight. The money filled his pockets.

He went back upstairs and searched through Skelton's clothes, taking pieces for himself. He still only owned what he stood up in. He took a bottle of scent from the dressing table and poured its contents on to the floor. Another photo of the children and grandchildren, more broken glass and scattered pieces. He doubted he'd even been in the house ten minutes.

Back downstairs, he pulled open the door to a cupboard beneath the stairs he hadn't seen before. Shoes and boots, umbrellas and walking sticks. And at the very back, against the wall and hidden beneath a sack, was a shotgun. He took this out and opened it. A search of the dark space revealed a full box of cartridges. He wrapped the gun back in the sack and put the cartridges in the bag.

After searching the pantry for more food – provisions to last him at least a week – he returned to the back door.

As he let himself out, he heard the noise of an engine and recognized the sound of Skelton's lorry approaching. The man had returned.

Devlin went to the gate and waited beside the low wall to see which way Skelton went. With a bit of luck he'd stay parked up on the road and let himself into the house at the front. More than enough time for Devlin to make himself scarce along the far side of the embankment.

He waited, listening for the gear changes as the lorry drew up, and then heard Skelton as he climbed down, the engine still running. The bastard was singing to himself. *You sing, mate,* Devlin thought, *because you're not going to have anything to sing about for much longer or for a long time to come.* Other people's worlds fell apart in an instant. Now it was Skelton's turn.

Skelton let himself into the house by the front door.

The instant the door closed, Devlin crossed the path, rose over the lip of the bank and dropped to the far side. Another track led away from the road and the houses to a path running through empty fields. Within a minute he was beyond all sight and sound of the house.

When he was safe, he stopped beside a tyreless, rusted tractor overgrown with brambles and looked back in the direction of the road. He neither saw nor heard anything. He imagined the man inside, running from room to room, unable to believe what had happened during his short absence. He imagined him grabbing and staring into the empty tins, scooping up the torn and scorched pages and the tiny black and white pieces of the scattered photographs. He imagined him pulling open the door to the cupboard under the stairs and finding the gun gone.

He waited for the tiny figure to climb the bank and come running towards him, but there was nothing. He could easily plan a route back to the prefab without anyone recognizing him.

An hour later, beyond Wigtoft, his new home only thirty minutes away, he stopped and counted the money in his pockets. A bit of good luck come his way at last. The couple had got all they deserved. He imagined Skelton's wife trying to piece back together all the smiling faces. He wondered what Skelton might be doing now, while he waited for the woman to return. Perhaps he might have hours alone with his misery. And perhaps then that misery would increase tenfold. He hoped so. Perhaps the woman hadn't even told her husband about her encounter with Devlin three weeks earlier. Perhaps the pair of them would sit down together in the sudden small ruins of their life and grow more and more anxious at the realization of just how many people might have taken pleasure in doing all this to them.

Devlin hid the jewellery and picture frames at the edge of one of the Drainage Board's abandoned work sites. Apart from the money, he took only the clothes and the food and the gun and cartridges with him back to the prefab.

Once there, he pushed the notes into a tin of his own and hid this beneath the raised floor.

Then he sat with the gun for an hour before taking it to one of the other buildings and hiding it inside an earthenware pipe that had been laid but never connected. He pushed earth into the pipe, pulling brambles over the open end.

Back inside, he poured himself a drink and toasted his success. He toasted Skelton and his fat, grasping wife and all they had just lost and would never retrieve for as long as the pair of them lived.

241

35

AS EVER, HIS SISTER HELD THE DOOR OPEN A FEW INCHES and spoke to him through the gap. The same old pantomime.

'*Now* what do you want?' And, as usual, her eyes flickered in every direction behind him but never once fixed on his own.

'You make it sound as though I turn up every other day,' he said.

'God forbid.'

'I just wanted to see you, that's all,' he said. A month had passed since their encounter in Lynn. He'd owed her money for years. Perhaps now was the time, in light of his recent windfall, to pay some of it back. Buy himself a bit of credit, so to speak. 'I know Morris isn't in,' he said. He'd waited until Morris had gone back to work after his dinner. A grown man going home to his wife every day. 'Smells nice.' Whatever it was.

'It's all gone. Pork chop. Morris knows a man – a farmer, a pig farmer.'

Of course he did. 'He's doing all right for himself,' he said. He put the tips of his fingers into the narrow space. Five hours until Morris returned. Six o'clock on the dot. 'You going to keep me standing out here all day? Besides, you're letting all the warmth out.'

The door closed, the chain rattled and then the door opened again, wider.

'How have you been keeping?' Devlin said. He cupped his hands together and blew into them.

'I don't see you for four years, longer, and then it's three times in as many months,' Ellen said suspiciously. 'Now I *know* you're after something.'

'What I'm after is paying you back some of what I owe you,' he said. 'I've had a good winter so far, better than usual. I'm renting a nice little place over Kirton way.'

'You look all right,' she said. 'I'll give you that.' Skelton's clothes.

'This old rubbish? You should see me on Sundays.'

She led him to the kitchen. It was warmer in there. Morris didn't appreciate her lighting a fire in the parlour until just before he got home. Waste of fuel, just for one. And Morris, Devlin guessed, no doubt knew a man who knew a man who had a contact at the coal jetty at Sutton.

The only thing different in the kitchen since his last visit was a television set standing on the table.

'That's new,' he said.

'Came yesterday. I was going to polish it before Morris wired it into the parlour. Not good for it in here – condensation, that sort of thing.'

'I can imagine,' he said. At least he was warming up. He went to the set and turned it on and then spun the two dials.

'It's not plugged in,' she said. 'We need to get an aerial fitted to the chimney.'

'A length of wire up the back wall and run to one of the stacks should do it. Save yourselves a bit of money.'

'Morris likes to have things done properly. It's a Murphy, best there is. You can ask anyone.'

The name was spelled out in curling cream letters across the front of the cabinet.

'Morris says you can count the number of sets in a ten-mile radius on the fingers of one hand.'

'He always was ahead of the game.'

Ellen smiled at this. 'Once it's up and running we'll be entertained every night of the week. Films, variety performances, sport, you name it.'

'What's "tone"?' Devlin said.

'Morris explained that one.' She watched him closely, relieved when he came away from the set. 'I'll give it another polish,' she said. 'Before Morris gets home. Mahogany. When the aerial's fitted we'll save a small fortune on newspapers and magazines. Morris says that in ten years' time, the wireless will be a thing of the past.'

'I've never seen you read a newspaper,' Devlin said.

'No need now. That's what I'm saying.' She sighed, as though he hadn't grasped a word of what she'd just told him. 'We're thinking of a twin tub next, separate washer and spin drier.'

'Woman over Grantham way had her arm broke in a drier. Stuck it in while the thing was still going round. Broke the bone in two places, lost a finger.'

'Morris said they had built-in safety.'

'What's that when it's at home? I could kill a hot drink.'

'I wish I hadn't heard that particular story,' she said, and he felt suddenly sorry for the lie.

'I'm pulling your leg,' he said. 'They wouldn't shift many if they kept breaking women's arms, now would they?'

She went to the sink and filled the kettle. A radio played on the shelf – voices, occasional music, applause.

'I only keep it on for the company,' she said.

Devlin tried to remember if she was thirty-one or thirty-two.

'You said something about the money you owed,' she said, her back to him. Money would be Morris's department. 'Only, I'm sure it would help, you know, if you showed a bit of willing in that direction.'

'Help what?' Devlin said.

'With Morris. You and him would get on better. You need to give yourself a chance to get to know him, that's all.'

'I'll try a bit harder,' Devlin said. He changed his mind about the money.

And because she thought he was being serious, she came back to him and put her hand on his arm.

'I saw Mother,' she said.

'Oh?'

'Last week. I called in on her. She said she might get over this way one day soon.'

It would never happen. Besides, she was only two miles away.

'She seen anything of *him*?' Devlin said.

'Not that she said. I doubt it. She'd probably keep it to herself if she had.'

'If she'd any sense she would.'

Ellen lit a gas ring and put the kettle on it. 'I've got a sort of coffee,' she said. 'Not the real thing, but not far off it by all accounts.'

'I never really got a taste for the stuff,' Devlin said. 'Besides, what's the point when you've got tea?'

As usual, there would be nothing stronger in the house.

'I should have thought and brought a bottle of something,' he said. 'A nice bottle of British sherry, something like that.'

'I used to like a drop of sherry. Port and lemon, that was me.'

She smiled at the distant memory. 'Morris says that women who keep drink around the house – even respectable drinks like port and sherry – he says they're prey to temptation, that they let other things go. Keeping yourself busy, that's the thing, especially this time of year. I suppose most women my age—' She stopped abruptly and Devlin wondered if she ever drew breath without in some way thinking of her lost child. She might have been another woman completely by now.

Breaking the silence, Devlin said, 'I can't think of anything better. Television, a nice relaxing programme that'd cost you five guineas up the West End, your feet up and a little drink in your hand.' As though he knew what a West End show cost these days, as though he'd even been back there since the weekend before his arrest ten years earlier.

His sister took the kettle from the ring and put it back on the drainer.

'So things are on the up?' she said.

He changed his mind again and took the folded notes from the inside pocket of Skelton's jacket and laid four on the table.

'Shall we say twenty? To be going on with. The rest won't be far behind.' He couldn't remember what he owed her, but it was considerably more than twenty.

She picked the money up and unfolded it.

'Hold them up to the light if you like,' he said.

'I didn't—'

'I'm joking. Good as gold, that little lot.'

She watched him fold up what remained of the money and push it back into his pocket.

'What sort of work are you at now that the drainage has finished?'

It was a week until Christmas, a fortnight until New Year,

and it would all come towards him and then pass him by without him participating in either event. It was beyond him to ask her what she and Morris had got planned. His family, most likely, over in Leicester, everything out of her hands, nothing left to chance.

'Bit of this, bit of that,' he said. 'I met some useful contacts on the drainage. Tell Morris I'm following his example. You know me – I can take an engine apart blindfold. Take it apart *and* put it back together.'

'I doubt if one would be any good without the other,' she said.

Devlin forced a laugh at the remark. 'Now you just made a joke,' he said. 'You should try it more often.'

'I don't really—'

'Don't tell me – not very ladylike.'

'Well, it isn't.'

'That what you're turning yourself into then, is it – a lady?'

She smiled again at this. 'No sense in *not* trying to improve yourself, is there? Besides, what's the alternative?'

'I suppose so.'

'Improve yourself, improve your chances. That's what—'

'I suppose so,' he said again.

An hour and three cups of tea later, the chill gone from his bones, Devlin said, 'I suppose I ought to make tracks. Don't want to outstay my welcome.'

And as usual, she stood up immediately and started the process of ushering him towards the door and back out into the world beyond.

'No,' she said. 'It was . . . you know . . . to see you.'

'My sentiments entirely,' Devlin said. Because – and he'd said it before – that's what proper families did – they saw each other.

Jesus fucking Christ. 'You tell Morris I'll be back with the rest of what I owe when I've earned a bit more. Don't want to leave myself short. Not with Christmas and everything.'

'Of course,' she said.

'Tell him to spend some of it on that aerial.' What did an aerial cost? A bit of wire, a few brackets.

Back outside, fastening Skelton's scarf over his mouth, he began to wonder why he'd gone, what he'd achieved, what purpose the visit had served. Keeping his options open? Prolonging the agony, more like.

He turned his back on the house and followed the road away from the sea. A line of recently pollarded willows stretched ahead of him like raised fists, the rounded tops already lost to sight in the falling cloud.

36

THE INSTANT SULLIVAN UNLOCKED THE DOOR, DEVLIN pushed it hard into the man's chest, causing him to fall backwards and to shout out in surprise and pain. Devlin went into the house and pulled the door shut behind him. In the narrow hallway, Sullivan made no attempt to get up. He wore a stained white vest and his braces hung at his thighs. He was unshaven and there were dark rings of sleeplessness around his eyes. The house smelled worse than Devlin's abandoned prefab.

'It's just that I'm getting a bit sick and tired of people peering through doors at me,' Devlin said, 'like they'd rather I just went away.'

'Oh, it's you,' Sullivan said from where he lay propped on his elbow.

'None other. Who were you expecting, Lord Mountbatten? I take it you do remember me?'

"Course I remember you. What's all this in aid of?' He held out his hand for Devlin to help him up, but Devlin ignored this and stepped over him, going into the small front room to sit by the fire.

Sullivan rose, pulled his braces over his shoulders and followed Devlin into the room, where he sat on the cluttered settee opposite him. Newspapers were strewn on the floor at Devlin's feet. Three ashtrays sat on a low table, all of them overflowing.

'You've let the place go a bit,' Devlin said, already starting to guess what had happened to him since their last encounter.

'How would you know?'

'You've got me there,' Devlin said.

Sullivan coughed and then struggled to regain his breath. 'As it happens, I've not been having too good a time of things lately.' He scratched both his armpits and then sniffed at his fingers.

'You and me both,' Devlin said.

'I've been laid off.'

'Sacked?'

'Laid off pending the outcome of a so-called inquiry.'

'Finally got caught doing something you shouldn't have been doing?'

'Nothing like that. We had a runner. The kid I pointed out to you at the drainage. Nasty little piece of work.' He rubbed his elbow where the door had caught him. 'I'm going to have a bruise there,' he said.

'You'll survive,' Devlin said. 'I read about it. They caught him.' He waited to see what more the man might reveal.

'They did indeed. And now the evil little runt's telling anybody who'll listen to him all sorts of tales about the place and about his time on the run. "On the run"? Don't make me laugh.'

'"Anybody" meaning . . . ?'

Sullivan searched through several empty cigarette packets before finding one half full.

'That's just it – they've shipped him off to Lincoln. Who knows what he is and isn't saying? But whatever it is, according to the Ministry, we're too slack. Too many backs being covered when we hold our own inquiries.'

'Stands to reason,' Devlin said.

'It might do, but it's still how things work best. Nearly thirty years I worked at that place. Ask me, the Ministry were just looking for an excuse to make the changes they want.'

'And all the new guards they were looking for – the job you told me I'd get just by turning up at the place?'

'Gone with the wind. Out of the Governor's hands. He's been given his own marching orders. End of the month.'

'So you're saying my interview counted for nothing?' Devlin said, feigning disbelief.

Sullivan sat staring into the low fire for a moment. 'Is that why you're here? To tell me what you think of me?'

'You said you'd let me know. Everything's been a bit up in the air of late. You're not the only one with problems.'

'I honestly didn't think you'd be that bothered,' Sullivan said. 'You never seemed particularly keen in the first place. I was doing you a favour, that's all.'

'Some favour,' Devlin said.

'And now they're talking about pressing charges,' Sullivan went on. 'Against me and some of the others. Apparently, all the things that were being done wrong were our fault, done at our "contrivance", whatever that means. The little bastard who ran off is staying in what amounts to a three-star hotel up in Lincoln. Got all sorts of bigwigs coming to talk to him. I can't even begin to imagine some of the tales he'll be telling them to save his own neck.'

'Yes you can,' Devlin said. 'How many have they laid off?'

'Twenty of us. The place won't even function. Twenty, and all of them good blokes, blokes who were good at what they did.'

'Blokes like you,' Devlin said.

'Exactly.'

'When will you know?'

'Know what?'

Devlin shrugged. 'The outcome of the inquiry, whatever the boy's telling them.' He almost said 'Egan'.

'Who knows? No one's said. Whatever the result, it won't be a good one. At least not for the likes of me and the others.'

'I read they caught him on a train somewhere,' Devlin said.

'On his way to start scraping up all that gold off the streets of London, by all accounts. Stupid little bugger. He should have stayed put, wherever he was.'

'Does nobody know where he went beforehand?'

'Not yet. I daresay he'll get round to telling them when it suits.'

'And then what?'

Sullivan considered the question for a moment. 'You seem very interested all of a sudden,' he said.

'Not particularly. He might have lost both of us a job, that's all.'

Sullivan rubbed his face. 'You might be right.'

Devlin looked again around the untidy room. A bottle lay on its side beside the settee.

'Go on,' Sullivan said. 'Have a good look.'

'I've seen worse,' Devlin said.

'I don't doubt it.' Sullivan stopped rubbing. 'Thing is, my wife's gone. A week ago, when all this blew up. It's been on the cards for some time – me and her – and everything got a bit much for her.'

'Where's she gone?'

'Doncaster. Her mother's. Woman's in her seventies. She

never liked me. Lives by herself. Council. The pair of them will be loving it.'

'And meanwhile . . .'

'And meanwhile I'm left to fend for myself, waiting for the axe to fall. We've been hung out to dry, the lot of us, that's the truth of it. Best I can hope for now is to cash in whatever pension I've still got coming to me. One of the lads said there was even talk of that being put on hold until everything's sorted. What am I supposed to live on until then?'

'You should have known something like this would happen one day,' Devlin said. 'You got away with things, that's all.'

'Thanks for your concern. I know we got away with things, bent a few rules here and there, but that's how places like that work. Nobody plays by the rules – not us, not them – because if you did, nothing would ever get done and the place would be even more like a holiday camp than the prison it's supposed to be. Rehabilitation – don't make me laugh.' Sullivan rolled the empty bottle across the floor with his foot. 'I'd offer you a drink, but as you can see . . . I fell asleep. You woke me up with your knocking. It's all a fucking mess. I don't know where to start.'

Devlin wondered whether to tell him all he knew about Egan, but quickly decided against this. There was little left for Sullivan to salvage, so why should he get involved? Why point the finger at himself and the McGuires when all those other pointing fingers already had a target?

'They probably won't believe even half of what he's telling them up in Lincoln,' he said.

Sullivan shook his head. 'Truth is, it hardly matters *what* he's telling them, because it will be enough. They've already decided who's to blame' – he jabbed a finger in his own chest – 'yours truly, that's who. That woman who showed up from the

Department for Prisons, she knew exactly what she was doing from the second she set foot in the place. Ask me, everything was a big sham.'

'Even my interview?'

'*Especially* your interview. Believe me, you can count yourself lucky on that score.' Sullivan paused and half smiled. 'I was thinking of applying at the nuclear plant down the coast. One of the blokes said there was a lot of building work about to start. Nuclear. It's the future. Electricity and all that.'

'First I've heard of it,' Devlin said.

'Same stuff as was in the bombs,' Sullivan said, his voice low now. 'We could go down there together, you and me, have a look-see. Unless you've got something better lined up, that is.'

'I'm not doing too badly,' Devlin said.

'Thirty years, me and her were married, solid as a rock.'

'You got kids?' Devlin said. He tried to remember what Sullivan might already have told him, but nothing came.

Sullivan glanced at the mantel as he considered his answer. A framed photograph of a boy in uniform.

Devlin stood up and went to look more closely. He brushed the dust from the glass with his sleeve.

'That was taken on his eighteenth,' Sullivan said.

'Did he see Active Service?' Devlin wiped his thumb across the boy's face. Smiling, trying not to.

'Put it down,' Sullivan said. 'Please. It's all we've got left. His name was Stuart – her choice, after her father.'

Devlin put the picture back in its pride of place amid the clutter.

'Was he killed, then?'

'Something like that.'

'What does that mean? Either he was or he wasn't.'

Like the trip to his sister's a week earlier, Devlin wondered what he'd expected to achieve from this visit. Loose ends, that's all. Letting all these others know where they stood, where *he* stood.

'What that means,' Sullivan said, 'is that the fucking Army, in all its fucking wisdom, put him on a troop carrier two days after that photo was taken and then sailed him straight to Singapore, down the gangplank and into a Jap prison camp. Seven weeks it took them to get there. Seven weeks, they had, to work out what was happening in the place and turn the boat back. Seven weeks and nobody lifted a fucking finger to do anything about it. Four years, he was held, best part of, camp after camp. Ended up in Japan itself. Ask me, only the Yanks ever had the first idea what that little lot were up to.'

After a long silence, Devlin said, 'Did he come home?'

'He did, as a matter of fact. One of the few. They sent us word of him. November time. Apparently, he went from Japan to Australia and then to India. Came through the Suez to Cairo and then on past Gibraltar to Southampton. Hospitals all the way. After Southampton they took him to a place down in Hertfordshire. He wrote to us, told us not to visit him, to wait until he was fully recovered and able to come back home under his own steam. Told us he needed to build his strength up, that sort of thing. I saw things in that letter she couldn't even begin to imagine. She cried solid for two days after.'

Devlin already heard the story's bad ending, like a gathering storm ready to break in the small room.

'What happened?' he said. It was probably what had scuppered Sullivan and his wife in the first place. He avoided looking back at the mantel.

'When he was finally ready to come home, I went to

Peterborough to meet him off the train. He called from London to say he would definitely be on it, but when it came in I couldn't see him. I waited an hour and then went back out to the car. I was crossing the road to where I'd left it and this bloke came up to me. It was him, Stuart. Apparently he'd walked straight towards me and I hadn't recognized him. He said he'd seen me waiting, but that he saw by my face that I hadn't spotted him and so he'd walked straight past me. Didn't want to cause a scene, not in the station. You know how it is with some people. Said he'd come out of the station and then waited for me to follow him. March time, that was, spring, seven months after the end of hostilities. His face was all altered. He hardly had any hair left on his head – some kind of skin disease he'd picked up, a lot of them had the same. Joked about it, said he was having trouble growing it back. Seven months and he was still all skin and bone. God only knows what he must have looked like to begin with.' Sullivan rubbed his eyes again. 'When we'd last seen him, me and her, he was just a kid. A kid in a uniform. By the time he got back to us . . . well, you can imagine the rest.'

It was why he hated the boys in the borstal so much. Hated them or felt something for them: it was all the same thing and it hardly mattered.

Tears ran over Sullivan's cheeks and gathered at his chin. 'Look at me,' he said. 'Eight years ago that was, nearer nine.'

'What happened?' Devlin said, guessing the tale had perhaps already ended.

'He killed himself. The following September. We found him hanging from one of those trees over there.' He gestured towards the window. 'I honestly didn't think we'd be able to go on living here after that, but it seemed to give his mother a bit of comfort, being so close to him. To be honest, it's probably the only thing that's kept us together these past few years. And now she's gone. Perhaps enough was enough. Perhaps it all just stopped mattering to her. She cried for a week when they found him. On her knees, she was; she could hardly stand. Everything that had happened to him, and then this. She spent half the time he was back home fighting with the Authorities to get him his back pay and whatever else he was owed.' He paused and wiped his eyes. 'I tell you, if anyone ever tells you that these bigwigs in Government and whatever are on your side, doing things for your good, then you can take it from me, they're lying to you. Every time he went out, she wanted to follow him. Not that he went out too often. The doctor said we should try to get him to talk about things – encourage him to "open up" – whatever that's supposed to mean when it's at home – but he wouldn't say a word. And especially not to me and her. He had a girlfriend before he went off, but she made herself scarce fast enough when he got back and she saw the state of him. Mind you, I can't say I blame her. If I'd had the choice, I'd have done the same. If only he could open up, they said, then he might be able to share things and lessen his load. That, and that *we*'d understand things better. All *I* ever needed to understand, I understood perfectly well the instant I saw him walking towards me outside Peterborough station.' He stopped talking and let out a long sigh.

Devlin felt uncomfortable sitting so close to the man. All the air had gone from the room. 'I'm sorry,' he said eventually.

'You? What you got to be sorry about?' Sullivan sounded suddenly hostile. 'You – you're nothing, nobody. You, me, her and him alike – all of us – we're all nobodies who count for nothing in the eyes of our so-called lords and masters. And once you've learned that particular lesson in this life, then there's nothing else left to learn.'

257

'I suppose so,' Devlin said.

Sullivan shook his head. 'You suppose so. You suppose so. You're as lost and clueless as the rest of us.' He waved at the door. 'Go on, get out. Get out, and do yourself a favour and *stay* out. You suppose so? You suppose so? Dear God.'

37

'I'M BETTING YOU'VE NOT GOT A LICENCE FOR THAT THING.'

The voice surprised Devlin and he turned to see Samuel, the old shepherd, standing behind him. He wondered how the man had come so close to him in the vast, empty space. It was not yet mid morning. He'd come there to fire the stolen shotgun, to get the feel of it.

'You've finally managed to get yourself a real gun, then,' Samuel said. He raised the barrels in his palm and stroked a thumb along the maker's name. 'This yours?'

'It is now,' Devlin said.

'Like that, is it? I had one similar when I was younger. Fired shot like sand. "Lark shot" we called it.'

'Besides, since when did I need a licence for a shotgun?' Devlin said.

'Since they changed the law. It's why I haven't got one any longer. I went to register my last one like they said, and they told me I was too old. Infirm.' He held out his arm and rolled back his sleeve, his hand close to Devlin's face. 'You see any tremor in that?'

'Tremor?'

'Tremble, then.'

Devlin watched the thin brown fingers. 'A bit,' he said.

'Enough to stop me firing at a duck fifty feet up?'

Devlin shrugged.

The old man lowered his arm and shook his sleeve down. 'Said if they caught me with a gun I'd get a fine *and* prison. Where's the sense in that? I'm nearly seventy.'

'You could have a shot or two with this if you like,' Devlin said. He handed the shotgun to Samuel, who took it, caressed its stock, balanced it on his finger and then opened and closed its barrels and looked along each. 'Somebody kept it nice and clean,' he said. 'What you shooting?'

'Not too fussy,' Devlin said.

Samuel raised the gun to his eye and turned in a half circle. He cocked the hammers and then pulled each trigger, the loud clicks echoing in the cold, still air.

'I thought I might get a few ducks,' Devlin said. He'd seen some birds earlier, out over the receding water, but too far away to shoot at. After that he'd aimed and fired at fence posts. He should have brought some bottles or cans with him. He found some fresh pellets in the posts, but not many. It was a disappointing exercise.

'You back at the chapel?' Samuel said, handing him the gun.

'I got a prefab. Kirton way.'

'The ones they put up and then never really filled? A real waste, that. The story at one time was that families from Coventry were coming out there, but those few that did eventually turn up took one look at the place and decided they'd rather take their chances with Coventry.' He laughed at the story.

'I won't be there long,' Devlin said. 'I'm just waiting for some money I've got coming. I like to keep moving.'

'I can see that. Some men never settle to anything, never settle in their lives, never settle in their own skins.'

'What's that supposed to mean?'

'I just see it, that's all – some men, all they ever want is to stand still, a bit of security, all the usual trappings. And others, all *they* want is to keep moving, to keep making up their lives according to where they are and who's listening to the tales they're telling.' There was no malice or judgement in the old man's voice.

'What makes you such an expert?' Devlin said.

'Nothing. I'm just saying, that's all. I saw it in you that time I first found you in the chapel. Some men, if they don't catch on to whatever it is they're meant to be in life, then it's almost like they make a deliberate point of *never* catching on.'

'I've been doing all right for myself,' Devlin said. He put the gun to his own eye and swung it in an arc across the empty sky. 'Why are you here?'

Samuel pointed to the distant inland embankment and the pastures running to the misty horizon. There was still snow in the dykes and up against the low hedges. 'They're wintering the sheep. Big time of year, this. They come out in lorries and spend a few weeks here.'

'Who pays you?' Devlin asked him.

'The farmers, mostly. Some want their animals on the marsh, some on the improved land. The cost depends. It's not much, but it's enough. I've never wanted much out of life myself.' He pulled at the thin rope which acted as a belt round his dirty coat.

They walked together towards a dry dyke, where they were able to sit out of the wind. The tin chapel was again visible towards the bank, its roof rising from the thin mist.

'They're talking again about pulling it down,' Samuel said.

'Roof's gone, walls have gone, hardly a full pane of glass in its window.'

'Good riddance, I say,' Devlin said.

'You would.' Samuel felt in the bag he carried over his shoulder and took out a bottle and a flask. 'Tea,' he said. 'Hot as when it went in four hours ago.' He poured some out and handed the cup to Devlin. 'My daughter bought it for me.'

The hot liquid burned Devlin's lips. 'Four hours?' he said.

'As God's my witness. It's a Thermos. She's a modern woman, my daughter. Forever telling me as much. Says she likes to keep up. Every week it's something new.'

'It's the way they are,' Devlin said, thinking of his own sister.

'Not that I blame her.' He passed Devlin the bottle and Devlin drank from it. 'She's just back from London. She went all that way just for the day to look at the new Queen's wedding presents. Apparently, they were all out on show for ordinary people to look at.'

'What's the point of that?' Devlin said.

'I suppose she thought it would make people think better of her.'

'The lot of them get handed everything on a plate as it is,' Devlin said.

'I suppose so.'

'No "suppose" about it. It's why the rest of us have got to do what we can not to get left behind.'

'*She* enjoyed it, anyway. Listen, you'll laugh, she said that in one room there was nothing but silver salvers on display, hundreds of the things – from companies, regiments, that sort of thing.'

'What's a salver when it's at home?'

'A serving dish, but made of silver.'

'Then why don't they call it a serving dish?'

'Never really thought about it, to be honest,' Samuel said.

'I'll tell you why – because it keeps them separate from us, from ordinary people.'

'If you say so.'

'I do,' Devlin said.

'Hundreds of the things. I told her I've still got the serving dish I was given as a wedding present. Full of cracks and chips, but still serviceable once or twice a year.'

'Exactly,' Devlin said. '*They*'ve got hundreds, all made of silver and never used, and you're making do with some piece of old tat.'

Samuel took back the bottle and blew on his own small cup of tea. 'My daughter said she'd seen a Sheffield plate dish in one of her magazines, said she was thinking of ordering it on the never-never.'

'What's Sheffield plate?'

'A kind of silver. Beats me why anyone would want to eat meat off a silver dish.'

Devlin kicked at a stone beside his foot and watched it slide down the slope. 'And then there's that husband of hers.'

'The Duke of Edinburgh? What about him?'

'Edinburgh? Don't make me laugh. He's a bloody Greek, practically an Eyetie. I'll bet there's not one in a thousand could tell you his real name. They got that one sorted out fast enough. Duke of bloody Edinburgh. When was he ever in Scotland?'

'I can see you've given it all some thought,' Samuel said.

'Because you need to know what's what in this world, keep your wits about you.' It occurred to Devlin that he was perhaps starting to sound like Morris.

Neither man spoke for a minute. The bleating of distant

sheep could be heard, and Samuel pushed himself up to look out over the top of the dyke.

'To be entirely honest with you,' he said, 'I came out to make sure you weren't shooting at the sheep.'

Devlin smiled at this. 'And here's me thinking it was a social visit.'

'We always lose a few each winter. Butchers looking for a bit extra.'

'Thought never crossed my mind,' Devlin said.

Samuel looked at him. 'I wish I'd never mentioned it now,' he said.

'Stop worrying; you're only doing your job. Besides, I've got enough on my plate without having the police after me for shooting sheep.'

'They give me a carcass or two when they come to take them back inland. I usually make a few quid selling them on. My daughter's talking about a refrigerator. A friend of hers has one. She can make ice cubes in a tray.'

'What for?' Devlin said.

'Search me. You put them in drinks.'

'I'll tell my sister,' Devlin said. 'It's the kind of thing she'd appreciate.'

'I don't know where it will all end,' Samuel said.

'That's the point,' Devlin said. 'It won't. You'll be getting the never-never like you used to get your wage packet before long. And not too long after that you'll be up to your eyeballs in debt. You can tell her that from me. I've seen how the world works.'

'I can see that. You finished with the tea? I need to keep an eye on the cups. They're just glorified lids really, but they keep the thing tight, see?'

Devlin handed back the cup and Samuel carefully screwed it on to the flask. He rose from the slope and looked back over the distant sheep, little more than whitish dots against the hazy green.

'I'd better get back,' Samuel said, picking up his bag. 'She'll start to wonder where I am.'

Devlin wiped mud from the barrels of the gun.

'Going to snow again soon, and worse,' Samuel said. He shielded his eyes to look out over the sea.

'See any ducks?' Devlin asked him.

38

TWO DAYS LATER, HE WENT BACK TO HARRAP'S FOR THE first time since his eviction five months earlier. It seemed more like five years to him.

Where the house had stood, there was nothing. The barn and all the outbuildings had gone. Even the vast concrete yard had gone. A few pieces of rubble lay here and there along the entrance track and beside the posts of the grubbed-out boundary hedge, but apart from that, nothing.

The previous day he had returned to the boatyard on the Welland and found the place abandoned. The McGuires had been busy. The place looked as though no one had set foot there since the war. He had broken in to the boatshed where everything had been hidden. Empty. Not even the boat builder's own debris remained. Not even a few spilled screws or piece of shining wire or pile of white shavings. Nothing. He might just as well have dreamt the whole episode. In Colchester gaol, a warder had warned him upon his admission that, whenever pushed, man turned wolf to man. Wolves, jackals, hyenas. Always those winners and always those losers, always those predators and always those victims.

He'd gone to the centre of the high, empty space and

shouted his own name, hearing it echo vaguely off the curved roof, like the flapping sound of a bird trying to find its way out of the building.

He went now to where the farmhouse had stood and searched for its outline on the ground. Nothing. It seemed impossible to him that something so substantial, something so permanent-seeming could have disappeared so completely. Even those ancient civilizations that collapsed and fell centuries ago – the Romans, he remembered from school, the ancient Greeks – still left their massive ruins standing today. But here there was nothing.

Where the surrounding land hadn't already been ploughed, it had been broken and turned. The rubble would have been carted away. The big mechanized ploughs – Canadian, he imagined; he did know *something* about farming – were too precious to risk damaging. Even amid the sparse detritus on the track there was nothing he recognized. A few whole bricks, but that was all. Shards of glass lay in the wet grass and reflected the winter sun. The deeply ploughed earth was blacker than any he had ever seen.

He looked beyond where the barn had stood. Even the few trees that had once grown there and shaded the building had been chopped down and their roots grubbed out. And if there was any truly hard labour in this world, then the grubbing out of tree roots was it.

And just as it seemed impossible to him that anything could disappear so completely and so quickly, it was also hard to believe that the new owner of the farm would have *wanted* to get rid of something so completely.

He went back to the road. Reaching where the gateway had once stood, he watched a car come towards him. It drew up beside him and a man got out. He wore a clean overall with a badge on the pocket.

'Can I help you?' he said to Devlin. He looked back along the track leading to the lost house, and then to the vast dark fields beyond.

'Help me?' Devlin said. 'I was just looking.'

'No, what you're *just* doing is trespassing.' The man still didn't look at him.

Devlin peered into the car and saw scattered paperwork on the passenger seat.

'Trespassing? I doubt it. It's a public road, this.'

'You were over there,' the man said, pointing to where Devlin had been. 'And that's private land, and the pathway's a private road.'

'Is it yours?' Devlin asked him.

The man let out his breath and finally looked at Devlin. 'I'm not here to argue the toss with you, my friend. I'm here to tell you that you're trespassing and that you need to leave, and sharpish, and then steer well clear in the future.'

Or what? Devlin thought, but said nothing. 'I was leaving. I came here to look – no law against that, is there, looking? – and now I'm leaving.'

'Look at what?' the man said suspiciously.

'I used to farm here.'

'Since when?'

'Until that bastard Harrap sold the place from under me, that's when.' It sounded a good, believable story.

'Never heard of him. Nothing to do with me, that side of things. I just act on behalf of the land management company.'

'What's that when it's at home?' Devlin said.

'Everything you're not, probably. I'd offer you a lift, but I'm not allowed. Company car, see? They're very strict on things like that.'

'I can imagine,' Devlin said. He looked back over the land. 'What happened to it all?'

'Cleared,' the man said. 'Landfill, probably. You can look in three directions from this spot and it's all the same land-owner for as far as you can see. Small farmers are a dying breed these days. That soil's going to be left to drain and then it'll be turned again before anybody even thinks of planting in it. Double ploughing, see? When did anyone round here ever double plough? It's all to do with science these days.'

Old farmers often said they could *hear* things growing in that soil, it was so rich, its fertility guaranteed as far into the future as it had been accumulating in the past.

'We've got people in the offices back up in Lincoln selling crops that haven't even been planted yet,' the man said, getting into his stride now.

All Devlin had to do was look impressed, interested at least.

'There's a spot over Boston way where they're building acres of greenhouses. Greenhouses the size of which you wouldn't believe. Salad crops.'

'It's winter,' Devlin said. 'Besides, who eats salads?'

'You'd be surprised,' the man said. He looked at his watch and frowned. 'I'm due somewhere else,' he said. 'I'm going to have to log this, so I'll need your name.' He took a pen from his pocket and stood clicking it over and over.

'My name? What for?'

'I just said. For my log. Everything has to be written down.'

'Since when?'

'Look,' the man said impatiently, 'I wish I'd got all day to stand around arguing the toss, but I haven't. What's your name?'

Devlin started walking away from him.

'I'm still waiting,' the man shouted after him.

'Then that's what you can do,' Devlin said, and continued walking. After a few seconds, he heard the man running to catch him up. Waiting until he had almost reached him, Devlin turned and held up his fists.

The man stopped running and stood panting, his eyes fixed on Devlin's fists. 'What's that for?' he said breathlessly. 'I'm only doing my job.'

'Let's just say that I'm getting sick and tired of being told what I can and can't do,' Devlin said. 'And where I can and can't go.'

'Still, there's no need for violence.' The man started to back away, suddenly more concerned, it seemed to Devlin, to find himself so far from his car, its door still open. 'All I asked for was your name,' he said.

'And all *I* told you was that you could whistle for it.'

The man considered this. He brushed the front of his clean overalls. 'I'm going to do you a favour,' he said. 'Just this once. I'm going to pretend none of this ever happened.'

'Pretend what you like,' Devlin told him, then turned and started walking again.

Behind him, the man returned to his car and drove off in the opposite direction.

39

THE NEXT OF THE SEASON'S STORMS ARRIVED, FOLLOWED only two days later by another. There had been little fresh snow over the past fortnight, and certainly nothing to match the heavy falls of the early winter, but the ground had remained frozen all that time and the drifts and ice had persisted. Now the storms were forecast. A third was due at the end of the week. A turn in the wind direction, high tides and a predicted surge along the North Sea coast, the newspapers said, would cause more flooding. Not as severe as that of the previous winter, but still bad. People needed to start taking precautions. People needed to remember.

For a week, the Army and the depleted workforce of the Drainage Board filled and stacked sandbags all along the Welland and the Nene. The Army set up a temporary camp at Spalding, and another close by the Hobhole drain. Lorries came and went along the narrow roads and tracks at all hours of the day and night.

Devlin regretted the lack of a wireless in the prefab to keep himself up to date. The storms and the likelihood of further flooding were all people were talking about.

During the first of the storms, the prefab shook and one of

its roof panels was lifted. When the wind finally fell after twelve hours, Devlin went out and stacked bricks on the roof to hold the panel down.

In the second storm the panel was lifted again, this time tearing free of the building's flimsy frame and scattering bricks across the rest of the shaking roof and over the nearby ground. There was nothing Devlin could do about any of this until the storm ended and so he sat up through the night hoping that no more of the roof would be torn away from him and that he would not be left completely exposed to the elements and drenched in the persistent rain.

In the respite following the storm, he left the shattered building and broke into another. He threw ropes over the flat roof and anchored these to stakes he drove into the soft ground. The continuing bad weather shook this second building but did little real damage to it. The small awning – useless anyway – was torn away from above the door, and a pane of glass was shattered, but the tethers held firm, and apart from a few places where the near-horizontal wind drove rain through dilapidated joints and seams, the building remained sound. There was little chance of any real flooding that far inland.

After the second storm, Devlin went out and inspected the remaining prefabs. Some of these had lost roof panels and whole windows. One of the structures had even been blown off its brick foundations and stood now at an angle in the grass and mud like a foundered ship.

He went further afield, beyond the Washdyke road, and saw the depth of the water lying in all directions. Everywhere, normally sluggish or empty drains and channels were filled and running with turbulent brown water. Any coastal surge, were it to materialize, was not expected until the third storm, and the highest tide of the month would also come in the middle of the night at the same time.

Soldiers visited properties that had flooded previously and tried to evacuate their inhabitants. Few went. Most, only just back on their feet after the previous year, insisted on staying where they were. People took precautions, moving furniture upstairs, stockpiling what food and clean water they could find. There were already tales of abandoned properties being looted again. Farmers and smallholders took their livestock inland. All around the Wash fishermen abandoned their work and moored up their boats. The sluice committees were convened. Plans were made. Past errors, people said, would not be repeated. Everyone waited.

Devlin read about all this in the local paper. There had been procedures and strategies before and they had all come to nothing in the face of the rising water. Water came and water went, and if it was stopped from either coming or going in one direction, then it invariably went in another and someone else suffered.

Returning from a visit to the petrol station at Langley, Devlin was about to enter his new home when a woman in waterproofs appeared from around one of the prefabs and called to him. She wore waders to her chest and her head was hidden in a broad hood. At first Devlin thought it was a boy shouting to him.

It was too late to hide from her and so he waited where he stood. It was no longer raining and there was even a rising brightness on the seaward horizon. Above him, low in the sky, he saw flocks of gulls flying inland ahead of the coming weather.

'Who are you?' the woman asked him. She pulled a clipboard from beneath her bulky jacket.

She was much younger than he had first thought, his own age perhaps, and her face was ruddy.

'I come from Kirton,' he said, nodding towards the distant buildings.

'I'm a special constable. We've been sent out to warn people about the possible flooding, the surge.'

'I know all about it,' Devlin said. He pointed to the row of isolated houses half a mile away on the raised road. 'I'm there looking after my parents,' he said.

She looked at the cans he was carrying, and Devlin put these on the ground.

'They've got a small generator. My father's just out of hospital.' He couldn't think of what else to add.

'You sound well prepared. What are their names? I can check them off my list.'

'They'll be all right. They're ten foot off the level. Even last year the water stopped six foot short at its highest. What, are you telling me this is going to be worse?'

She shook her head. 'But perhaps I could come back up there with you and put everyone's mind at rest.'

'You'd only scare them,' he said. 'It's why I'm here. My mother's a worrier, always has been. Sixty-three. Seriously, I'll make sure they're all right. Your time would be better spent somewhere else. Besides, there was only me to look after them last year when nobody else gave a toss.'

The woman was offended by the remark and took several paces away from him.

'The worst of it's expected later tonight, elevenish,' she said, her voice different, 'but it should have passed by dawn, say eight or nine.' Her every word added unnecessary drama to the situation. She was making herself important, Devlin understood that much at least. It was what people did these days. She motioned to the surrounding prefabs. 'This lot will be under two foot of water, according to the boffins,' she said.

'They've never been occupied,' he said.

'I know. Someone in Sutterton thought a few tramps might have been living here. We've had reports. The last thing we want this time round is an unnecessary loss of life.'

Devlin wanted to laugh. 'No,' he said. 'I haven't seen anyone.'

'Why are you here?'

He motioned to the lane end. 'I got a lift. The petrol. This is the quickest way back to the houses.'

She looked from the lane to the distant buildings. 'It makes sense, I suppose,' she said.

'I should be getting back,' Devlin said. 'They'll be wondering where I am.'

'They're expecting the worst of the flooding from the Scalp all the way up to Welland House. The land on either side of the channel will be under water for at least the next few days.'

Devlin avoided looking at the prefabs.

'I'd offer to help you,' she said. 'But, as you can imagine, we've got our hands full.' She walked even further away from him.

He wondered if there were others nearby waiting for her. Had she already looked through the windows of the prefabs and seen that someone had been living there? He knew that anything he said would only raise her suspicions further. He picked up the cans and started heading away from her.

He walked a hundred yards from the prefabs. He put down the cans, pretending to rest, surreptitiously looking behind him to see what the woman was doing. She was wandering among the buildings, but making no attempt to search inside any of them. Eventually she went back to the road and continued along it in the direction of Kirton.

Devlin waited where he stood, cursing her for every step she had made him take carrying his heavy load.

The third storm came soon after dark and was, as forecast, considerably more violent than the first two. The rain was heavier and lasted longer, and the wind blew harder. The prefab rocked and shifted on its foundations and the water continued to come in at the seams. Every window rattled in its frame.

Towards midnight the note of the wind changed, and Devlin heard the splash of water all around him. He looked out and saw the few inches which already covered the ground. Rain mostly, he guessed. Any surge would have come in a more pronounced wave. He could easily judge the depth of the water by the rubble scattered around the buildings. Only one of the two concrete steps beneath his door was so far submerged.

He put pans and bowls beneath the worst of the leaks. Parts of the floor started to come loose and to rise, pushing up the thin linoleum. He stood a chair over this. During the last flood, the water had been inside the buildings within minutes. Nothing at the start of the hour and then a foot of dirty water washing around each room by ten past. By twenty past everything was lost. He had ignored all the warnings and advice then, such as it had been.

By five in the morning, the sky still black and the wind still blowing, the water was up over the second step and starting to appear in damp patches across the whole floor. He took the two cans of fuel outside and stood them on his coal bunker.

He watched the waves rolling across the land between the sea wall and the embankment. The lights of the houses still shone in the distance. The waves grew in size briefly and then subsided.

By six the water was calmer and the sky had brightened to a heavy grey. The sun – if it came – was not due for two more hours. Looking at the sky, Devlin guessed the worst was over.

He went back inside and waited. He even slept fitfully for a few hours.

When he finally woke, the sun was up and the storm had passed. The land was still under water, but this had already started to fall and to thicken to mud.

He went outside and watched a succession of lorries pass along the bank road. Men were already at work on the slopes, more soldiers.

In the distance a boat moved in the direction of the sea, appearing to vanish completely in the molten glow of the rising sun.

That's that, then, Devlin thought to himself. He watched the distant men for a few minutes, knowing that even if they had seen him come out of the prefab, he was of no concern whatsoever to them. He guessed the water was sitting no deeper than two feet, probably less over much of the surrounding land. With any luck most of it would drain away with the ebbing tide later in the day.

40

HE WATCHED DUGGAN UNLOADING THE LORRY IN THE half-light: a roll of chain, a few folded tarpaulins and a solitary empty drum, which fell and then rolled noisily over the hard ground in front of the barn. He turned to look at the house, where, mid afternoon, lights already showed. He went closer.

Duggan was talking to himself. He stopped briefly and then resumed. And then he straightened and stood looking back at the empty lorry.

'I know you're there,' Duggan said without turning. 'It must be the smell.' He raised his face, sniffed deeply and then laughed. 'And I imagine that if you think you're brave enough to come back here and get this close, then that's Skelton's gun you're pointing at my back. Just about your mark, that – pointing a stolen gun at an innocent man's back in the dark. Are your hands trembling? Because they should be. And they will be by the time I turn round and you get to look me in the eye.'

'Stay where you are, then,' Devlin said.

Duggan turned slowly.

Devlin watched his empty hands.

'Very wise,' Duggan said. 'Keep watching.' He held up his palms.

'Who's in the house?' Devlin asked him. 'The old man?'

'He's my father – call him that. Him and my wife. Why – you think the pair of them are going to come out shooting?' He nodded at the gun. 'Nice bit of steel, that. I've offered to buy it a dozen times.'

'Then you'll know to stay away from it,' Devlin said.

'Whatever you say.' Duggan raised his hands briefly before lowering them. 'You made yourself a bad enemy there, boy.'

'I can handle Skelton.'

Duggan laughed. 'No, not him. Though I daresay he'd still like to have a few words with you. No, I'm talking about his wife. Old Skelton's very much a let-sleeping-dogs-lie kind of man. But his wife – she's something else completely. She hasn't stopped yakking in his ear, by all accounts, ever since you paid them a little visit. You shouldn't have done that to the pictures. She's like a woman possessed. She just won't rest. I can think of a dozen blokes I'd rather get on the wrong side of than her. Last thing *you* want is her on your tail.'

'She isn't *on* my tail,' Devlin said.

'No, that's right – you keep on moving around, don't you? According to the tales I've been hearing, you've been keeping yourself busy, popping up here, there and everywhere. What, did you think I'd forgotten all about you? Forgive and forget, is that it? Now, that's not very likely, is it?' He reached slowly into his pocket and took out his tobacco tin. 'All right by you? Condemned man and all that?' He rolled a cigarette while Devlin watched. 'I'd offer you one, but that would mean me holding the gun while you lit it.'

A silhouette appeared at the farm doorway and the old man shouted out to Duggan.

'Just a bit of business, Dad. Go back in. I'll be there in a minute.'

The old man stood watching them for a moment and then went back inside.

'Don't worry,' Duggan said. 'He won't have seen the gun. He can barely see his own hand in front of his face these days. What are you here for? To settle up what you owe me?' He laughed. 'Oh, and I suppose I should thank you for returning the carving knife. One of our wedding presents, that. Meant a lot to my wife. Not as much as the Bible meant to the old man perhaps, but . . .'

'That wasn't me,' Devlin said.

'You do surprise me. I *know* it wasn't you. But the thing is, from where I'm standing, you're still the one who took it. And without you taking it in the first place, it would never have come back to me like it did. You can see my reasoning. Oh, I know exactly who pulled that little stunt, don't you worry.'

'Have you seen them?'

'The Flying Zambinis? Once or twice. Naturally, they're still insisting it was you, and, for the moment at least, it suits me to go along with that. Unfinished business is always that until it reaches some happy conclusion in one direction or another. In this case, hopefully, mine.'

'They told me—'

'I don't care what they told you. They did what they always do, and believe me, I'm going to keep that pair close and you looking the other way until I decide to do something about it all. They're like you – they probably think they've got away with everything just because nothing's happened yet. At least so far they've stopped short of trying to sell me back my own stuff. Even *they're* not that stupid.'

Devlin tried to understand the implications of all this and how he might in some way benefit.

'I know where they took everything,' he said.

'Me and you alike,' Duggan said. 'But then they took it all somewhere else and told no one. Next thing, you'll be offering to help me look for it.'

'Part of it's still mine,' Devlin said.

Duggan laughed. After rubbing out the last of his cigarette between his fingers, he said, 'According to the weather men we've got more bad weather to come. Even a bit more flooding. I daresay those rickety prefabs over Kirton way will be on their last legs before too long.'

Devlin felt suddenly cold.

'That's right,' Duggan said. 'Like I said, I keep my ear to the ground. You wouldn't credit some of the things I've been hearing. Turns out you're a regular little Scarlet Pimpernel.'

'What's that when it's at home?' Devlin said.

Duggan stretched his arms and yawned. 'Like I said, you need to keep an eye on Skelton's wife. She's been weeping and wailing to everybody who'll give her the time of day. Your problem now is that every nasty little piece of work between here and Lynn – and a fair few there – are going to be keeping their eyes peeled to make money on your neck.'

'What money?'

'Oh, didn't I say? She's put it about that Skelton will pay good money to find out where you are. I've been wondering about having a word in her shell-like myself.'

'So why haven't you?'

Duggan pulled a face. 'Let me think. Because it's not in my nature? Or perhaps, like with the McGuires, I'm best suited by keeping you exactly where I want you, especially if I'm the only one who knows where you are. What do *you* think?'

'Most of the prefabs are already under two feet of water,' Devlin said. 'You don't know where I am now.'

Duggan laughed again at the remark. 'You should hear your-self,' he said. He rubbed his forearms against the cold. 'Getting chilly again,' he said. 'They're even forecasting more snow. You want to find yourself a nice cosy little billet somewhere.' He pretended to think. 'I hope that's not why you're back sniffing around here again.'

'I wouldn't come back here in a hundred years,' Devlin said.

'And yet here you are.'

The farm door opened and this time Alison Duggan appeared and called to her husband.

'Tell her to go back in,' Devlin said.

'You tell her,' Duggan said. He watched Devlin closely for a moment. 'You see, what you're doing now is trying to remember or work out if I've got a gun of my own in the house. And whether or not she knows how to use it. "He was going to shoot my husband, officer. I had to do something to protect him. He's shot others before now."'

'Tell her to stay where she is,' Devlin said.

'Make your mind up. Besides, all she's doing now is being a witness to you turning up here out of the blue and waving a stolen gun in my face. I can just imagine the courtroom. I can even see the McGuires in their Sunday best turning up to scratch my back by telling the judge how you'd had everything planned from the very start.'

An hour ago, Devlin had had a plan, but now he didn't. Most of that plan had involved telling Duggan what had happened with his carving knife and everything they'd stashed at Dove-cote Farm. But now that plan – such as it had ever been – had evaporated.

'I just wanted to set a few things straight,' he said.

Duggan laughed. 'I'll bet you did. Trouble is, you see, as far as

I'm concerned, everything *is* straight.' He tapped his forehead with a finger. 'As straight as it can be. And from where I'm standing, you look exactly like what you are – a pathetic little excuse for a man waving a gun around.'

'She shouldn't have started shooting her mouth off,' Devlin said.

'Who shouldn't? Skelton's wife? It's in her nature – she shoots her mouth off about everything. I take it you're talking about the happy couple and the kid that might be yours, God help it. Are you trying to tell me that if she'd kept shtum in the first place then you wouldn't have broken into her house, smashed everything up and torn the pictures of her with her kids and grandkids to smithereens?'

'Perhaps,' Devlin said.

Duggan shook his head. 'I don't believe you. You'd have wrecked the house whatever. Just like you did here.' He nodded back to his wife in the doorway. 'Not much of her best dinner service left, by all accounts. What was *that* revenge for? Christ, you're even more pathetic than I thought you were. Always somebody else's fault, always somebody else to blame, that it?'

'Skelton and his wife were the start of it,' Devlin said. They were unformed thoughts turned to words, but he saw no need now to hold them back.

'Harrap's place?' Duggan said. 'You should see it now.'

'I did.'

'Two hundred years, more, and then that.' He held out his hand and drew it across the space between them.

He seemed suddenly much closer to Devlin.

'What, making you nervous, am I?'

Devlin took a step back from the man.

'Gun like that,' Duggan said, 'you'd need to be further back still to get the best spread.'

'And you think I'd miss from this distance?'

'You won't miss because you're not going to fire the thing.'

When Devlin glanced at the farmhouse, the doorway was empty.

'Same company made me an offer for this place,' Duggan said. 'They're buying up land left, right and centre.'

'And?'

'And I'm giving the offer some serious thought. Half the land's back under water again. This new company, they've got drainage equipment and machinery the likes of which this county's never seen.' He nodded at the house. 'He's not too happy, but she's keen enough. Already started looking for somewhere new. Farming's turning into something of a mug's game, you ask me. I'll get myself a proper garage, yard, set myself up properly. Always money in scrap.'

'Is that why you're letting the McGuires off?' Devlin said.

'What makes you think that? Just because I've likely had a windfall? The McGuires know exactly where they stand, and they know exactly what they've still got coming to them from this particular direction.'

It had grown much darker in the time they'd been standing there. Darker and colder.

Neither man spoke for a moment. Duggan swung his arms across his chest and blew out plumes of cold air.

'I think we're just about finished here,' he said. He nodded to the gun. 'Your best plan now, boy, would be to give that thing to me and then turn around and vanish back into that darkness you've started to favour. Give the gun to me and I'll make sure Skelton gets it back. I could also tell him I'd given you what you deserved on his behalf. Be one less thing for you to have to worry about, at least.'

'And why would you do that?'

'The goodness of my heart? Besides, all these others looking out for you and then doing what they're likely to do – it makes things messy. I like things done nice and tidy, you know me, one thing at a time. Who knows, perhaps Skelton and his wife have managed to finally gather up all those tiny scattered pieces of paper and bits of shattered glass and fitted them all back together again until they're good as new. Granted, it's not very likely, but it would be something.'

Devlin wondered why he was saying all this.

'Like that, would you – retracing all those steps and making everything good again?' Duggan said. 'I bet you would.'

'None of this—' Devlin began to say.

'I'm still talking,' Duggan shouted at him. '"None of this" what? Oh, don't tell me – none of this was supposed to happen? Well, that's life, boy. All of this *did* happen, and most of it happened because you – *you*, nobody else – made it happen. Anything you got coming to you now, you brought it all on yourself.'

Devlin took several more steps away from Duggan.

'Where you going?' Duggan said, and even before he'd finished saying this, he ran several paces to one side and then threw himself to the ground beside the parked lorry, shouting something Devlin couldn't make out. After that there was an explosion in the darkness somewhere close to the house and Devlin immediately felt the sudden sting of pellets against his face and arm.

'Again,' he heard Duggan cry out from under the lorry.

A second explosion sounded, and this time Devlin saw the

cone of bright light and cloud of smoke produced by the gun. There was no further stinging, but he could feel the blood already flowing over his forehead and cheeks and chin where the pellets from the first shot had struck him.

Instinctively, he turned and fired towards the house. There was nothing to see there except the outline of the building in the darkness, the blocks of light at its windows and doorway – nothing to aim at, and no response to his shot to let him know if he had hit anyone.

He ran away from the house into the surrounding night, stopping briefly beside the scattered ropes and tarpaulins to fire again at the ground where he imagined Duggan now lay. He heard Duggan call out and then go on shouting after him as he ran out of the yard and into the surrounding fields. He felt the blood on his face and in his eyes and tasted it on his lips, blinking wildly and wiping his mouth on his sleeve as he ran stumbling over the wet, uneven ground.

41

HE TWISTED HIS NECK AND PINCHED HIS CHEEK INTO THE small pockmarked mirror. He counted eleven spots of rising blood, another seven on his hand and forearm. Prodding each red bead, he felt where the pellets remained beneath his skin. Those which had struck his hand and arm had penetrated the flesh enough to draw blood, but had not lodged. On his cheek and neck, eight of the lead balls remained, and nowhere had the deeply coloured blood yet stopped flowing. He squeezed at those pellets which felt closest to the surface, but none of them appeared and he succeeded only in tearing the flesh further and causing the blood to flow faster and to smear across his skin. He cursed Duggan with every fresh stab of pain.

Having returned only briefly to the prefab, he was now in a caravan at the edge of one of the camps in which he had worked with the McGuires during the autumn. He had hurriedly gathered his few belongings and left the place before Duggan showed up there. The journey to the empty holiday camp had taken him almost two hours through the same sodden darkness. He had stopped frequently to wipe his bleeding face and arm, but knew instinctively that the wisest course of action now was to get beyond Duggan's reach.

Apart from a solitary watchman at the site entrance a quarter of a mile away, the camp was deserted. The storms of the past few weeks had finally put an end to all the repair and maintenance work. He remembered the caravan from when he'd worked there – close to the perimeter mesh fence and with a broken lock. The camp owners had used it as a makeshift store and canteen for the out-of-season labourers.

The mirror had been on the door of a cabinet in the cramped toilet. He'd pulled the door off its feeble hinges and propped it close to the basin's single cold tap. He doused his face with water, numbing it and diluting the blood which still flowed from most of his wounds. One of the holes was on the side of his nose, another close to his lips, and a third less than an inch from the corner of his eye. He saw for the first time how close he had come to being blinded.

He watched the blood drip into the basin. As he managed to stem one flow, another reappeared because of the pressure from his clumsy prodding fingers. He wondered why nothing from the second barrel had struck him. It was a small consolation. And he wondered too if what Duggan had said was true and the man had known all along where he'd been and what was happening to him.

Beyond the perimeter fence lay a wide verge and then the grass-topped dunes. Beyond these lay only the broad open space of the beach, the flats and the distant sea. He could hear the tide and the wind from where he stood in the caravan. He could see the lines of distant foam breaking on the shore, phosphorescent in the darkness.

One of the pellets in his cheek was deeper than the others, perhaps half an inch into his flesh, and this bled the most and caused him the most pain as he tried unsuccessfully to work it to the surface. When he was a boy he'd broken a tooth on the tiniest grain of metal lodged in a pigeon his father had brought home. He cut into his flesh now using the smallest blade on his pen-knife, and after ten more minutes of painful probing, dousing the wound with Skelton's whisky and biting hard on a piece of cloth, he finally heard the pellet fall into the sink, where it lay barely visible against the blood on the stained surface of the bowl. Most of the other pieces of shot, he knew, would work their own way to the surface over the coming weeks.

After an hour, by which time he had drunk what remained of the whisky, most of the lesser wounds had finally stopped bleeding.

There was no lighting in the caravan, no heating, and he was careful not to make any noise. He might have been a good dis-tance from the entrance, but the smallest sound carried in that empty place. Devlin guessed that the watchman stayed where he was on such nights. The light from the man's room lay in a strip across the driveway, and Devlin could hear the man's radio when-ever he opened his door to look out into the darkness.

Only the torn and gouged flesh of his cheek refused to stop bleeding and he was forced to pack it with a piece of torn curtain and then to hold this in place with a strip of the same material fastened around his head, clamping his mouth shut. He looked at himself in the mirror and saw that he looked comical and ridicu-lous in equal measure. He doubted if Duggan would see it like that. The problem now, he knew, would be staying out of the man's sight until the bleeding had finally stopped and his wounds had started to heal. Wherever he went and however he now appeared, Duggan would be looking for him, and coming closer all the time, his vicious intent honed and sharpened even fur-ther by everything that had just happened.

42

'HE CAN STAY WHERE HE IS.'

Devlin tried to push the door open and force himself past Morris. He called to his sister, who stood a few yards behind her husband in the dark hallway of their home.

'You're nothing but trouble,' the man hissed at Devlin. 'I told her you'd turn up here. And I told her what kind of reception you'd get when you did, when you were finally desperate enough to show your face.'

It was again night, four days after he'd been shot, and during that time he'd eaten only a loaf of stale bread he'd found in the bins behind the camp entrance.

He'd walked all the way, through the darkness and the sleet, having waited until the early dusk to start his journey. It was almost midnight by the time he'd arrived and shouted for his sister to come down to him.

Morris made no attempt to stop Devlin once he was inside and Devlin went immediately into the parlour, where he took off his coat and then carefully unwound the scarf wrapped around most of his face. The wounds had started to heal during those four days, but both the deeper gouge on his cheek and the hole at the side of his mouth had continued to swell and to ache. There was still occasional bleeding from both wounds, diluted now by smears of yellow pus. Devlin tried hard to convince himself that it was how all wounds healed and that soon there would be nothing left to see.

The marks on his arm and hand had already started to scab over and caused him almost no pain now. But the pain in his mouth was as bad as any toothache he had ever suffered and he wondered if the pellet was still deep and undetectable in his jaw somewhere. Sometimes he was able to jab his mouth and feel nothing whatsoever, and at other times he cried out with the unexpected pain of the slightest touch.

His sister was the first to see him like this. 'Dear God,' she said, and held her hands to her face. 'What's happened to you?'

'An accident,' Devlin said.

'We *know* what's happened to him,' Morris said, coming to stand beside her. He wore a dressing gown over his pyjamas and thick socks inside his slippers. He went briefly into the kitchen and returned with a rolled newspaper that he slapped hard into Devlin's chest. It was what men in films did. Perhaps it was the same on the television set which now stood in the parlour in its glossy wooden cabinet.

The three of them stood for a moment and watched as the paper fell to the floor.

Morris picked it up and gave it to Devlin. 'Read it,' he said.

Devlin unrolled the paper and read the headlines. An accident with a shotgun had left a well-known local businessman wounded in the foot and leg following a foiled armed robbery at the man's house. The businessman's wife was the hero of the hour, having come to the rescue of both her husband and his ailing, terrified father, a man of over seventy and another well-known local character, scaring off the would-be thief by discharging a gun into the air.

'There's even a description,' Morris said, pulling the paper from Devlin's hands. 'But why don't you just look straight in the mirror instead?'

Involuntarily, Devlin lifted his eyes to the mirror hanging on its chain above the mantel.

'There are some long words in the report, but even you should be able to get the gist of it,' Morris said. 'Besides – Ray Duggan? You went back there with a gun and threatened Ray *Duggan*?'

'He won't—' Devlin began to say.

'He won't what? The police have already been here looking for you. They came the morning after, in full view of everybody. I told them that neither of us had seen you for years. They told us what to do when you finally showed up. According to them, you had nowhere else to go.' He looked hard at Devlin's face, at the swollen wounds. 'They didn't say anything about all this.'

'The paper said Duggan's wife fired into the air to give you fair warning,' Ellen said.

'And *she* said that you ran faster than a rabbit at that first shot,' Morris added.

'She fired twice,' Devlin said, turning away from the mirror. 'And she fired *at* me. And she fired first.'

'If you say so,' Morris said.

Devlin looked at his sister. 'What else did you tell them?' It was clear to him that she had said nothing to her husband about his recent visits. He let her know by his glance that he would reveal nothing now.

'What did we tell them?' Morris said. 'It was the police. What do you think we told them? The truth, that's what we told them. It might be an alien concept to people like you, but most of us still know how to do the right and proper thing when called upon.'

Devlin read the rest of the article. 'It doesn't mention me by name,' he said.

'Of course it doesn't. But that doesn't mean that Duggan won't have told them exactly who it was. Besides, how long do you think it would have taken for them to work it out for themselves?'

'It could be anyone,' Devlin said.

Morris shook his head. 'What did I tell you?' he said to his wife. 'He hasn't got the first idea. He's still living in his own little fantasy world; has been ever since he was drummed out of the army and we were all expected to treat him like the homecoming hero. I've been telling you this for years. And now this.'

'I know,' Ellen said. She led Devlin into the kitchen and told him to sit at the table. She helped him off with his coat. 'Who's Harold Edwards?' she said, reading the label in the collar.

'Just a mate,' Devlin said. The watchman at the camp.

'Mate?' Morris said. 'What mate?'

Ellen brought a bowl of warm water to the table and started to examine his wounds. She unrolled a length of lint and took several small bottles from a cabinet, shaking these vigorously as she arranged them on the table.

'What do you think you're doing?' Morris asked her.

'What does it look like?'

'It looks to me like you're aiding and abetting a wanted criminal – I believe that's the phrase – *that's* what it looks like.'

'No, I'm just doing what anybody decent would do.' She opened and sniffed each of the bottles.

'And that's what you'll be telling the court, is it?' Morris went to the window, lifted the curtain and looked out. 'It's the middle of the night,' he said. 'Somebody's bound to see that the lights are on.'

'So?' Ellen said.

Devlin flinched at the first of his sister's dabs. She picked away the dirty scabs and washed the raw flesh beneath. There was surprisingly little fresh bleeding as she did all this.

'I know what I'm doing,' she told him, and he believed her and was grateful both for what she did and for her faith in him.

'They'll know it was you, us,' Morris said. '*Me* – they'll think *I* was a part of it all.' He let the curtain fall and then tugged at its sides to ensure that no light showed.

'I can clean him up and *then* he can go to the police,' Ellen said, surprising both men.

'I can't,' Devlin said.

'Yes you can,' she said. 'You can tell them that Duggan's wife fired first. You can tell them that the robbery story was made up by Duggan. Tell them everything that's happened between the two of you. They'll listen to you. Surely they must know Ray Duggan for what he is and not what the paper makes him out to be.'

It made a kind of sense to Devlin, but he still knew that what she was suggesting was beyond him, that everything would continue to work in Duggan's favour.

'It'll be his word against the woman's,' Morris said. 'And Duggan's and the old man's. We'd all get dragged into things. You, me, him, everybody.'

'He's right,' Devlin told his sister.

'He always is,' she said quietly, firmly, surprisingly, turning his face to dab at the swelling beside his mouth.

Morris, who had been about to say something else, fell silent at the remark.

'I can say I did all this myself,' Devlin said. 'There must be first-aid kits all over the camp, stands to reason.'

He started to consider these new possibilities.

Ellen told Morris to put the kettle on and to make them all a drink. She told him to make Devlin something to eat.

'So I'm his skivvy now, am I?' Morris said.

'No, you're just another one of those decent human beings doing something for his fellow man.'

There was no argument to this, and Morris began to gather together food from their cupboard. He put this on the table in front of Devlin and Devlin ate everything he was given.

When he'd finished, his sister said, 'You need to see a proper doctor. It looks to me as though the wounds on your cheek and your mouth are infected. They'll only get worse. You need that new miracle drug they have these days.'

'Antibiotics,' Morris said.

After that, the three of them sat in silence for several minutes.

Then Ellen said to Devlin, 'Morris told the police he'd call them the minute you showed up. They told him that if we could keep you here, that would be for the best. Or if not, then to let them know before you'd gone too far. They said it was all for your own good.'

'It always is,' Devlin said.

'They said they didn't know how long it would be before your name appeared in the paper.'

'What difference would that make?'

'He's right,' Morris said. 'They probably already know everything there is to know about what happened. All he's doing now – all this – is getting us involved.'

'Have you got a telephone, then?' Devlin said.

'One day,' Morris said. 'Meanwhile, there's one at the road's end. It's half a mile. I can—' He stopped talking.

'What is it?' Ellen said.

'The gun,' Morris said.

'What about it?' Devlin said.

'For all we know, he could have brought it with him,' Morris said, 'hidden it somewhere close by.'

'Have you?' Ellen asked Devlin.

'It's miles away,' Devlin said. 'Miles.'

It was outside, pushed into a bundle of garden canes beside the outhouse. For the first time in his life, Devlin felt guilty for lying to his sister.

'The wound by your mouth is infected on both sides,' Ellen said. 'Inside and out. Your gum's gone black. It could be a lot worse than you think.'

Devlin had tried to convince himself that the pain in his mouth was growing more bearable each day.

The police would already have alerted the local hospitals and doctors' surgeries. Wherever he went, the outcome would be the same.

Morris finally left them and returned to the parlour, where he sat alone in the dim light.

Ellen leaned closer to Devlin. She started to gather up the bottles. 'A man called Sullivan was here,' she whispered to him.

'Sullivan? What did he want?' What did Sullivan have to do with any of this?

'He said you'd worked together and that he owed you a favour.' She glanced at the open door of the parlour.

'And?'

'He told me to let you know that the boy – he said you'd know who I was talking about – was blaming you for everything.

He said the police had already been to see the gypsies and that they were backing this boy up and saying that they hadn't even known he'd been to see you. Do you know what I'm talking about?'

Devlin nodded.

'He told me to wish you good luck with it all, said he was finally leaving and that if he never saw you again then it would be too soon. He was only here for a minute, didn't even come in.'

Morris returned to them and asked them what they were whispering about.

'You,' Devlin said. 'But then again, you must get that a lot, people whispering behind your back. You're that kind of man.'

'Which makes you what?' Morris said, pleased with the remark. 'She's right about you needing to see a doctor. Or perhaps the next thing we'll hear is that some local surgery or other has been broken into and medicines stolen.'

'That was my next move,' Devlin said, attempting to smile.

'It says in the paper that you even stole the gun. Ray Duggan said he recognized it and that he knew the man who'd had it taken. The police said they were looking into it.'

'They look into a lot of things,' Devlin said. Besides, who recognized guns when they were pointed at you from ten feet away in the dark?

'A man I know,' Morris went on, 'said Duggan had got a bandaged foot and a bit of a limp, so you must have hit him.'

'Probably twisted his ankle when he fell and tried to crawl away,' Devlin said.

'It's not what he'll be telling the police, or what his wife and father will be confirming,' Morris said.

'He's right,' Ellen said. 'You should turn yourself in before all this gets even more out of hand. It might just be your word against Duggan's, but you're still the one who's been wounded. It's got to count for something in the eyes of the law, surely?'

'Unless Duggan presses charges of attempted murder,' Morris said. He shrugged. 'I'm only saying.'

'Another twenty years and I could probably get to like you,' Devlin said.

'Fair enough,' Morris said.

'So what *will* you do?' Devlin said.

Ellen held his arm for a moment. 'In the paper, they're telling people to be vigilant, to keep an eye out for you. They make you sound like something you're not.'

'It's how they work,' Devlin said.

'They talk about your "known haunts".'

'Meaning here,' Morris said. 'Us.'

'"No fixed abode" it said,' Ellen said. 'That never sounds good. They use the word "armed" three times, warning people not to approach you.'

'Put like that, half the men in this county are armed,' Devlin said. He wondered how swiftly he had become this other man, how swiftly and how completely and how unknowingly.

'Perhaps if you let Morris call them – not now, necessarily, but first thing in the morning – then we could arrange something,' Ellen said. 'I could even go with you, help you explain things.'

Devlin shook his head at the words. 'And that's what you think would happen, is it, that we'd all sit down over a cup of tea and sort things out?'

'We could try,' Ellen said.

'The best thing now,' Devlin said, 'is for me to go and for you two to deny ever having seen me. Or you could tell the police that I came, but that you wouldn't let me in. I'll go over Sutton way and break the surgery window there, tell them I cleaned my-self up.'

'They won't believe you,' Morris said.

Devlin could think of no answer.

For the next hour, Ellen dried the stolen coat in front of the low fire, its embers stoked and fed to give some warmth in the winter night. Then she made them all more tea and wrapped what-ever food remained for Devlin to take with him when he went.

An hour after that, three before the late dawn, Devlin stood at the door ready to leave.

'Where will you go?' his sister asked him.

Devlin shook his head.

'We'll tell the police you were here,' Morris said, 'but that we refused to let you in.' He made the words sound almost like an act of kindness.

'And if they don't believe you?' Devlin said.

'We'll *make* them believe us,' Ellen said. She ran her hand over Devlin's arm. 'I *know* you're not the way they make you sound in the papers.'

And again it seemed like an act of almost unbearable kind-ness to Devlin.

He left them a few minutes later, walking away from the house briefly before doubling back to the outhouse to retrieve the shotgun.

Later, as he neared the empty holiday camp in the already brightening dawn, he started to wonder about all the half-chances and vague opportunities that had just been revealed or suggested to him, and which had then, one by one, all been just as swiftly and as completely taken away from him.

43

ANOTHER HARD FROST COVERED THE WINTER COMPOUND and its caravans and trailers and dismantled rides. A solitary light shone above the entrance to the distant stables.

Devlin poured the petrol beneath the trailer and then splashed what remained against its sides. The can was heavy and difficult to hold with his one good hand. He went in a full circle around the trailer, throwing the liquid as high up its sides as he could manage. When the can was almost empty he dropped it beneath the axle.

He waited for a moment, looking around him. He had gone first to Maria's caravan and had gently tried the door. It was locked. All the curtains were drawn. The McGuires' lorry sat where it was usually parked at the compound entrance.

He had already gathered a ball of dry straw beside the trailer steps. He went to this and struck a match, which was instantly extinguished in the light wind. He crouched closer to the straw and struck another. This time the match flared and he dropped it into the waiting fuel. It smoked for a moment and then the straw caught light, erupting close to Devlin's hands and causing him to move quickly back from it. He picked up the ball of burning straw and carried it to where he had splashed the petrol, blazing stems falling and floating behind him. He threw the straw close to the can. For a moment there was nothing, and then the blue vaporous flames appeared everywhere at once, liquid across the hard ground and starting to catch against the lower edge of the trailer, where the blue turned to yellow, took further hold and started to burn. The air felt suddenly warm and he backed away from the flames.

The trailer burned. A crackling sound gave way to a succession of small explosions. And then he heard noises from inside, the panicked shouts of both brothers.

Devlin retreated further, hiding himself beside the shuttered ride where Egan had been found. He remained mesmerized by the spreading flames, watching as they rose above the roof of the trailer, peeling the paintwork from its sides and burning in lines along its wooden trim. Sparks erupted from the rear of the structure and then a pane of glass exploded. The next moment the door was pushed open and both Patrick and Colm ran outside shouting. Patrick appeared to have flames on one of his arms, but he quickly rubbed these out. Both men were dressed but barefoot and they ran back and forth across the frozen ground in front of their blazing home.

Devlin went on watching.

A light appeared in Maria's trailer and she too came outside. Beyond, along the far boundary of the field, others emerged to see what was happening.

Maria went to her brothers and stood beside them.

There was nothing anyone could do now, except stay clear of the rapidly spreading flames and watch the trailer burn.

It seemed to Devlin that the inside caught fire even faster than those parts on to which he had poured the petrol, and that every surface and fitting and piece of furniture had turned yellow in an instant. Dark smoke poured out of the doorway and broken window. A second window shattered, causing Maria and her brothers to cover their faces. People from the other caravans and trailers came closer.

Devlin could hear the brothers shouting at each other.

People tried to pull them away from the blaze, but both men resisted.

Only Maria, Devlin saw, left the fire and walked to the centre of the compound. She stood there and looked all around her. It stood to reason that whoever had started the fire could not be far away, a fact that seemed not to have occurred to either Patrick or Colm. There was a sharp smell of petrol in the night air and the empty can still lay in view beneath the axle.

A louder explosion sounded and one of the gas canisters attached to the trailer flew a few feet into the air before landing close to Patrick and Colm. Seeing this, and knowing a second canister was still in place, the brothers finally moved further from the flames. And then they too started to look all around them, making short barefoot dashes into the darkness as though they might flush Devlin from his hiding place and then set off in pursuit of him.

But no one came close to him where he stood and watched all this.

Light from the flames spread across the open ground and played on the sides of other trailers. A solitary man threw buckets of water into the flames from a nearby tank, until he saw the futility of this and stopped.

The second gas canister exploded and the rear of the trailer seemed to crumple. Flames rose into the night air higher than before, and as these swiftly fell and faded the whole structure collapsed, deflated almost, like a slowly punctured balloon. The sides fell inwards and then the floor fell away to the ground. Every new draught formed new flames and every collapse fanned the fire and smoke in new directions.

After ten minutes of burning, only the thin metal outline of the trailer remained, and the flames now ran only along those pieces where glue and pitch still burned fiercely. The interior of the structure was lost completely, every shape and outline blackening and then disintegrating to dust and ashes.

A few minutes more and the blaze finally lost its force, the flames subsiding into glowing mounds, sparking and smoking occasionally but with nothing of the power and energy of only a few minutes earlier.

Knowing now that only this single trailer was destroyed and that the fire could not spread, some of the night's urgency was lost. People went back to their own homes. Several men went to check on the horses at the rear of the compound.

A small group of women came closer to where Devlin stood, but no one saw him there and they were soon beyond his hearing.

Maria went back to her brothers and the three of them walked together to her caravan. Devlin expected one or other of the men to turn and shout that they knew who had done this and that they would find him soon enough. But neither man did this.

Besides, the thought only then occurred to him, they probably considered Duggan a more likely culprit than himself, and this cheered him briefly.

He stayed where he was for a further ten minutes, watching the remains of the all-consuming blaze finally subside and die. And when there was nothing left to watch, he left his hiding place and went back through the hedge on to the open land beyond. He retrieved his gun and followed the line of the old bank in the direction of the sea.

He climbed a plank bridge and looked back at the distant compound before dropping below all sight of the trailers and rides. He imagined the smouldering wreckage and its disturbed embers rising and scattering occasionally in the night air.

Ahead of him, Devlin saw the first bright stripe of the rising winter sun across the eastern horizon, and it seemed to him almost a portent: both an ending and a new beginning in one; a sign, perhaps, of better things to come.

Only a minute later the rising sun was lost to the falling cloud, but the loss went unnoticed by Devlin, who kept his head down and who now walked without looking.

44

THE FIRST DEVLIN KNEW WAS THE VAGUE PULSE OF BLUE light on the wall beside him. He'd had another sleepless night and had slept only intermittently and lightly through the previous day, waking at every sound. It was mid afternoon and the daylight was already failing.

He went to the window and looked out. Between the rows of caravans he saw the police car parked at the camp office. Two constables stood beside it, talking to the watchman. Devlin wanted to laugh at the idea of a man calling the police over a missing coat.

Both constables carried torches, which they occasionally shone towards the nearby caravans. A faint cloud of frosted air quickly formed above the three men.

And then the watchman pointed directly to where Devlin sat watching them and the three men started walking, disappearing and then reappearing amid the lines and rows of caravans.

Devlin grabbed the coat, the gun and the holdall containing his few other belongings, and then, waiting until all three men were again briefly out of sight, he left the caravan and stood behind it. His instinct was to get away from it, but he knew that if he left his hiding place there was a good chance that one of the men would see him as he crossed the open ground. The three of them had now moved further apart and were coming towards him separately.

Dropping what he carried, Devlin pushed the bag and gun beneath the caravan and then crawled into the space himself, pulling behind him the empty gas canisters and water drum. It was dark at the centre of the restricted space, but he knew that a torch shone there would reveal him to any searcher, and that when that happened he would be trapped. He might somehow evade a single man, but not three men already on their feet and waiting for him to run like a rabbit from a hole.

He watched his own breath cloud in the cold air and covered his mouth.

He heard the voices of the men as they came closer and again joined company.

An elongated circle of yellow light moved jerkily across the grass and came to rest beneath the caravan door.

Someone knocked, metal on metal, and the watchman shouted uncertainly that he knew someone was in the van.

'Not very likely,' one of the constables said.

Devlin watched a pair of booted feet walk around the van. The man stood on his toes to look in at each of the windows.

'When did you last see him?'

'There was definitely somebody here three days ago. My coat was stolen the day after. I've been freezing ever since.'

'Let's just say it went missing, shall we?' the second constable said.

Devlin heard the man's scepticism in every word.

'*You* say what you want,' the watchman said angrily.

'All I'm saying is that I think we ought to consider one thing at a time. Sir.'

'It's the only one I've got. I was demobbed in that coat.'

'I'm sure.'

Devlin heard one of the men go into the van and walk its full length. He felt the tremors above him. He felt the whole surface sway slightly.

'Nothing,' the man said, going back outside. 'It looks as though *someone*'s been there. Might be him, might not be. We get reports like this every closed season.'

'Whoever it was,' the watchman said, 'I didn't recognize him.' The man, perhaps fearing for his poorly paid job, was now watching his words.

'And the camp's been empty for the past month?'

'At least that. The winter came early. Like I said, the van was used last by some of the contractors when they were working here.'

'And not since?'

'Not until I saw him three days ago.' Then something occurred to the watchman. 'You're only here on account of that man you're looking for,' he said. 'This has got nothing to do with my coat.'

'Everything is of interest, sir.'

'But some things are more interesting than others, is that it?'

'He's a dangerous man,' one of the constables said.

Beneath the van, Devlin held his breath for a few seconds.

'Where do you want me to start?' the other constable said. 'So far we've got allegations of trespass, non-payment of rent, robbery, aggravated assault using a firearm, wounding, illegal possession of said firearm, housebreaking, wilful destruction and possibly arson with intent to endanger life on the Charge List. How much more do you want? So, as you can see, from where we're standing a stolen coat isn't too high on the agenda where our priorities are concerned. Oh, and did I mention the aiding and abetting of an escaped prisoner from the North Sea Camp? I'm telling you, with this one, the longer you look, the more you find.'

'But, presumably,' the watchman said hesitantly, 'when you do finally catch up with him, you'll find my coat at the same time?'

Neither man answered him.

'Sounds as though he's been a busy boy,' the watchman said.

'We're still receiving reports of this, that and the other from every two-man police house between here and Spalding.'

'So why didn't you do your job properly and pick him up sooner? He sounds a regular little one-man crime spree.'

'Because sometimes these things just never add up,' the constable said. 'It's only when somebody starts making all the right connections that we actually get somebody in our sights. You can rest assured that now we know who we're looking for, he'll be in the bag fast enough.'

'And is he?' the watchman said.

'Is he what?'

'In your sights? It seems to me that all you're doing here is running around in the dark.'

The two constables laughed awkwardly. 'You sound like our Chief Super,' one of them said. '*He* wanted to know why Jimmy Devlin hadn't been arrested months ago.'

'The point now,' the other man said, 'and especially with all this firearm and arson stuff, is that everything gets pushed up a notch.'

'So you're going to do nothing whatsoever about my coat, then?' the watchman said.

'We can add it to our list of reported thefts, if that makes you feel any better. It might take some time. This character seems to have had his fingers in everything going. A list of known associates as long as your arm.'

Devlin listened intently to everything that was said. He saw what a neat, clear and well-defined picture all these others had drawn of him.

'Believe me, we'll be doing a lot of people a lot of favours when we catch up with this one.'

'I don't suppose there's any reward,' the watchman said.

Both constables laughed again at the question.

'Not that we know of. But we'll keep you informed.'

Devlin heard the change in all the men's voices.

Beside him, the beam of light moved along the skirt of the caravan and then disappeared.

'Ask me, whoever it was, he's long gone,' the watchman said.

Devlin heard the caravan door being closed above him.

'By rights, I should lock that,' the watchman said.

'Have you got the key?'

'Somewhere. Not on me. I'll come back.'

'We'd appreciate you letting us know if whoever it is turns up again.'

'And we strongly advise against trying to come the hero and do anything by yourself. Leave it to the professionals.'

'Who's that, then?' the watchman said. 'You pair?'

'I mean it. Where this character's concerned, things might be about to take a very drastic turn for the worse any day now.'

'What's that supposed to mean?'

Devlin turned his head to better hear what was said.

'The other man he shot,' the constable said. 'Not shot, exactly.'

What other man?

'Duggan Senior. Our boy Devlin fired at the house, at Mrs Duggan, I suppose. The old man was in the room behind her. He wasn't actually hit, not as such, but he had a bit of a turn at everything that was happening. Weak ticker, by all accounts. The ambulance boys settled him after they'd looked at Ray Duggan and he seemed fine. But then he had another turn early the next morning. Heart attack, they reckon. His second. If he dies, we'll probably have a murder charge to add to that list. And when that happens, then the county and the national boys will get involved and the rest of us here will be relegated to swinging sticks through the long grass.'

'Again,' the other man added sourly.

Devlin struggled to take in all that was being said.

'The old boy's in Boston hospital. We're keeping an eye on things.'

There had been nothing of this in the newspaper article.

The voices grew fainter as the men finally started walking away.

Devlin crawled to the edge of the space and watched them as they went, occasionally pointing their torches into other caravans, but with no real sense of purpose. The pulsing blue light of their car still shone in the distance.

Waiting until the tiny figures arrived at the camp entrance, Devlin pulled himself out of the low space and squatted on the grass to watch them. Then he took a circuitous route through the caravans until he was again close to them. He raised the unloaded gun and sighted the watchman along its barrel before lowering it back to his feet. He tried to hear what else was being said, but this was impossible. One or other of the men laughed occasionally.

After a few more minutes, during which the constables went into the small office, the two men emerged, got into their car and drove away.

The watchman came back out and watched them go. He stood with his arms wrapped across his chest, shivering.

Devlin wondered if everything that had been said about Duggan's father was true, or if the constables were exaggerating to make everything sound worse than it was to the watchman. He knew this was unlikely.

And then he wondered what would happen if he raised the gun again and walked out of the darkness towards where the coatless man stood shivering and shouted to him that he was the man they were all looking for, and told him to drop to his knees and start saying his prayers.

45

DUGGAN'S FATHER DIED THREE DAYS LATER.

Devlin saw the headline on the hoarding outside the small shop at the Surfleet Bank close by the Welland. He'd spent the past two nights in the abandoned boathouse where he and the McGuires had hidden Duggan's haul. It was at least half a mile from the nearest inhabited building, a farm on the Drove road.

He'd gone to the shop for provisions. He put on an accent and told the girl who served him that he was from Suffolk, working at the nearby brickworks. She paid him hardly any interest, adding up what he'd bought and holding out her hand for his money.

Back at the boathouse, he read the front-page article and saw that he was mentioned by name three times. The police were still considering their response to the old man's death. Duggan himself was demanding action; his wife was still too distressed by everything that had happened to make any comment. Everything possible was being done, the article said, to bring the perpetrator of the robbery and shooting to justice.

There was a photograph of Duggan's father as a much younger man – apparently he'd won trophies and rosettes at various agricultural shows; hadn't they all? – alongside a drawing of a man who was supposed to be Devlin. The Assistant Chief Constable was convinced that it was now only a matter of time before he was apprehended and charged. This time the word 'armed' was used five times. The Assistant Chief Constable said that anyone knowing of Devlin's whereabouts should report this immediately to the police. Under no circumstances should anyone attempt to approach or tackle him themselves.

Devlin saw again how he continued turning from one thing into another in the words. He saw how his last remaining choices and options had disappeared in the article's changing shades and inferences. Dangerous – *armed* – no true threat to ordinary members of the public, but dangerous. What were people supposed to think? What was *he* supposed to think? Perhaps this was how things always worked. Devlin's sister – they called her 'Helen' – said she was appealing to her brother's better nature and that he should hand himself in so that everything might now be sorted out. The boy she knew wouldn't harm a fly. She couldn't believe half of what was being said of him. Only half? Every sentence sent another chill through Devlin. He searched for whatever Morris might have added, but there was nothing.

Soon, he guessed, others would be looking for him – not like the half-hearted search at the holiday camp – and the last of all those uncertainties would be gone for good.

Possible geriatric heart failure brought on by the shock of recent events.

Everywhere he looked there were these victims – *his* victims, supposedly – and everywhere he looked there were those same fingers pointing directly at him.

The wound at the side of his mouth had started to heal, but the swelling on his cheek remained painful and continued to ooze. He wiped at this, but it was difficult to keep the sore clean. He wondered if the infection had started to spread – both up towards his eye and deeper into his mouth. His gums close to the wound throbbed occasionally and both his gums and teeth were sore to the touch. He was careful to chew on the other side of his mouth.

He washed in drums of collected rainwater. He slept on wooden pallets with pieces of old sail for blankets. When he went out he took the gun with him, but was careful to hide it whenever anyone appeared, however distant. He walked for miles in the half-light, never visiting the same place twice. There were times when he wondered if he might freeze to death in the night, or if not to death, exactly, then something close to it. He developed a sore chest and a painful cough. His clothes felt loose on him and he was forced to punch a new hole and then a second in his belt.

It seemed to Devlin that he was a changed man – not that he was doing this to himself voluntarily, willingly, but as though an irresistible outside force were working on him. He was changed in his own understanding of himself, and now he was changing in his appearance. Perhaps it was a thing that happened sooner or later, for better or worse, in the lives of all men.

After two more days of this spartan existence, a man came to the boathouse, knocked heavily on its giant door and then waved a shotgun. He shouted that he knew Devlin was in there, that he'd informed the police and that they were already on their way.

Having heard the man's approach, Devlin was standing closer to the door than this stranger realized and was watching him through a gap in the planking.

The man pushed open the door and looked inside.

'I know this boathouse,' he shouted, as though this added weight to whatever he might be about to attempt. 'You're the man in the papers, I'm certain of that much.'

His voice came back in a broken echo. Birds flew unsettled in the high space of the corrugated roof.

From where he stood in the shadows, Devlin could see that the man was already starting to have his doubts. He swung the gun he held, but loosely.

Devlin's makeshift bed was at the far corner of the space, and, seeing this, the man came forwards into the shed.

'You should just come out now,' he shouted. 'Put your hands in the air and show yourself to me. I'm ex-military, so you needn't think I don't know how to use this thing.'

Devlin wanted to laugh at the words, but instead of laughing he started coughing uncontrollably, and, hearing him, the man swung towards him and pushed his gun out in front of him.

'I can see you,' he shouted. 'I know you're there.' Everything he said continued to betray his uncertainty. He looked hard into the half-light in which Devlin stood. 'Believe me, I don't want to hurt you. Just come out and we can get all this sorted. I know you're ex-forces yourself – Other Ranks. I can help you. You just need to give yourself up. For God's sake, man . . .'

Devlin took a silent step backwards, hiding himself even further from the man. He was finally out of sight behind a stack of empty crates, but was then betrayed again by another bout of coughing.

'You're not well,' the man shouted. 'Another hour and all this could be over. You need a medic to look at you.'

Devlin's coughing finally subsided. 'Put your gun down,' he shouted to the man, his voice dry and cracked.

The man was surprised by this. 'I've just told *you* to do that,' he said.

'And now I'm telling you.'

'Why should I? What's stopping me from just going back outside and securing the door and waiting for the police to arrive?'

'If they're even coming,' Devlin said, testing.

'My wife went to telephone for them. They'll have heard by now.'

He was probably telling the truth, but what neither of them knew was how quickly the police would arrive.

For an instant, Devlin considered doing what the man was telling him to do. Folding open and throwing down Skelton's gun and then walking out from where he hid with his hands in the air. It was how people surrendered. It was how things ended. He started coughing again, struggling to control his breathing.

'I'm going,' the man shouted. 'Like I said – I can bar the door from outside. There's no other way out. The slip door's been padlocked since last August.'

He started walking backwards to the door.

And seeing that any small opportunity that might still remain to him was about to be lost, Devlin stepped out of the shadows and revealed himself. He held his own gun at arm's length, raising the barrel.

'Throw it down,' the man shouted, suddenly confident.

'It's loaded,' Devlin said. 'I don't need to be throwing it anywhere.'

'*Put* it down, then,' the man said. 'Where I can see you. Nice and slowly.' He was warming to his role now.

Devlin took several more paces towards him, indicating a clear space on the shed floor midway between them.

'That's right – there,' the man said.

Devlin crouched, as though he were about to lay the gun on the ground, but then he started coughing again, holding a fist to his chest.

'That sounds nasty,' the man said. 'I'm still watching you. I know your sort.'

And at those words, Devlin let the barrel of the gun slide through his hands until he was grasping it at its tip and he swung the stock hard into the man's shins, causing him to half scream and half shout – as much in surprise as in pain – and to drop his own gun. He fell to one knee, and then his other leg gave way beneath him and he sprawled on the ground, feeling around him for where his gun had fallen.

Devlin quickly regained a proper grip on Skelton's gun and took a step closer so that he was able to stamp hard on the man's scrabbling fingers, causing him to cry out again.

'My "sort"?' Devlin shouted at him. '*My sort?*'

'I only meant—'

'I know what you meant.'

The man pulled his hand to his mouth and started sucking on it. With his free arm he tried to protect his head. He began pleading with Devlin not to shoot him.

'Why not?' Devlin said. 'It's what *my sort* do. Go on – beg me.'

'I am,' the man said. 'I'm begging you. I've got a wife and children. Two daughters. One of them's expecting her first child at Easter.'

'So what?' Devlin said. 'What does any of that have to do with me? Perhaps you should have thought about all that before you decided on this.'

The man was weeping now. 'Don't shoot me,' he said. 'Please, don't shoot. You could just go, leave. I'll tell them all this was an accident, my fault. I'll tell them I must have made a mistake about you even being here. They know me, I'm well known, they'll believe me. I'm talking about senior officers, magistrates.'

'What difference do you think any of that makes?' Devlin said. 'Perhaps you should just shut your mouth while you've still got the chance.'

'I only meant—'

'You stopped begging me,' Devlin said.

'What?'

'You stopped begging for your life. I'm a violent, vicious man, remember? All the papers say so.'

'I *am* begging you,' the man said. He clasped his hands together. 'Look, I'm begging you. I'm begging you with everything I say. I've got some money in my wallet – take it.'

'Because that's what my sort would do, is it? Rob a man who was already on his knees and begging for his life and *then* shoot him?'

The man unclasped his hands and pressed them to the ground. He started sobbing convulsively, and then he wet himself and the dark stain seeped quickly along the length of his trouser leg and pooled beneath him. He considered this for a moment and then resumed crying. Then he covered his head with both his arms and drew up his legs, kicking in the dirt and turning himself in a clumsy circle, as though he might yet somehow run away from everything that now so suddenly confronted him.

46

DEVLIN WOKE AND STRUGGLED TO HIS SENSES. A DRY FILM held his eyes closed and it was painful for him to open them. His lips, too, were stuck together and his tongue felt coarse and heavy in his mouth. He struggled to breathe and then to raise his arms. He imagined for a moment that he was being held down. Neither his arms nor legs possessed any strength. And above all else, the pain in the side of his face and mouth was now sharper than ever, pulsing through his whole head every few seconds.

His first thought was to wonder how he had slept with so much pain. He coughed, trying to clear his throat, but this only added to his agony.

He became aware of someone beside him in the dimly lit room. But which dimly lit room? There had been so many of them over the past few aimless, unsettled months.

'You need to take it steady,' a voice said.

Someone drew a blanket from his arms and he was finally able to raise one of them to his face. He pushed himself half upright, resting on his elbow. He held a hand to his cheek and then flinched and cried out at the slightest touch.

'You'll need to get that seen to.'

The man leaned closer to him. The voice was familiar. Devlin looked around him.

He was in the abandoned tin chapel.

'Getting your bearings at last?' It was Samuel, the old shepherd.

Devlin tried to speak, but only choked, and this, too, added to his pain.

Samuel held a hand to the back of his head and tilted an enamel cup to his lips.

Devlin drank, most of the water running down his chin. He pulled his other arm free and pushed the blanket and sacking which covered him to his waist. He motioned for more water and Samuel went to refill the cup from the drum by the altar.

This time Devlin was able to hold it himself and spill less of the cold liquid.

'I'm in the chapel,' he said.

'Where did you think? Ely cathedral?'

Devlin looked around him, trying to remember how he had come to be there.

'I put the gun over by the altar,' Samuel said. 'I took the cartridges out.'

'How long?' Devlin said.

'How long you been here?' Samuel shrugged. 'I found you here yesterday. It's been snowing hard again. I came to look at the sheep. The door was hanging open. I came in and found you on the floor. You were frozen. I covered you over the best I could. I tried to wake you. You were groaning in your sleep. You should go to hospital.'

Devlin shook his head and felt suddenly faint, dropping the cup and pressing his hand to the floor in an effort to steady himself. He felt as though he were going to be sick and then started to retch, producing nothing but a bitter watery bile and causing himself more pain.

'You were already sick,' Samuel said. 'Over there. You can still smell it, despite the cold. The snow's been coming in through the broken window.' He refilled the cup and held it again to Devlin's lips.

Eventually, Devlin felt able to push himself up into a sitting position. His nausea faded.

'You've got a bad infection, by the look of things,' Samuel said, holding a finger to Devlin's chin. He pulled his knapsack to him. 'I brought you something to clean it. And something to eat when you're up to it.'

'Who else knows?' Devlin said.

'That you're here? Nobody. Everybody knows *who* you are, though.' Samuel took a folded newspaper from his jacket and laid it beside the food.

Devlin started to remember. He remembered the story of the death of Duggan's father. He remembered the police at the holiday camp, and then the boathouse and the man who had confronted him there.

'Recognize him?' Samuel said, showing the man's face alongside Devlin's in the paper. 'He says you knocked him down while he was going about his business, robbed him and then attacked him with the gun. He says the last thing you did before leaving him was to break his shinbone with the gun. Says he was screaming for help for three hours. A woman on a passing boat heard him and went in to investigate. Your face was back on the front page the next morning.'

'So are people looking for me?'

Samuel laughed. 'Here, there and everywhere. Truth is,

321

they've been looking these past few weeks, but not like this. Not that it'll amount to much in this weather. Snow's drifted four foot deep across the marsh and most of the roads. It's stopped falling today, but there's already another gale forecast for tonight, an inshore shipping warning.'

Devlin considered all this. He looked at the altar and saw the gun propped against it.

'It wasn't like that – the boathouse,' he said.

'Hardly matters, I don't suppose,' Samuel said. 'There's always two sides to a story, and in my experience people usually choose right from the start which one they want to believe. The man in the shed said he pleaded with you to spare his life. He says he was certain you were going to kill him.'

'His wife had already gone for the police.'

'I doubt that. It says in there that they didn't show up until two hours after the woman on the boat. What does that tell you? He's in Boston hospital now. Same place they got the old man's body. *His* son's already complaining that they won't release it for burial until they've finished all their prodding and poking. There's talk of the man you hit walking with a limp for the rest of his life. It says in there he's supposed to be walking his daughter down the aisle in a few months.'

'And people will far prefer his story to mine?' Devlin said.

Samuel shrugged. 'They've already got a lot of other things to consider where you're concerned, I suppose.' He filled the cup again and gave it to Devlin. 'You do even half those things they're accusing you of?'

'One way or another,' Devlin said. A sharper jolt of pain than usual caused him to cry out and he was unable to go on speaking until this subsided. '*Have* you told anyone I'm here?' he said eventually.

'I already said – no. I didn't even say anything to my daughter when she started going on about how worried she was that I was coming out here alone, and in this weather. I told her it was my job. What else was I going to do? Besides, I'm an old man; look at me, what threat am I to anybody?'

Devlin almost smiled at the words. 'What did she say to that?'

'What could she say? She jumps at her own shadow, that one. A lot of them do these days.'

'I don't even remember coming here,' Devlin said. 'I remember the boathouse now, and the start of the snow perhaps, but nothing else.'

'Hardly matters,' Samuel said. He lit two cigarettes and gave one to Devlin. 'You were shot,' he said, looking more closely at the swellings, scars and wounds on Devlin's cheek and neck. Then he rose to his feet and went to the small altar, sitting beside it on one of the few remaining benches. 'Finally got the go-ahead to pull the place down,' he said. 'Eyesore, see? No call for places like this in the modern world. The congregation – eight of us by my reckoning, and that was two years past – can do its christenings and burials somewhere else. Been nothing like that here for at least fifteen years. My daughter says good riddance. Good riddance to me, more like.' He turned back to Devlin. 'What will you do?'

'I don't know.' When had there ever been a plan? 'Leave, I suppose. London, somewhere like that.'

'That place? They'll be looking for you, pick their spots.'

'I never killed the old man,' Devlin said. 'He died, that's all.'

'And that's what you'll tell them, is it?'

'Tell who?'

'The police, the court.'

'You think they'll listen?' Devlin started to cough, holding a hand over his mouth, the other pressed hard to his chest.

Samuel waited. 'You're in a bad way,' he said, his voice low. 'How on Earth did you come to this?'

'Things just—' It was as much as Devlin could manage.

'Seems to me,' Samuel said, 'that half the trouble with this world is that nobody ever really knows where one thing ends and another begins, not really. It's just one thing after another, for-ever crowding in on you. It confuses people, gives them no chance to stand still and take stock, makes them lose their bear-ings. I sometimes wonder—' He stopped abruptly, rose and turned to the chapel door. He put a finger to his lips and told Devlin not to speak.

Devlin's coughing finally subsided.

Then Samuel went to the door, opened it a few inches and looked out. A shaft of vivid winter sunshine fell into the chapel. The old man remained where he stood for a moment and then pulled the door shut and came back to sit beside Devlin.

'What is it?' Devlin asked him, his voice barely a whisper.

'You know what it is,' Samuel said. 'There's a police car at the lane end. Four men. One of them looks to be making his way towards the pumping station. The other three are coming here.'

Devlin took a deep breath and then let it out slowly.

'This is the first real break they've had in the snow for the past three days,' Samuel said. 'What are you going to do?'

'You could go out to them,' Devlin said.

'And tell them what?'

'That there's nobody here. Give me a chance to hide.'

Both men looked around the small space. It could be checked in seconds by a man standing at the door. There were no hiding places.

'I doubt they'd believe me,' Samuel said. 'I've never seen the local police this serious about anything before or working so hard.'

'Go back to the door,' Devlin said. 'See how close they are.'

Samuel looked towards the altar and then returned to the door. This time he opened it wider.

'Don't,' Devlin said to him.

'They're following my tracks,' Samuel said. 'They know *some-one's* here. Besides, you need to get your face seen to.'

And before Devlin could respond to this, the old man pulled the door wide open and went outside into the snow. Devlin heard him calling to the approaching men.

More light fell into the chapel, reaching in a solid stripe across the full width of the floor to where Devlin lay, running over his covered feet and legs and then continuing beyond him. He looked at the shotgun and his few other belongings scattered beside it. He tried to remember how many cartridges remained in the box he had stolen.

A strange voice called in to him, telling him there was no-where left for him to go and to stay where he was. There was both excitement and anxiety in the voice.

Then one of the constables blew hard on his whistle and afterwards shouted to the others. The noise of the whistle lasted a long time in the cold, sharp air.

Devlin imagined the four men running to join each other at the chapel to share and applaud their sudden good fortune.

A silhouette appeared in the light at the doorway and Samuel returned inside. He came to where Devlin lay and knelt beside him. He straightened the sacking over Devlin's legs and then pushed more of this behind his head. Devlin felt the old man's hands caressing the top and sides of his head.

'They said for you to stay where you were,' Samuel said to him. He rested Devlin's head against his leg and then stroked aside the hair which fell over his forehead and eyes. 'I told them I'd stay with you. They know you've got the gun.'

'Get it for me,' Devlin said.

Samuel shook his head. 'What good would that serve?'

'It'd be something,' Devlin said, his final hope evaporating on the breath of the words.

'It wouldn't be half of what you imagined,' Samuel said, and before Devlin could say anything else, the old man rose to his feet, went to the altar, picked up the shotgun and went back outside with it.

A further whistle sounded, followed by another and then by several shouting voices.

Devlin heard the clacking sound of the gun being opened and closed and then opened again. This was followed by relieved laughter. He imagined the men outside already celebrating their victory, or whatever it was they considered it to be.

Eventually, Samuel came back inside and returned to where Devlin lay. 'It seems to me you got no choice now except to let events run their course and hope for the best,' he said. There was affection in his voice and he smiled at Devlin as he spoke.

'And what would that be, do you imagine – the best?' Devlin said.

'You know that as well as I do,' Samuel said. He again laid his hand on Devlin's head. 'Do you want me to go back out to them, tell them it's safe to come in? They're only lads themselves.'

'Save your legs,' Devlin said. He felt comforted by the old man's hand resting on his head, the gently moving fingers.

He watched the door. Shadows came and went across the shining snow and someone rapped at the thin, corroded side of the chapel. He looked all around him. Soon, just as at Harrap's, just as at Duggan's, there would be nothing left of the place. A vague and fading outline on the open land between the embankment and the sea, perhaps; a few scattered pieces of rusted iron and shattered glass, perhaps; a lingering note in the air and a richness in the ground beneath, perhaps. But apart from that, nothing. Only an everlasting emptiness where once men and women and their children had gathered to worship and to sing and to pray, where they had come to rejoice and to mourn and to remember, but whose names were now long forgotten, whose voices were long since silent, and who would never again return to the place and say it was their own.

The Devil's Beat
Robert Edric

'We must prise opinion from fact, belief from supposition and guesswork from whatever evidence must exist . . .'

1910. THE EYES OF THE country turn to a Nottinghamshire town where four young women allegedly witness a terrifying apparition. Has the devil really revealed himself to them? Are they genuine victims of demonic possession? Or, as most suspect, does their real purpose lie elsewhere?

A panel of four men must examine the substance of the girls' story and decide their fate: a minister, a doctor, a magistrate, and Merritt, an investigator. But even with a perfect mix of the rational, sacred and judicial, their judgement will be called into question as the feverish excitement around the case grows ever more infectious and hysterical . . .

'A connoisseur of shadows. Edric is excellent on what is truly "devilish" in human beings'
SUNDAY TIMES

The London Satyr
Robert Edric

1891. LONDON IS SIMMERING under an oppressive summer heatwave, the air thick with sexual repression. But a wave of morality is about to rock the capital as the puritans of the London Vigilance Committee seek out perversion and aberrant behaviour in all its forms.

Charles Webster, an impoverished photographer working for famed actor-manager Henry Irving at the Lyceum Theatre, has been sucked into a shadowy demi-monde which exists beneath the surface of civilized society. It is a world of pornographers and prostitutes, corralled under the sinister leadership of master manipulator Marlow, to whom Webster illicitly provides theatrical costumes for pornographic shoots.

But knowledge of this enterprise has somehow reached the Lyceum's upright theatre manager, Bram Stoker, who suspects Webster's involvement. As the net tightens around Marlow and his cohorts and public outrage sweeps the city, a member of the aristocracy is accused of killing a child prostitute . . .

'Sharply written, wholly engrossing . . . not just an Edric novel, but the *Edric novel'*
GUARDIAN

Sanctuary
Robert Edric

Haworth, West Yorkshire, 1848.

Branwell Brontë – unexhibited artist, unacknowledged writer, sacked railwayman, disgraced tutor and spurned lover – finds himself unhappily back in Haworth Parsonage, to face the disappointment of his father and his three sisters, the scale of whose own pseudonymous successes is only just becoming apparent.

With his health failing rapidly, his aspirations abandoned and his once loyal circle of friends shrinking fast, Branwell resorts to a world of secrets, conspiracies and endlessly imagined betrayals. But his spiral of self-destruction only accelerates his sense of destiny as a bystander looking across at greatness and the madness which that realization will bring . . .

> 'A work of art . . . Edric is one of the most
> remarkable novelists writing today'
> ALLAN MASSIE, THE SCOTSMAN

> 'Stunning and ambitious . . . Branwell's close relationship
> with Emily, the love he feels for consumptive Anne and the
> disintegration of his bond with Charlotte who looks on him
> with resentment and hostility are vividly explored . . .
> Moving and imaginatively reconstructed'
> PAULA BYRNE, THE TIMES

> 'The book succeeds in poetically entering into the destructive
> world of a young man of modest talent who finds himself
> born into a household of genius'
> JANE JAKEMAN, INDEPENDENT ON SUNDAY

> 'Robert Edric has written some of the most interesting and diverse
> historical fiction of the past thirty years . . . An extraordinary
> portrait of a man lurching towards self-destruction'
> NICK RENNISON, SUNDAY TIMES